Wicked Magic

HARPER SHADOW ACADEMY: BOOK THREE

LUNA PIERCE

Alt Book Cover Design by EmCat Designs
Book Cover Design by Mibl Art
Editing by https://studioenp.com
Editing by Cruel Ink Editing
Proofing by Tiffany Hernandez
Formatted by EmCat Designs
First Edition 2020
ISBN 978-1-7332322-5-8 (paperback)
ISBN 978-1-957238-14-2 (alt paperback)
ASIN B08F4PQD94 (ebook)

Mom and Dad… listen, I know you're super proud of me and all, but could you just do us both a favor and skip this one? Thanks, love you bunches <3

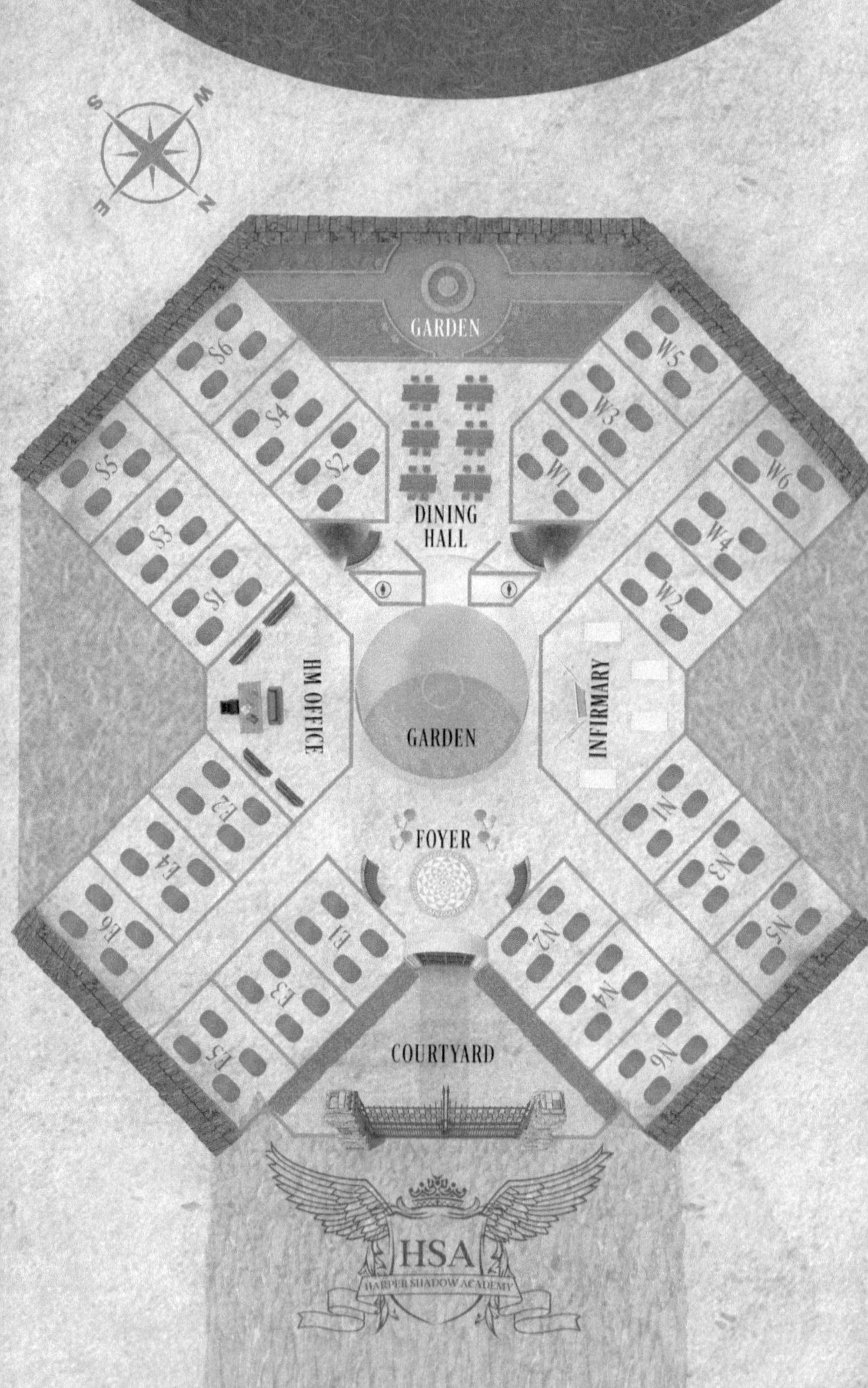

S
W
E
N
GARDEN
S6
S4
S2
S5
S3
S1
W5
W3
W1
W6
W4
W2
DINING HALL
HM OFFICE
GARDEN
INFIRMARY
N1
N3
N5
F2
F4
F6
FOYER
N2
N4
N6
E1
E3
E5
COURTYARD
HSA
HARPER SHADOW ACADEMY

Basement/Library

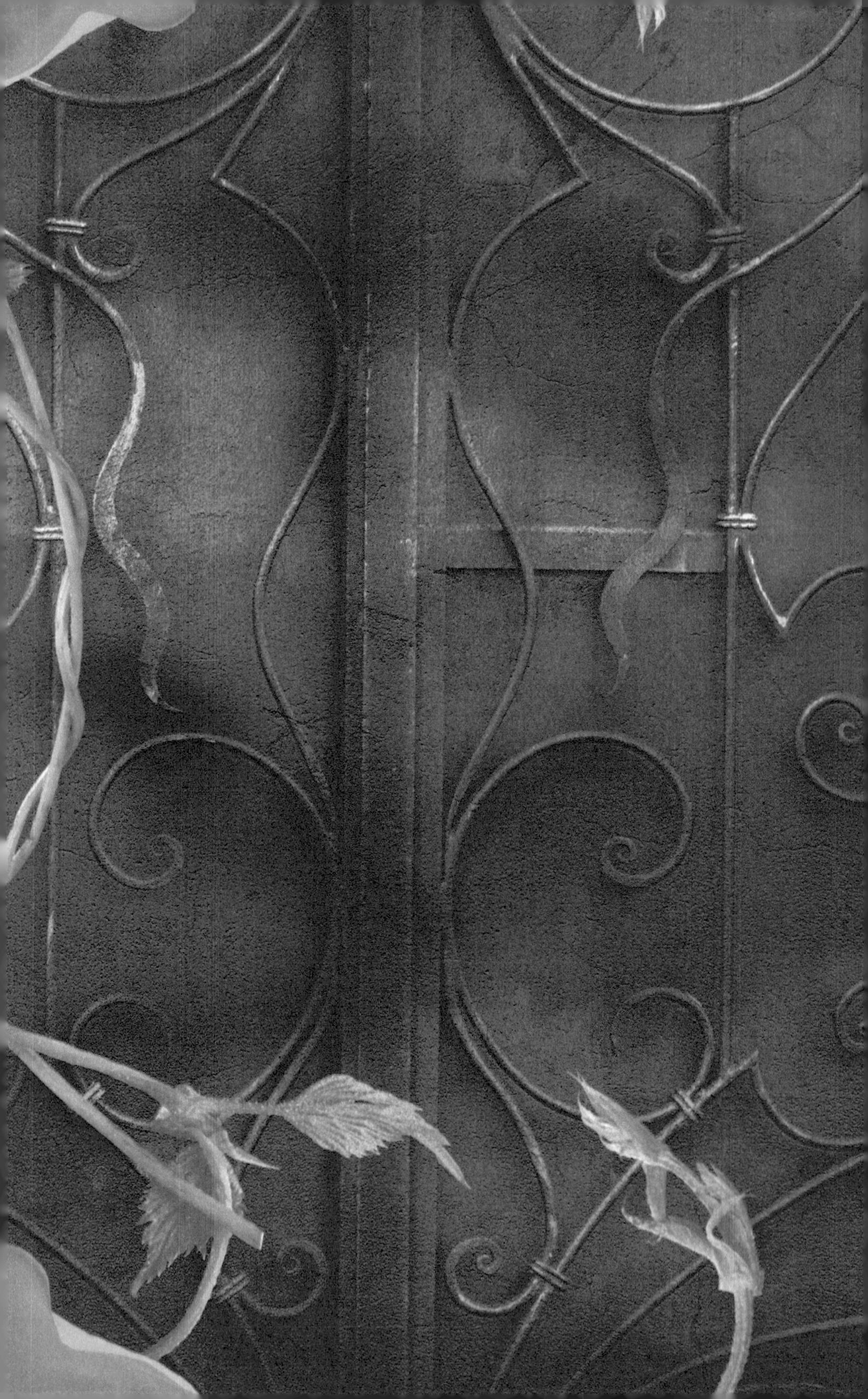

CHAPTER 1

I have no fucking clue how I'm going to get through the next week.

Don't get me wrong, I have enough to keep my mind occupied: four hot guys around at all times, friends who genuinely care, and this whole learning magic thing I have going on, but it never seems to be enough.

I'm always dragged right back to the endless thoughts of whether or not my mom is okay.

I guess when you become someone's caretaker, it sort of makes you feel pretty damn responsible for them, so if they go missing, it's only a natural reaction to go into panic mode.

Deghan rubs his thumbs into the tight knots in my neck and shoulders. "Damn, Will, your back is a mess."

I sigh, blinking myself into this reality. I glance across the table to Remi.

She frowns. "Have you listened to anything I've been saying?"

"Ugh, I'm sorry." I really am. I don't mean to be so scatter-brained, but pretending I'm fine when I'm internally freaking out is proving to be rather difficult.

"You done eating?" Deghan points to the food sitting in front of me. A half-eaten cheeseburger and some French fries growing cold by the minute.

"It's all yours," I tell him.

"Do you have everything for classes tomorrow?" Cameron asks me while grabbing a fry from the pile.

I shake my head. "I think I still need to get a math book."

"Me, too. Want to go get them?" His gaze meets mine, those blue eyes glistening.

Somewhat forcing a smile, I stand. "Yeah."

"Cool," Cam adds.

"I'll see you guys later." I offer a weak wave to the rest of the group.

Kyra nods and Remi scowls.

"Don't forget Wednesday." Remi narrows her eyes at me.

"Okay, I won't," I respond, despite having no idea what she's talking about. Not wanting to awkwardly admit that I'm clueless, I keep my mouth shut. I have a few days to figure it out.

Cam's warm hand grazes my lower back and guides me away from the dining hall.

I sink into his embrace and allow it to temporarily soothe me.

"Do you want to talk about it?" he whispers into my ear on our walk to the library.

For some reason, Cam is always the easiest to open up to. His personality is calm and welcoming—totally non-judgmental. It's one of the many qualities I love about him. He's truly such a likable person without a bad bone in his body.

"I can't stop thinking that I'm not doing enough, that I should be doing more, doing something, you know?" My words are quiet so only he can hear. I flick my gaze to him and then focus ahead. Maybe if I get downstairs, the lack of prying eyes will lift some of the pressure weighing so heavily on me.

"I understand, but acting irrationally won't help you find your mom. You're doing the right thing by waiting, even though it's hard."

"How can you be so sure?"

I take a few steps down the stairs, and then suddenly, my feet are tangling up under me and my entire body falling toward the concrete floor.

Cameron grabs my hand with lightning speed, righting me just as I'm about to smack face-first on the hard surface. He yanks me up and toward him, settling his grip on my shoulders. His baby-blue eyes dart back and forth on me. "Are you okay?"

Without giving it another thought, I wrap my arms around his torso and press myself against him. The hug is something I wasn't aware I desperately needed until now. My hair mashes into my face, and I don't bother moving it. Instead, I breathe him in, his calming scent reminding me of a sunny day at the beach.

Cameron holds me close, and moments pass with us standing there, glued together at the entrance to the library.

I'm so damn thankful that this area isn't traveled often.

All too soon, he breaks the perfect silence. "Come on." He plants a soft kiss on the top of my head and takes my hand, leading me to our destination.

We find the math section, and I scan the shelf.

"You're taking statistics, right?" He runs his finger along the spines in search of the right textbook.

"Mmhm. What about you?"

"Yep, second period."

A wave of relief floods over me. "Same."

He nudges my arm with his elbow and smirks.

"Shit, there's only one left," I mutter, pulling it free. Dust bunnies scatter all around.

Cam shrugs. "We can share. No biggie."

I hand it to him. "Here, you should have it. I'll ask Abigail if she can snag me one."

He crosses his arms and huffs. "You don't want to share with me?"

"Fine." I hold the book to my chest and shake my head.

"But this means late-night study sessions." He grins.

"I see what you're up to." I pathetically attempt to wink at him, but it comes out like I have no control over half my face.

Cameron laughs. "That was cute."

His near proximity and gorgeous smile steal my focus, and I find myself staring at his lips. He must think I'm an idiot.

Time slows down. I look from his mouth to his eyes, noting his gaze mimicking mine.

Cam's face turns serious, and his hand reaches up to graze my cheek. He tucks an unruly strand of hair behind my ear.

Sucking in a breath, I inch myself forward, testing the waters.

He hesitates, but then moves, closing the gap between us. His hand tangles in my hair, and his lips firmly crash onto mine.

If I thought his hug was what I needed, I was wrong, *this* is something on a completely different level. It's passion and desperation and longing—and it is *everything*.

Cam wastes no time, his tongue twirls into my mouth, dancing gracefully. He backs me against the shelf, and I fumble to rid myself of the book I'm still clinging to in my hands.

Once it's tucked away, I run my fingers through his silky blond hair, not daring to break our kiss.

He presses his body to mine, and his growing hardness becomes apparent.

I allow him to lift me onto a table we've somehow knocked into, and I position myself to wrap my legs around him, consuming the pleasure from his mere touch.

A loud throat-clearing sounds, and I nearly fall off the table, bumping Cam's face in the process.

"Shit," I stutter.

"Umm, sorry to interrupt what's going down in here, but you

two are aware there are cameras, aren't you?" Deghan points to the ceiling where, lo and behold, a blinking red light flashes.

I smooth out my shirt, taking a deep breath and hopping down from the table. I rush over to the shelf, grabbing the randomly stuffed away book, and bolt from the library. Embarrassment warms my neck.

"Willow, wait!" Cameron calls out.

I run up the stairs, taking them two at a time, jogging through the foyer, along the garden, and up the west wing stairs. I reach the top, my breath growing ragged with each step.

I'm almost to my room, and a person speaks.

"Hey, are you okay?"

I turn toward the sound, my sights finding Ruby standing near her door.

I nod quickly, then realize how stupid I must appear. "Yeah, I'm good."

She tilts her head and squints. "You sure?"

"Yep."

"Okay, well. I was going to ask you, what are you wearing Saturday?"

"I have no idea, that's forever away. Probably jeans and a T-shirt, why?" I do my best to calm my rampant lungs.

"No, I mean, to the formal. You're going, aren't you? You practically already have four dates."

What the hell is a formal?

"You have no idea what I'm talking about, do you?" She shifts her weight to her left leg.

I rack my brain in an attempt to piece together whatever puzzle this is but come up with nothing. "No?"

"The annual Harper Academy Formal. There's this fancy event, and everyone dresses up. It's *this coming weekend.*"

"You're shitting me."

"I am, in fact, not shitting you." Ruby smirks, and the dimples on her round face show. "And before you even try, you can't get out of it. Not with Remi and Kyra on the committee."

Maybe that's what Remi was talking about earlier? Maybe I have to help her with something on Wednesday. Something for the event...

"So, I'll ask again, what are you wearing?"

"I don't have evening dresses laying around. I'm not exactly knowledgeable when it comes to clothes and fashion." I wave my arm down my body, drawing attention to my faded leggings and grey tank top.

"I think some of the girls are going shopping in town this week. You should go. I'm pretty sure Remi is organizing the whole thing. Surprised you don't know."

Shopping? Now maybe *that* is what Remi was talking about.

"What day?"

"Wednesday," she responds.

Oh, Ruby, you saved the day. Yeah, you dropped a bombshell, but this spares me from having to tell Remi I wasn't listening to anything she said at breakfast. It wasn't that I was purposely ignoring her, I've just been having trouble concentrating on anything other than my mom lately. I need to make more of an effort in paying better attention to my surroundings, because focusing on something I have no control over is going to ruin what I have going on here at the school.

Ugh, but then it dawns on me.

"I don't really have the extra cash to blow on a dress." I glance to the floor and bite at my lip. I have a little left in my savings from working at the coffee shop, but most of it was spent making sure the bills were paid while I'm away at school.

"Oh, don't worry. Remi found six different thrift and consignment shops." She exhales. "We're all on a budget, girl, don't stress."

Her words relieve some of the tension in my chest, but then I recall a few minutes ago when Deghan walked in on me and Cameron about to do the dirty in the library.

My face flushes, and I inch toward my room.

"I have to run, but seriously, don't forget." She latches her door shut.

"Okay, I won't."

I clutch the handle, backing into my room and closing the door. I lean into it, resting my head against the frame, letting the solitude of my space wash over me.

Although, I can't help but be drawn to the pulsing energy that fills the room. Without turning around, I'm certain I'm not alone.

CHAPTER 2

"What's wrong?" His voice pierces through the air, a hint of something I can't decipher hidden within it.

I face him, studying the way his body tensely rests on the spare bed.

Silas stands but doesn't come any closer.

"The usual," I admit and stroll over, tossing the math book onto the mattress across from him. "And apparently there is some dance I wasn't aware of, which sounds all kinds of terrible."

I slump down, and when he continues to stand, I tug him to sit beside me.

"Are you sure that's it? Nothing else happened?"

Um, other than Deghan walking in on me and Cam? No? Well, except...

"I sorta fell down the stairs."

Silas's eyes widen, and immediately he's scanning for any sign of injury. "Are you hurt? Did someone instigate this? Is it the next curse?" He spits out one question after another.

"I'm fine, really. It was just embarrassing." Especially with everything else that went down. "It's not a curse; I'm naturally clumsy. I tripped over my own feet, and I was lucky that Cam grabbed my arm, stopping me from faceplanting."

His interrogation continues. "You didn't notice anything? No weird energy or anything?"

"No." I lay my hand on his shoulder and calm him down. "It was only me and my dumb feet."

Silas's body relaxes, but not quite all the way. Something is *off* about him, and I can't quite put my finger on it.

"What about you? You doing okay?" I scan him, not really picking up anything else but not being able to shake the feeling that *something* is wrong.

He ignores my inquiry. "Will you please tell me if you observe a change? Willow, you're all I have...I can't lose you." His voice is raw and crackly like he might cry. Not the strong man everyone sees on the surface.

It breaks my heart to watch him be so afraid of the unknown.

"I promise," I mutter, sliding my fingers around his, giving them a gentle but firm squeeze.

We lock gazes, and his energy bubbles through me, the sadness and aching darkness almost too much to bear.

What has this world done to you, my sweet Silas?

I lean forward, grazing my cheek along his and wrapping him into my arms.

He stiffens but then allows me in.

His jacket pokes me in the arm, and I reach down, maneuvering my way inside to remove it. His skin a beautiful fire against mine. Not too long ago, our touch caused him unbearable pain, and now, the high from the slightest hint of closeness drives me wild in all the best ways.

Silas does what he's instructed and takes the coat off.

I'm immediately drawn to the shades of black and grey tangled all over his body. It really is a breathtaking sight, such a masterpiece on his skin.

I reach up to his face but he stops me from my next move, scooting back and holding out his arm.

He gives me a look that says, *lie with me.*

So, I do exactly that.

I'm not sure who finds comfort in who, but I settle in with him and take advantage of this calm before the storm that I call my life.

I must doze off at some point because I wake to the sound of knocking at my door.

I blink myself to life and find that I'm alone.

"I'm coming," I grumble while jumping from the bed.

I turn the handle, and Deghan pokes his head inside.

"Wills, time for lunch." He looks me over. "Were you *snoozing*? Without me?" He clutches his chest. "I'm hurt."

"You really are so dramatic, you know."

He ruffles my hair. "Yeah, but that's why you love me."

It's definitely one of the reasons.

"Shoes, I need shoes." I skim the room and finally spot a pair of sandals tucked by a nightstand. Those will do.

"Do you wanna hit the library when we're done? Do a little studying?" He pauses and then breaks into the biggest smile ever. "For real studying, not whatever you and Cam were doing." His brows raise. "Not that I wouldn't be interested. But maybe somewhere a bit more private."

I rest my head in my hands. "You're never going to let me live this down, are you?"

"Umm, let me think about it. Yeah, no. Absolutely not. The

image is burned vividly in my memory." He leans against the wall, waiting for me to finish.

I glance up to him from my spot across the room. "Are you mad...about what happened?" I hold my breath for his response.

"Mad? Why would I be?"

I shrug. "Angry, jealous, any of those?"

He shakes his head. "No, Will. I think it's safe to say we all have some super-secret silent agreement of whatever this is, and somehow, we're all on the same page. For me, and probably everyone else included, we just care about you. We want the best for you. And if that involves all or none of us, that's what goes. Although we'd prefer the former. We've been through a lot together, all of us. No sense in breaking that up over territorial issues. If they're treating you right, that's what matters to me. I'm good—no, I'm great—with what we have, our tiny group of superheroes."

My heart swells with emotion. I'll never be able to comprehend how I got so fucking lucky with the four of them. They all have rare and wonderful qualities I adore and have grown fond of. I can't imagine a life without the guys in it, and from what Deghan is saying, maybe I won't have to.

With all the crazy shit going on, how can I be so sure that they're getting what they deserve from me? I need to pay more attention to their individual needs and leave them feeling as loved and cared for as I do. Maybe this will help me focus on something other than the ticking clock until I can use the Reperio stone again to try to locate my mom and dad.

"You're too good to me, you really are." I make my way across the dorm, stepping close to Deghan.

He cups my chin in his hand. "You're worth it, little one."

"What're we eatin'?" I say without taking my eyes off his.

His grin beams wider. "Are we talking about food now?"

I laugh and shove him.

"Okay, okay. Sorry. Speaking of Cam, though." He flinches in anticipation for another swing. "He's made us sandwiches, and we're eating in Sydney's room."

That has to mean that Silas is not joining us. Where could he have run off to? Maybe he's *feeding* in his own style.

We make our way from my place, heading across the common area, walking next to the glass floor of the garden below. I tense and step away.

Deghan pulls me close to him in response.

"One of these days, that thing is going to bust." I eyeball the greenery and its encasement suspiciously.

"You afraid of heights?" he asks.

"I'm more skeptical of unexpected thirty-foot drops onto a tree."

"At least it would break your fall."

"Not helping."

"That thing is rock-solid and probably spelled with magic. How else do you think those plants flourish so well in there?"

I have always wondered about the complexities of the garden and all its glory. Magic does make sense to how it's possible.

Without knocking, Deghan opens Sydney's door and waltzes inside like he owns the place. "Sup?" He heads straight to the food splayed out on the small table.

Sydney looks up from the book in his hand and waves, going right back to the text.

"Hey, Wills." Cam blushes and averts his gaze.

"Oh, righttttt," Deghan says with a mouthful. "You two haven't seen each other since..."

At this, Sydney perks up. "Since what?"

"She fell down the stairs," Cameron speaks up.

I internally thank him for not letting Syd in on our library shenanigans.

"You did?" Syd furrows his brows.

I nod. "Yeah, but I'm fine." I eye the selection of food and take one of the sandwiches that Cam was kind enough to make. I settle into one of the chairs and dig in, thoroughly enjoying the deliciousness. How can someone take something so ordinary and make it taste so good? "Is this another one of those sauces you're experimenting with?" I glance over to Cam and catch Deghan's wide stare boring into me.

I roll my eyes at him.

"My own spin on honey mustard," Cameron confirms.

"It's quite tasty." I take another bite and reach for the pitcher of tea. "You guys don't have to suffer through unsweet on my behalf."

"I prefer it," Sydney chimes in.

"Really?"

"Yep." He closes and sets aside his work, coming over to sit with me. "What are you doing after you eat?" Sydney peeks at me while he sips from his cup.

I make eye contact with Deghan briefly. "Degs wanted to study in the library."

"Oh cool, mind if I join you two? I have a few things I need to research and was going to see if you wanted to come along."

"The more the merrier," Deghan answers.

We finish our lunch and help Cameron clean up until he insists that he has it under control.

"Watch your footing on your way down," he whispers to me as he takes the trash out of my hands. "Seriously, be careful."

"Right, of course." I bob my head up and down in understanding.

"Can we...can we talk later?"

I swallow, the uncertainty of the situation growing. Does he regret kissing me? Here I thought I was living on cloud nine with the guys, but maybe Cameron doesn't feel the same. I should have never assumed any of them did.

"I'm going to make a cup of coffee. Do either of you want one?" Sydney looks to me and then points to Deghan.

"Sure," I say, but it ends up answering both of the questions at hand.

"My man." Deghan slaps Sydney on the back in a bro kind of

way. "Here." He holds his arm out for Sydney's bag. "I'll take that for you and meet you in the library."

I use the opportunity to mutter to Cam, "When we're done studying?"

"Okay." His expression is unreadable.

It's everything I can do to not assume the worst.

"Will, do you need to stop by your room, or are you good?" Deghan stands near the door.

"No, I left everything down there." I exchange one last look with Cam and leave his side.

The burning analyzation consumes me to the point that it's all I can think about on our way downstairs.

Deghan said we are all on the same page, but maybe we aren't?

CHAPTER 3

I manage to get to the basement without almost falling on my face, which is a huge improvement from earlier. I let Deghan lead the way since he has a better understanding than I do of where the room that Abigail secured for me is.

Usually, I have the beacon on me, but this time it's sitting on my nightstand next to the book Silas loaned me that I haven't had the chance to read yet.

Deghan is unusually quiet, so I break the silence. "What are you working on today?"

We funnel into the room, and he places Syd's belongings on a nearby chair. "Wolf stuff."

Is he more shut down than normal? "Do you need any help?"

"Nope." He smiles. "But I'll be right back. I have to get a couple books from a different section."

"Okay..."

He leaves, and my loneliness grows super noticeable. I'm becoming too damn dependent on the guys, and I'm not sure if that's a good or bad thing. It's not that I can't handle being alone, it's that there is such comfort with them around, that the void of their absences is that much more evident each time it happens.

Luckily, though, Sydney comes strolling in at the same time I'm trying to find a book to occupy my thoughts.

The aroma of freshly ground coffee beans and vanilla fills the air.

I take one of the three cups he holds tightly in a triangle. "Thank you."

He sets one on the table and takes the lid off another, blowing lightly on the steamy liquid.

I can't help but stare at his lips and reminisce on our time here not too long ago.

Apparently, I have an itch that needs to be scratched, because every time I glance at any of my guys, I want to pounce. I need to focus.

"What's going on in that head of yours?" Sydney asks.

Shit. Am I that obvious?

"Umm..." *Come on Willow, think of something.* "Nothing. Zoning out." *Good one, idiot.*

"You're lying." He brings the mug to his mouth, testing it to see how hot the drink still is.

I have to look away to stop myself from gawking.

For once, I force my mind to think about my mom, the endless curse, anything other than what I'd rather be doing at this very moment. Typically, that's all that's on my brain—my mother and how to end this living nightmare—but with Sydney giving off copious amounts of sex appeal doing barely nothing, it's a growing challenge.

"You zoning out again?"

I snatch a book off the tall stack in front of me. "Yep."

Flipping it open, I relax into a chair, eager to escape my own mind.

For a while, I read about cosmic witches and how they use celestial things to fuel their powers. Some of them use the entire cosmos, while others practice specifically with the stars or moon or certain planets. For each type of emphasis, it's broken down even further to types based on exclusive constellations or planets —like Pluto or Saturn. Apparently, the ones that deal with Jupiter are deemed Jovian witches, and their emphasis is on good fortune, prosperity, and luck.

Seems I could use some Jovian magic in my life.

I turn the page, glancing over at Sydney and Deghan who are both face down in their books. I hadn't detected Deghan had come in.

Next up are green witches. Something that Abigail and Walker have said that I am. A green witch is one who uses natural and living things. They think that, because I have a connection with flowers, that they *speak* to me, or offer me guidance, that I am one with the earth.

If that is a hereditary trait, it would make sense, considering my mother always had a garden and often put a lot of emphasis on maintaining its success.

According to the text, if I am in fact a green witch, it would help me to start bottling rain and snow and bits of soil to use for casting more powerful spells I can't conjure on my own. I should be on the lookout for rocks and animal fossils, too.

"Whoa," I accidentally say out loud.

"What's wrong?" Sydney says.

"Are fairies real?" The words exit my mouth, and I can't help but feel silly for asking.

Sydney leans back. "Well, according to legends, yes."

"Seriously?"

"Vampires are real. So are witches and werewolves. Why wouldn't you believe in the fae folk?"

"I guess when you put it that way..." I pause. "But you haven't seen one? Or heard of any instances?"

"My family is more traditional, and if I'm not mistaken, that's a green witch specialty."

But they think I'm a green witch.

"I've heard rumors," Deghan adds. "Talk in the pack is that they're randomly making appearances here and there."

"What?" I say to him.

"I thought it was a joke." He shrugs. "But maybe with all this curse business and the fact that you're potentially green and all." He rubs his chin. "Maybe they're coming back for you, to help you or something."

First the angels, and now fairies. What else could I possibly be tied to?

I let my gaze fall back on the book and look at the following page. The image sends chills down my spine. Black horns attached to a floating creature with even darker wings, nothing comparable to those flowy powder-white angel wings I'm so familiar with. To this figure's right is another creature, one with a goat-shaped head and a long, wavy beard. It resembles the form of a man but half of him has animalistic features. In its arms is a limp baby, a haze going toward the being like it's sucking the life out of the infant.

The words *demonic witch* come into my line of sight. Descended from the Devil himself, these types of witches are fueled by stealing the power of others. They perform wicked magic, often to gain more influence and clout to take advantage of weaker witches. Over time, their spell work became more sophisticated, and they better learned to disguise themselves from others. Most of the time, hiding in plain sight.

For a short period, there were demonic witch hunts, and ordinary witches were falsely accused and executed. On only a few occasions were actual demon witches found and executed.

Elizabeth Howe and Susannah Martin were two of the innocents who were taken and killed. A few months later, it was found out that they were wrongly slain. At that point, the hunts stopped, in fear that more harmless people would die.

Over the many years to follow, occasions of withering crops and plague-type illnesses were tied to demonic witches, but because they were always one step ahead, they were never found and punished. To stay undetected, they prey upon witches who want to convert, to gain the kind of strength the demonic one's harbor and have them do their bidding.

"You look like you've seen a ghost, Wills," Deghan says calmly, concern coating his voice.

I shake my head to rid myself of the nasty images. "Was reading about some terrible things that happened."

"Why don't you call it quits for the day? You're a little pale."

My mind wanders to those angel wings that often pop up in my vision.

Angel wings.

Silas had told me that he thought I was descended from the angels. And that other witches were descended from all sorts of other things...including the Devil.

And these demonic witches *steal* the power of others.

I'm cursed, and with that, demons are trying to take my power. The Oliver witches have had their power suppressed and stolen for decades.

I've been going in circles trying to figure out how and why, and never once getting close to *who*...but maybe, just maybe, we're cursed by a coven of demonic witches.

That would make sense, especially with how they're able to channel and tap into our powers. They've had that ability for as long as they have been in creation.

All along, I never considered the drastic opposite of what being created by the angels meant.

This is a blood feud.

A blood feud between the angels and the Devil.

And here I am. My birthright is that I have to fight the battle to free my kind.

I thought this was strictly an Oliver witch thing, but no, this is much bigger than that.

"Yeah, good idea." I grab my cold coffee off the table and tip it back. The lid buckles, flopping to the floor, and the rest of the contents dump all down the front of my shirt. Jumping up, I mutter obscenities and shove the books away so they don't get soaked, too.

Deghan and Sydney are at my side in an instant.

"Here, let me take those," Sydney offers.

Deghan rips his shirt off and dabs mine to help clean me up.

It's all I can do to not stop and stare at his chiseled form.

"I'm fine, really. Don't ruin your clothes on my account."

"I'm not a huge fan of this shirt anyway." Deghan winks and continues to wipe me down, ridding my arms of the coffee mess.

First, falling down the stairs, and now spilling my drink all over myself? What is this?

Sydney gets all the texts to another table and somehow appears with a roll of paper towels. "Why don't you go get a shower? I have this under control."

"Are you sure? I'm sorry I'm so clumsy." My shirt sticks to my chest in a totally uncomfortable way.

"Yes, Will. Go." He does another pass over my chair.

I scan him for any irritation but all I sense are good intentions.

"I'll walk you back," Deghan adds.

We make our way out of the library in awkward silence until I glance over at him.

"Are you going to stroll through the school topless?"

"Is that a problem for you?" He grins and nudges my arm.

"Maybe," I mutter.

I get across the foyer in a hurry, not wanting to draw any more attention than normal. I jog up the west dorm stairs with Deghan following close behind.

We enter my room, and I head straight to the shower, turning the water on to heat up.

"You good in there?" Deghan calls through the half-open bathroom door. "I'm going to head out."

A bolt of uncertainty flows through me. "Umm."

"What is it?" He pokes his head inside. "What's wrong?"

I avert my gaze to the floor—for some reason, a heavy nervousness devours me. "Do you mind staying?"

"Yeah, sure, absolutely. Whatever you need." He steps into the room. "Want some help?" He points toward the coffee-soaked shirt clinging to my body.

I nod, and he strides toward me.

He places his hands at the hem of my top and looks into my eyes for approval.

I raise my arms in response, letting him remove the ruined garment.

It gets tangled in my hair, and we both have to squirm around a little for it to come free.

When it does, we accidentally fall into each other, both of us giggling.

The steam from the hot water fills the room and attaches to our bodies.

Both of us go quiet.

Without thinking, I reach out and lay my hand on his chest, over his heart. The rapid thudding matches my own pulse.

He trails my face with his gaze, hesitating on my lips and making his way back to my eyes. Deghan runs his fingers up my arm, along my shoulder, landing on the side of my face, gripping it firmly. His thumb rubs a small spot on my cheek, and he whispers, "Oh, Willow."

His words are my undoing. I give in to the stress of life, the stupidness of the day, the unending desire I have raging through me. I stand on my tiptoes to reach him, and he leans down to meet me.

His luscious lips weave their way onto mine, and our breath becomes one.

All at once, he lifts me, and I wrap my legs around his torso.

How is it possible to have so much fucking chemistry with each of my guys?

Deghan sets me on the counter, and I go to unbutton his pants.

He pulls back. "Are you sure?"

I reel him in without skipping a beat. "Mmhm," I mumble.

He smirks against my lips and kisses me more intensely than a moment ago. His grip finds my waist, tugging my leggings and panties at the same time over my bottom and onto the floor.

I shove his jeans down, and he fumbles behind my back to unsnap my bra. He tosses it to the side, and a second later, he wiggles out of his shoes and we're stark-ass naked together.

I scoot closer to him and look into his golden eyes. His wolf instincts shine through in a fucking magnificent way.

He merges our mouths again, only pausing slightly to take his index and middle finger and slip them into my mouth in the most seductive way ever.

He reaches down, sliding the same hand between my legs, running it up my thigh slowly, slowly, slowly, until I shift myself forward, nearly begging for the touch.

He lightly caresses me, gradually twirling his digits around my entrance.

I extend my arm, taking him into my hand and nearly gasping at his rock-solid size.

Panic and excitement flow through my body.

I encourage him toward me but stop with him practically in place, bracing for what comes next.

Cautiously, he inches himself nearer, until finally, he breaks through my barrier.

I bite down on his lip when he enters, breathless and full of him.

He continues to move unhurriedly, our bodies melting into each other.

"You okay?" he says against my mouth.

I lace my hands through his dark hair. "I'm great. Are you?"

He stiffens his arm around me, lifting me off the sink top and carrying me into the still-running shower. The hot water pours down all around our entangled bodies, and we lose ourselves in each other.

Magic appears—pink and gold sparkles glitter against the droplets of water in a beautiful symphony called us.

CHAPTER 4

Despite having a mind-blowing evening with Deghan, I slept like complete dog shit last night.

Once we had both finished, we sat and stayed in the shower until the water ran cold. It was perfect post-sexual bliss.

But night finally came, and all I did was toss and turn, never able to get comfortable enough to fall into a deep sleep. I was either too hot, too cold, too *something*. A constant distraction, the floor creaking or wind rattling on the window, one thing followed by another kept me awake for hours on end. It was as though I was having growing pains, my body aching constantly.

And now, standing in front of the mirror in my bathroom with freshly brushed teeth, I can't help but observe the dark circles under my eyes. Great, that's exactly what I wanted on the first day of the new term. Fresh classes, first impressions...and I want nothing more than to crawl back into bed for the next seven to three hundred hours.

Coffee calls to me something fierce.

I yawn widely and stretch, the black oversized T-shirt sliding down my shoulder. I run a brush through my hair. That'll have to do.

Grabbing my bag from the table, I make my way to the door. I head straight for the teachers' lounge, desperate for something stronger than the java they supply us in the dining hall. Maybe some espresso and sugar will kick my ass into gear.

I jog down the stairs, waving to Ruby when she smiles at me from across the foyer.

Sydney's sights land on me. "You look rough, Willow."

"You're telling me. I didn't get any sleep last night." I motion to the elaborate machine next to him. "Make me something potent?"

He immediately turns and gets to work. "Of course." Sydney takes a carton of milk from the fridge, pouring some into a metal cup. "You sure you're down for first period?"

"What do you mean?" I drop into a seat nearby.

"We have Walker and Abigail during first for this term. We're supposed to be working on the shadow realm repair." His last few words are quieter than the rest. "Have you even gone over your schedule?"

"Uh...not really." I fumble through my bag in an attempt to find the paper. "I've been a little mentally preoccupied."

The sound of the brewing heaven fills the room, along with the glorious aroma. Damn, I freaking love coffee.

"They're optimistic that we might be able to start regular lessons by the end of the week. And that the other supernatural students can, too. Our classes will be a little different, though, because we'll have to spend two days a week maintaining the realm and making sure it's solid. It will be a constant effort, but I think we can do it." With his back to me, he continues making my drink and talking. "They think we have something *special* together. The way our powers mix into each other, it's out of this world."

I shuffle between a few notebooks. "I can't find it." I let out a huff.

Syd places the steaming cup on my desk, plopping a few ice cubes into it and putting on the lid, taking extra care to make sure it's secure.

We don't exactly need another repeat of yesterday.

"You have Walker first, then stats, speech, lunch, marketing, and intro to management." He rattles them off one by one without hesitating.

My jaw drops in response to him having this memorized.

"I'm not sure if I should be impressed or creeped out." I hold the steaming cup between my hands, blowing through the small hole and taking a blisteringly hot sip. The warmth alone manages to wake me up a little.

"Do you want to get breakfast or head to class?" He puts on his backpack and then grabs his own drink, his shaggy hair toppling down onto his forehead as his emerald eyes glow radiantly. He tucks a thumb under one of the straps.

"Yeah, I could use a muffin." I weave my fingers through the handle on my bag and stand, the contents spilling on the floor. The stitching is completely ripped out, and because I hadn't zipped it all the way closed, my books spilled out haphazardly. "Seriously?" I mutter, kneeling to pick up my stuff.

Sydney gathers the few writing utensils that managed to make their way over to him, and hands them to me. "You're having a pretty bad time lately, aren't you?"

"I'd say so." I let out an exasperated sigh.

"Hmm."

I shift to look at him. "What?"

"Could this have anything to do with your curse?"

I continue to study him. "You can't be serious? I'm just having some bad luck."

"You're not wrong. But it seems awful sudden, doesn't it?"

I shrug. "I think it's me, not the curse. Or maybe Mercury is in retrograde. I heard that's a thing."

"I'm familiar." Sydney's gaze wanders aimlessly like he's lost in thought. "Anything else weird happening? You fell down the stairs yesterday, and then dumped that coffee on you, now this."

"And I slept bad, lost my schedule. I'm going to assume there aren't any blueberry muffins left, either." Something is going on with Silas, too.

"This is serious, Willow. We have to stay on top of any changes and prepare ourselves for whatever your next curse is. We need to be vigilant. This could very well be the precursor to something much bigger." He steps forward, using his free hand to lightly tap my arm. "I care about you, okay? I'm not going to let something else happen to you. Never again will I be so foolish."

He still blames himself for what happened with his parents, and I can't say I wouldn't either if I was in his position. He didn't know what they were up to, but that doesn't mean it sucks any less for him that he fell right into their trap and put me in danger.

How fucking strange is it that they've made no attempt at contact with him, though? The whole blindside happened, and he came back here, as did Silas and I, and he hasn't heard a word about them or what they're doing.

For all we know, they're scheming up other weird bullshit and using their son like a pawn in whatever game they're playing.

At least he managed to steal the stone. Now we can use it to find my mom and dad. Well, once it's charged and ready to go again. The passing minutes drag by while we wait until the time is right.

"Let me carry your coffee. I don't want you to burn yourself if a freak accident happens again." Sydney grasps the cup without letting me protest.

"Thank you." I shove the fabric handle into the bag and put the backpack over my shoulder gently in case it decides to burst open again.

We arrive in the dining hall, and Remi waves us over.

"You go ahead and sit. I'll see what the muffin selection is." Sydney places the drinks on the table and slides his bag near my feet.

I lower my head into my hands and rest my elbows on the table.

"Listen, girl, I'm all for the natural look, but if you need some concealer, I gotchu," Remi says from her seat a few chairs down.

"Is it that bad?" I sigh.

"No, I've seen worse. You feeling all right? You're not getting sick, are you?"

Kyra glances up from her phone where she was using the front camera to apply a coat of red lipstick. "She's not wrong. Maybe you should see the nurse."

"I'm not sick. I didn't sleep last night. You two act like I'm dying." I lean up, scanning the rest of the crowd. "Where's Lills?"

Kyra points, and I follow her finger to spot Lillian and Ethan flirting with each other near the food.

They really are so damn adorable together.

"Bad news," Sydney says from behind me. "You called it. No blueberry." He holds out his hands. "Banana nut and apple are your choices."

I take the former, and he tugs the wrapper down on the latter, biting into his breakfast and sitting next to me.

Deghan and Cameron stroll toward us.

"Morning." Deghan's tanned skin blushes.

My mind flashes to last night, my body pressed against the wall of my shower by his, water cascading down our intertwined bodies. I have to blink to clear my vision, and this time it's *my* cheeks that get rosy.

"Hi." I peek around the room even though I'm certain Silas isn't here, his presence not filling the space whatsoever. Where could he be, and why is he being so distant again? Maybe he's not as okay with me and the other guys as he lets on. I have to get to the bottom of it so it doesn't drive a wedge between us. If he wasn't okay with it, he shouldn't have told me that he was. That only leads to confusion and unfair expectations.

Sydney tosses the remaining part of his muffin into his mouth. "You want to get going? You can eat in the room."

"Sure, yeah." I stand, getting my things and waving a weak goodbye at everyone. "See you guys later."

Once inside the north wing room, Sydney leads me to a place to sit and have my breakfast.

Ten minutes later, Abigail and Walker arrive, chattering to each other about nothing I can comprehend.

"How's everyone doing today?" Walker asks from his spot at the front of the room.

I glimpse at Sydney out of the corner of my eye.

"Great, we're great." Sydney answers. "How are you?"

"Good to hear. I'm just peachy." Walker pulls a notebook from his bag. "Now, excuse me for getting right down to business, but if our calculations are correct, we should be nearing a stable shadow realm. What do you think, Abby, another session or two and we can experiment with crossing over?"

She studies her own pad of paper. "I'd say that's accurate. We've made wonderful strides. You two are something else. We couldn't have done it without you." Her red hair is in beachy waves today, and it really brings out the blue in her eyes.

"You wouldn't be in this mess without me, either." I rip off a piece of my muffin. "I'm glad to help." I toss it into my mouth, hoping it fuels me to get through this day.

"Actually, Willow, the accident only brought to light what weaknesses the shadow realm did pose. So, if anything, you did us a favor. I'm only sorry that it put you and your friends in danger in the manner in which it did." Walker leans on a desk. "Whenever you're ready we can get started."

I ball up the muffin wrapper and brush my hands together. "I'm good to go."

Taking the headphones from Abigail, I slide them over my ears.

Sydney drags a chair over and holds his hands out toward me.

I place mine onto his, like we had done in the past, allowing my magic to flow into him and his into me.

The surge is electric at first, the connection vibrating and pounding, then calming into a steady stream of sheer power. Crackling shades of green and pink orbit us, but I don't dare take my eyes off of Sydney's, not wanting to weaken the connection and make it any more difficult for Abigail and Walker to do their thing.

"*Hey,*" Sydney's voice floats into my head.

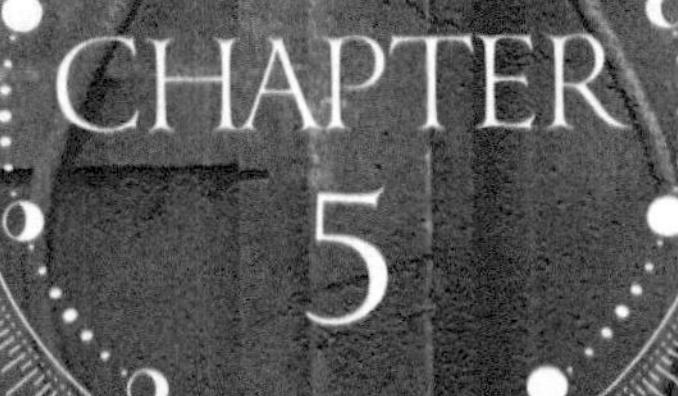

CHAPTER 5

The realm repair goes exactly like all the rest.

Syd and I sit, hand in hand, gazes locked, nearly oblivious to our surroundings as we hold a conversation in our heads.

It's romantic and fun and honestly a nice break to focus on him and the power we create together.

Although, the topics of our chats do vary.

"I missed this," Sydney says.

"Me, too."

"I know it's going to take you some time...but I hope you'll trust me again someday." His eyes sparkle, and his energy is wholesome.

"Have you heard from them?" I ask.

His head shakes faintly.

"I hope they're okay at least..." Regardless of what they did to me, they're still Sydney's parents.

"I don't." He says it so matter-of-fact.

My eyes widen. *"But..."*

Sydney cuts me off. *"But nothing. Their actions are inexcusable. I can look past how they've treated me; I always have. They screwed up by putting you in danger. I won't ever forgive them, or myself, for letting that happen."*

"You're going to have to realize that wasn't your fault. If you want me to be able to move past what happened, you should work on forgiving yourself, too."

He nods. *"You're right. I'll do a better job. But that doesn't mean I'm going to stop worrying about you. I don't think any of us will."*

"Until I break this curse, and then you guys are going to have to acknowledge that I can keep myself safe."

"We'll see when it happens. Speaking of, are you making any progress?"

"Not really, no." I force away any rampant thoughts that attempt to give away what's going on in my mind. It's not that I don't want to talk to him about every single detail I learn, it's that I hate not knowing the things fully before involving someone else.

"What aren't you telling me?" He reads me like an open book.

Without me getting a chance to reply, a wave of nausea hits me. I rip my hand away from his and grasp at my mouth, dissolving our magical connection. I frantically look at Walker and Abigail, who pause with their hands near the ceiling.

"What's wrong?" Sydney says out loud.

Jumping up, I run for the door, desperate to get to a toilet so I don't puke everywhere.

I jog down the north wing hallway, the sound of Sydney on my heels, and bust through the foyer and into the girl's restroom to find the nearest stall. Once inside, I quickly hug my newfound best friend and empty the contents of my stomach.

"Willow!" Sydney calls through the door. "I'm coming in."

Oh God, no, no, no. Please no.

I can't even object when another surge takes hold. I flush in an effort to lessen my embarrassment.

Creaking fills the space, and I know it's too late.

Hands weave through my hair, pulling it back and away from my face.

"I got you." Sydney clutches my hair in one hand and rubs gently on my back with the other.

I am absolutely mortified.

It's one thing for him to see me take on a demon or almost die…but to witness me puking up my guts is a whole new level of humiliation.

He sits with me for a few minutes, waiting until the heaving stops. I finally relax against the wall.

"You coming down with something?"

Is that his sly way of asking if I'm pregnant? Because that would be a definite *no*. Silas is a vampire, and I only slept with Deghan yesterday. It would be nearly impossible.

I did just find out fairies are real, though, so I guess I shouldn't totally rule anything out. Especially with the whole Bella and Edward honeymoon fiasco. Wouldn't that be some crazy shit?

"Probably food poisoning," I finally mutter.

"Willow." Silas's voice rings through the bathroom.

Can this get any worse?

"Are you in there?" he asks loudly.

"Yeah, she's in here," Sydney answers.

Not a second later, Silas rushes into the area. "What did you do to her?"

I weakly put my arm up in protest. "Stop always blaming him. It was a bad muffin."

He reaches my side, scooping me into his arms without letting me or Sydney protest.

"What are you doing?" Sydney asks.

"Taking her to her room where she can rest privately," Silas says, walking out the door.

"I'll bring up some tea." Sydney follows us.

I lose track of him while Silas carries me up the west wing stairs. I take in a breath and relax into him, willing myself not to hurl all over his extravagant leather jacket. "I can walk."

"And I can carry you."

We reach my room, and he turns the handle without setting me down.

Inside, he sets me down on my bed and goes to the bathroom, coming back out a moment later with a damp rag and a wastebasket. He places the cold cloth on my forehead and tucks my blanket around me.

"I'm not staying in here. How long until second period?" I ask with my eyes closed.

"A little over an hour."

"That should be plenty of time. I'll take a quick nap and be golden."

"Fat chance." His voice is stern.

I peek through one lid at him. "You've been different lately."

He repositions his body somewhat. "How so?"

"I'm not sure...but something is off. I can *feel* it."

"I could say the same thing about you." He blots my face to cool it down. "You still think this has nothing to do with your curse?"

"I don't see how that's possible. How would that make sense? I'm cursed to have an upset stomach?"

"You should rest." Silas saunters to the oversized window and closes the curtain to block out today's bright sun.

"Promise me you won't let me oversleep."

"Shh."

It doesn't take long until I doze off, the sound of Sydney's voice waking me.

"Hey," he speaks softly. "Drink this."

I sit up on my elbows, eyeing the steaming mug. "What's in it?"

"A little family recipe. Some ginger, chamomile...fennel. Some other stuff that helps with nausea."

My gaze shifts to across the room where Silas stands, clearly keeping his distance from Sydney.

Taking the cup into my hands, I hold it tightly near my face, letting the steam rise and caress my sinuses. For such a weird combination, it seems to smell pretty good. I take a hesitant sip, and the warmth courses through my body.

A few swallows later, I'm surprisingly feeling much better, my energy levels rising and the heavy exhaustion disappearing.

I suppose his family isn't good for nothing.

I swing my legs off the bed and pause, worried I might get dizzy from standing too quickly.

Sydney reaches out to steady me and helps me to my feet.

"How are you feeling?"

"Better, much better." And it's not a lie. It's a surprise, but if I didn't know better, I'd never think that I was sick just an hour ago.

"You have statistics next. I can accompany you there." Sydney keeps one hand on my arm like I might topple over.

"Not necessary. I'll take it from here," Silas interjects.

Sydney steps back. "If that's what you want."

Is that sadness I sense from him?

"We'll catch up at lunch, okay?" I graze his arm with my fingertips. "Thank you for taking care of me."

"Always."

Silas carries my backpack and escorts me to my next class.

It's a silent venture and only gives me more time to think about the disconnection I have to Silas lately.

"Can we talk tonight?" I finally ask.

"Okay." His response is short, and it makes me grateful that we'll get a chance to talk this out later on.

"Thanks." Is it me or is there a weird tension? Typically, the invisible thread to him is beaming with energy, and now it's almost like there's a thick haze covering it. It's still there, the original line, but there is something else, too.

"I'll be out here when class is over." He kisses my cheek, hands me my bag, and leaves.

My heart aches for him to come back so I can piece together whatever has happened to us.

I stroll in, and Cameron is there to greet me.

"What was that all about?" he questions.

"Um..." Do I really have to relive the humiliation? "I kind of got sick in first period. But I'm better now, don't worry. I think it was something I ate."

He frowns and holds out his arms, wrapping me into them. "Aw, you poor thing. Tell me if you start to feel bad again, okay? Do you want me to go grab some crackers? A Gatorade, maybe?"

I smile into his chest. "Sydney made me a witchy tea, and Silas sat with me while I napped."

He leads me to my seat. "Well, don't be afraid to speak up if you want anything."

"Thanks, Cam."

Professor Tremont walks into the room, his dark hair flowing almost to his shoulders.

We've interacted on occasion regarding supernatural things, but I've never had him for a teacher.

He supervised me a couple times during the whole constant surveillance thing, but my guys insisted on taking over the majority of the shifts, so his help wasn't necessary. And even in those instances, we didn't talk much, so I barely know anything about him.

Tremont clearly knows about supernaturals, and from our handshake the first time I met him, his energy imprint has me leaning toward thinking he's a witch.

"Good morning, students." He scans the room, pausing and nodding toward me and Cam. "Today we'll be going over the syllabus and diving right into our work. This course isn't for the faint of heart. Most come close to failing it on their first attempt, so here's to a new start and an opportunity to pass on the initial go."

A collective gasp fills the room, and I glance around, taking in some of the familiar faces.

I'm not exactly an outgoing person, but outside of my guys and the girls, I haven't really gotten acquainted with anyone else. Not that that's a bad thing. I have my hands full with balancing my friendships and relationships as it is, especially because I'm a newbie witch—and there's that whole curse thing.

Still, though, I can't help but think I should be doing a better job at being social. This college experience may be my last shot at making friends, even if it's only short-lived. Maybe this formal will be a good opportunity to do exactly that.

"If you pay attention, there shouldn't be an issue, but if you get behind by just one lesson, you will struggle. Each skill builds on the next, so you have to master each one and *then* move on." Tremont reaches into his briefcase and retrieves a stack of papers. He motions to the girl with bright-blonde hair sitting in the front row. "Hailey, will you pass these out?"

She cheerfully stands and does as she's told, handing them out one-by-one.

"Your final exam will be thirty-five percent of your final grade, and you will be tested on *all* of the material learned up until that point. I highly encourage you to make sure the entirety of your assignments are turned in on time and accurate to get any credit you can."

I take the sheet and look it over. Words including *probability, plots, histograms,* and *null hypothesis* stare back at me.

Cameron sighs heavily and meets my gaze. "We're gonna need some extra buddy study sessions."

Math was always my strong suit, but this class might pose a challenge.

Here's to hoping I can balance it with everything going on. Fingers crossed my life doesn't blow apart like the seams of the shadow realm.

CHAPTER 6

"That was brutal." Cameron sighs while shoving his stuff into his bag.

"You're telling me." I secure mine onto my shoulder carefully, not wanting yet another spill.

We take off toward the door, and a voice calls out.

"Miss Oliver, a moment, please."

I nod to Cam and walk across the room to Professor Tremont, who sits on the chair behind his desk.

He glances at the empty room. "I wanted to reach out, to tell you that if you need anything, don't hesitate to ask."

His deep-brown eyes strangely stare into mine.

"You're doing quite the service for the school. Well, you and Sydney both. So, should something come up, whether it be for statistics, the repair, or related to your curse, I'm here to help." He pauses and then laughs faintly, his dimples showing. "I don't mean to come across so overbearing. I'm sure this is all incredibly daunting. If I can be of assistance, don't waver."

"Thank you, I appreciate that." It is nice to know that if I find myself struggling in his class he might offer some leniency or guidance in getting back on track.

"Of course." He pauses and shifts his head to the door. "Better not keep your escort waiting."

It doesn't take long to comprehend broody Silas is there. I felt his presence arrive prior to the period ending.

When I get out of the room, Silas says, "What was that about?"

"He was telling me if I need help to reach out."

"With what?" He takes my bag, carrying it for me.

"Anything that comes up." I shrug. "I think he was trying to be nice."

We pass the dining hall, where the human students are beginning to eat lunch. We continue along and finally make it into the west wing for speech. Luckily, Silas leads the way because I'm still a bit rocky on my schedule, something that is *so* not my style.

Typically, I'm well put together. Totally organized and on top of everything. On time, fully prepared, and all that jazz. But now? Now, I'm a hot mess. I can't even *find* my schedule; I certainly don't have it memorized yet. What is going on with me?

Oh, right...my life is chaos.

"You should be cautious of people being nice out of the blue." Silas motions for me to sit and then claims the desk next to mine.

Apparently, we're in this class together. Something else I was unaware of, not that I'm complaining.

"I will be."

He grabs my hand, startling me but remaining serious. He holds it with a gentle firmness. "Promise me?"

I meet his gaze. "Yes, Silas, I promise."

Something is so off about him. He's typically reserved and stern, but this takes on a new level of extreme for him. He's hurting, more than usual, and it eats at me from the inside. I have to figure out what's going on, and when I get some alone time with him tonight, I hope like hell I can solve this new mystery. Here's to hoping he doesn't shut down and not talk to me.

I take the moment with his hand still on mine to push a little calming energy into him, anything to ease whatever it is he's experiencing.

Oh, Silas, I long to take all of your torment away, to free you of your demons.

Speech goes by quickly, considering it's during a lunch period. Those two time slots are allocated for the shorter classes that have fewer credit hours.

Silas walks me toward Deghan, handing him my pack. "I'll be back. Watch over her."

Confused but willing, Deghan does what he's told, side-eyeing Silas and then me.

Silas kisses my cheek softly and leaves, not bothering to explain where he's going.

"I get that you two are in love and all, but damn is he strange sometimes." Deghan clasps my hand, leading me toward the food.

My heart flutters at his words. In love? Silas is fated to one true love, but he's never fully admitted it to me. Maybe he's fated but the love part comes over time? I wonder what makes Deghan so sure.

"I'm starving. They really should let us eat first." Deghan drags me along, only dropping my hand to get a plate and extending it to me. "Ladies first."

"Thank you, sir." I curtsy and then pluck a cheeseburger from the metal tray ahead.

"Mmm, yeah, me, too." He takes two burgers, some fries, a slice of pizza, and onion rings. Sadly, he looks at his food. "I ran out of room."

"You're pathetic. What else do you want? I have space on mine." I grin at him.

"You are an absolute princess. Surprise me. You know what I'm into." He winks.

My mind flies to the time our bodies melted into one another, and it takes me longer than I'm proud to admit, to focus on the task in front of me. I decide on a massive BLT, two brownies, one for each of us, and a yogurt parfait—hopefully, that should satiate him, for now at least.

I make it to the table without tripping or losing any of the food along the way, each step more careful than the next.

"You okay over there?" Sydney asks. His gorgeous green eyes meet mine.

I'll never get over what a brilliant shade of green they are. It's comparable to someone chiseling an emerald and plopping it right around his pupil. Even the nearly black ring around them stands out beautifully.

"Accident-prone lately. Just being careful." I relax once I'm finally sitting. I place the extra food in front of Deghan, and you'd think I'd handed him a puppy.

He wraps his arm around me and squeezes tight.

The way to that man's heart is definitely through his stomach. No wonder he and Cam are so close—Cam being a bomb chef and all.

I steal a fry off Deghan's plate and munch on it. "Hey, Syd, have you talked to Tremont lately?"

Sydney wipes his mouth. "No, why? What's up?"

I shake my head. "Nothing. He um…" I pause to look around the room. "He held me back to tell me to get ahold of him if I needed anything. He mentioned what you and I were doing for the school, so I wasn't sure if he offered the same to you."

He shrugs. "Nope, not a peep. I don't have him until later, though." Sydney takes a drink of his tea, reminding me that I forgot drinks. Like he can hear into my mind, he says, "You good with tea?" He stands and points to Deghan. "Sweet for you?"

Through a mouthful of cheeseburger, Deghan mutters, "I love you, guys."

Sydney laughs. "I'll take that as a yes."

I focus on my food, my stomach growing more and more impatient by the minute. Shadow realm repair really does do a number on draining me, not to mention the whole barfing up my breakfast thing I did earlier. I should probably avoid the greasy meal, but damn does it look good.

"How are you feeling?" Sydney returns with full glasses.

I hold a napkin over my mouth while I chew what's left in there, bobbing my head to somehow speed the process up. "Much better. Whatever was in that tea did the trick."

Deghan reaches out and takes a long swig of his drink, then hands the cup to me with his nose wrinkled up. "This one is yours."

"Oh shit, I'm sorry," Sydney calls out.

"It's fine, really, just wasn't expecting it."

I swap the cups and pat Deghan on the back. "You're not a fan of dirty sock water."

Ruby comes toward us, tray in hand. "Mind if I sit with you?"

She's so tiny and shy, and it's kind of adorable.

"Absolutely." I point to Sydney. "Scooch over."

"Sup, Rubes," Deghan says with another stuffed mouth.

To an innocent bystander, one would assume Deghan hadn't eaten for days.

"Hey, Degs." She unwraps her sandwich. "I hear we're going to be back to work by the end of the week. Is that true?" She eyes Sydney and then me.

Sydney speaks up. "That's what they're saying."

I latch on to my burger, and right when it's almost to my face, a big ol' blob of ketchup falls onto my lap. "Shit." I frantically find a napkin. "Seriously?"

Why does dumb shit keep happening to me? I mean, totally ridiculous stuff that seems so silly and small but at the same time, conveniently keeps adding up.

It's like I'm cursed.

Oh, wait.

No? Is that possible? I think it's safe to say that *anything* is, but maybe I shouldn't be blaming my bad luck on some ancient curse. Maybe it's nothing other than a temporary crap time.

I wipe the substance off my leg. Luckily, my pants are dark, so even if it does stain, it won't be obvious. Regardless, though, it's hella annoying to smell of ketchup the rest of the day. Maybe if I hurry and eat, I can run to my room and change out of my pants quickly.

Yeah, that's what I'll do.

"Did you get it?" Syd hands me a napkin, this one wet.

"I think so."

He frowns. "And you think this is only another *accident*?"

I exhale, sitting closer to the table and over my plate this time. "Probably." I continue to eat my lunch, robbing Deghan of a fry here and there.

Despite his obsession with food, he doesn't seem to mind sharing.

I give Deghan what's left of my meal and grab the brownie and my backpack. "I'm going to swap out my pants. I'll see you later."

"I'll tell Psycho you went to your room," Deghan adds.

Taking a bite of the chocolatey heaven, I exit the dining hall and make my way to my room. It's only one left turn and then up the stone stairs, and into the west wing hall. My dorm is the last one of the left, and I'm pretty sure the biggest of all of them.

I open the door, and my eyes are immediately drawn to the massive, curved window along the far wall. The cushy seat calls to me, begging me to skip next period and curl up with a book. But the responsible side of me reins in my attention to my messy situation.

I set my treat on the nearby table and toss my bag on the floor, freeing up my hands to rid me of these pants. I haphazardly remove them and head to the bathroom to soak them in the sink.

They might not stain, but with my current luck, that's not something I want to risk. I only have so many clothes at the school, and I can't afford to get any more if I ruin them.

A loud sound startles me, and I accidentally fling the cold liquid all over myself.

Double shit.

CHAPTER 7

Silas rounds the corner. "Are you okay? Why are you alone?"

I point to the tiny pool of water. "Um, I spilled ketchup."

His gaze wanders down, like it's finally clicking into place for him that I'm pants-less and partially wet.

Now I'm going to have to change my top, too. Great.

He stands there silent for an awkward minute and then asks, "Do you need help?"

"Could you get me a change of clothes?"

In a flash, he leaves and is right back, the garments secured. He approaches me slowly.

I let go of the now soaked bottoms and turn to him.

Silas tugs at the hem of my shirt and pulls it over my head.

My heart seems to pound out of my chest. I'm only in my black bra and matching panties, inches away from him. Desire fills my entire body, and the connection we share thrums between us, begging to be smothered.

"Here," he whispers, holding out the new shirt.

Oh.

I take it reluctantly and pop it over my head.

He kneels, holding the pants open for me to step into. His hands graze me on their way up, sending figurative sparks flying. He stops, his face so close to mine. "I was worried about you."

"I'm worried about you, too."

Silas's brows crinkle. "Why?"

I fiddle with a stray string on my top. "You're..."

I'm cut off by a knock at the door. "Ey, you love birds decent?"

"We'll talk later, okay?" Silas runs his thumb along my cheek and across my lip, tugging it down in that drive-me-wild kind of way.

"Yeah." At least he's willing to talk tonight, that's a good sign...isn't it?

Silas vamps out of the bathroom and turns the handle, letting Deghan into the room.

"I can walk her to class." Deghan peeks around the corner at me and waves.

"I need to get my shoes."

"I'll be there when it's over to get you to last period." Silas's posture stiffens. "Be safe."

"Aye, aye, captain." Deghan holds two fingers to his forehead and salutes Silas.

I haven't gotten both shoes on, and Silas is already gone, taking a part of me with him like he always does. I'll never quite get used to that. I feel it with all my guys, but it physically manifests itself the strongest with him.

"Cute outfit." Deghan scans me up and down.

"You ready?" I ask him.

"Yep, what are you doing with that brownie, though?" He bites his lip waiting for a response.

"Half, you can have half! But I want the rest, you ravenous boy."

"I can't help it. I think I'm still growing."

At this, my eyes go wide, my gaze going all the way up his body and landing on his head. "You're already five hundred feet tall."

"Oh hush, I'm six-four." He ruffles my hair. "We can't all be tiny."

Deghan walks me to fifth period and joins me in finding a seat. I guess we have this class together. Now I can't help but wonder what I have next and who with.

"Psst," I whisper.

"All right, class," Professor Strong calls into the space with her raspy smoker's voice.

Deghan goes to speak, but I cut him off. "Never mind."

"Welcome to marketing class. I see some familiar faces from last term." She squints and examines the crowd. "The emphasis of this class will be to learn what marketing is, why it's important, and teach you how to conduct research and strategies to help scale business growth. We're going to study customer behavior, pricing, product management, and so on and so forth. Is that understood?"

The class collectively mumbles an agreement.

My final lecture of the day is intro to management, which to my pleasant surprise, is filled with Remi, Kyra, and Lillian. Honestly, I've been blessed with my lineup of courses and classmates, so maybe I'm not cursed with bad luck after all.

Although that's what I think until Allie walks in and sits at a desk.

Ugh. I really hate to be petty, but damn do I dislike that girl.

She could have potentially got me killed by pouring that booze all over me. Had I wandered off or been left alone, the demon could have easily weaseled its way in and stolen my magic, or whatever it had planned for me.

Plus, she's bitter as hell for no apparent reason. Even prior to the whole Silas thing she was rude to me. I'm not sure what crawled up her ass and died, but she needs to knock it off.

Her annoying side-eye isn't helping either.

Does she think I can't see her blatantly looking my way?

I raise my hand and wave, making sure she knows I see her.

Remi whacks my arm lightly. "You little instigator."

"She won't stop staring at me," I say with a groan.

I pull the notebook out of my backpack and flip it open, ready to jot down whatever the teacher is about to tell us. If I'm going to stop myself from smacking Allie upside the head, I'm going to have to keep my mind occupied.

Thirty minutes into the class, Kyra nearly falls out of her seat. She had nodded off, her head resting on her hand, until she moved slightly and did that thing where your arm goes out from under you and your head drops.

Remi immediately swoops in, asking her if she's okay.

Kyra yawns widely and folds her arms across her chest, leaning back into the seat.

The rest of the time goes by pretty uneventfully, minus the few times I caught Allie gawking at me. It makes no sense why she's so damn weird to me, maybe I should ask her and get it over with. I have enough problems I'm dealing with, though. Perhaps I'll keep my mouth shut for now.

"Which one of your hunks is escorting you to the formal?" Remi clicks her pen shut and tosses it inside her bag.

"Oh god, I have no idea." I have to choose? Why? And how? I want each one of them to be there with me...is that too much to ask?

Remi shakes her head. "Better figure it out. Less than a week away."

"Who's your date?"

Her eyes flicker to Kyra and back to me. "Not sure yet."

Kyra breaks her conversation with the redhead next to her and joins us. "What are you two talking about?" She wraps her arms around us and tugs us toward the door.

"Do you have a date for this weekend?" I ask, knowing damn well Remi is going to murder me.

"Um, no, no yet. One of Ethan's friends, I think his name is Noah...he asked me." Kyra continues to drag us along.

Remi tenses but doesn't say anything.

"So, are you going with him?"

Kyra scowls. "Hell no. He's pretty and all but he only wants in my pants, no thanks."

Remi lets out an almost silent breath she must have been holding.

"Plus," Kyra reaches across and pokes Remi in the side, "screw boys. I thought we could do a girl's date instead."

Remi doesn't speak, not a single word, clearly in shock from getting the very thing she was desperately hoping for.

I push my calming energy into her, and her body relaxes ever so slightly.

"Yeah, of course," she finally manages.

Kyra loosens the grip I didn't realize she had on my arm.

Was she nervous that Remi would say no? Maybe those two are more on the same page than they think.

The familiar influence calls to me from across the foyer.

I steal a glance around, my gaze settling on Silas, keeping his distance but close by. I mouth, "I'll be okay."

His gorgeous face frowns.

I offer him a weak smile.

He taps his wrist and holds up one hand to signify five o'clock.

Apparently, he's holding true to having our talk.

"Think the dining hall has anything out? I want some snacks," Kyra whines.

"If they don't, I know where we can find some." And that's exactly where I take them.

I lead us through the big open eating room and around to the random door. I knock, and the girls stare at me like I'm an idiot, waiting for something to happen.

"Trust me," I add.

I lose a little hope, but then the door swings open, and those two cheerful faces I expected to see smile at us.

"What's up, princess?" Deghan beams.

I inhale something sweet and crane my head to see inside. "What's lover boy making you?"

He grins and extends his arm to fully give us room to enter. "Pancakes."

I shake my head. "I knew I'd find you here."

"He's hungry, literally *all* of the time," Cameron teases and smacks Deghan's arm.

If anyone is in love, it's those two. What Silas and I share is special, but what Cameron and Deghan have is absolutely precious. I have no idea if either one of them are actually into guys, but damn do they have some chemistry.

"You have your own personal chef?" Kyra asks Deghan. "No fair."

Cameron looks up from his post near a skillet and winks at me. A white hand towel is thrown over his shoulder. The confidence he has in the kitchen is so sexy. He nods to the counter where he's stationed.

I walk over, putting my hands down to steady myself, and hop onto the cold metal surface. I immediately flash to the memory of us in the library, him pressed up against me as I sat on top of that desk.

"You having a little déjà vu?" His voice is quiet, and the others don't hear.

"You could say that." I blush.

He flips one of his heavenly creations and takes a step toward me, leaning in to graze my cheek with his lips for the softest and sweetest kiss. He breaks away, and our eyes meet, his waves of ocean blue stealing my breath.

"You hungry?"

More like insatiable.

Cam divvies the food up between us, giving Deghan a massive serving. He made a blueberry sauce, too, and the combination is good enough that it doesn't need syrup. That's how you know something is freaking awesome—you don't have to drench it to choke it down.

Deghan hums along while he eats, his cheerfulness making me that much happier.

If only Lillian, Sydney, and Silas could be here, then it truly would be perfect.

"I wonder if Syd is hungry?" I glance at the clock on the wall. If I hurry, I can take him leftovers and sit with him until it's time to see Silas.

"Pretty sure I saw him heading to the library." Cameron sets his plate on the counter and starts to clean up.

I join him, gathering the dirty dishes from the girls.

"Your secret is no longer safe, you realize that, right?" Kyra looks from Deghan to Cam. "You should totally expect me to randomly stop by for free food." She giggles and then stops. "I'm going to gain fifty pounds." She reaches out and pokes Deghan in the arm. "How do you stay so jacked with how much you eat? I mean, no offense, but you're like a garbage disposal."

Deghan shrugs, his mouth full. "Metabolism," he mumbles.

"So," I say, leaning down against the counter. I can't even get my next word out before scorching pain slices through me, and I reflexively pull my hand away.

"Shit." Cameron slides to his knees in front of me. "Let me see it."

"No, I'm okay." I bite my cheek and bob my head rapidly. "I'm good."

"Willow, please." He cups his palms around mine, waiting to assess the damage.

I stop clutching it tightly and cringe when I hold it out.

"Did you put your hand on that skillet?" Remi's eyes go wide.

Okay, so that wasn't a counter, that was a blisteringly hot surface.

Cameron winces during his inspection.

Then, out of fucking nowhere, the door to the room bursts open. Silas rushes in at a quick human speed, considering the girl's presence.

"What happened?" His jaw is rigid, his voice harsh. "I said, *what happened?*"

"I burnt myself. It's all right." I reach to him with my unharmed hand in an attempt to calm him down.

"*All right?* I can't leave you alone with them for *five* minutes without something happening." Silas focuses on Cameron. "Get off her. You'll only make it worse."

Cameron stands, a look on his face I'm unfamiliar with. "*You,*" he shoves his finger into Silas's chest. "You are what makes it worse."

I take a hesitant breath.

What the fuck is going on?

CHAPTER 8

"D on't start with me, Cooper." Silas stiffens. "You guys can't be trusted to keep her safe," he adds.

I've never known him to use Cameron's last name.

"Trusted? Are you serious? She's an *adult*, Silas. You treat her like a fucking child. I'm pretty sure she's..." Cameron glances toward the girls.

Deghan perks up. "Yeah, so this might be a good time to leave, it's sort of a family matter now. Not that y'all aren't family...we just need a minute, please." He pushes them toward the exit.

"Uh..." one of them says.

"Are you sure? Willow, you good?" Remi asks.

"Mmhm," I say through gritted teeth, the residual stinging still taking place on my flesh.

The door closes, and Cameron doesn't skip a beat. "She's taken on demons and saved *all* of our asses. Stop pretending she isn't capable of taking care of herself."

"I'm done with you." Silas turns, but Cameron grabs his arm.

"No, you don't call the shots. I'm sick of this bullshit attitude from you."

I feel the surge moments prior to it happening. Fierce aggression boils up inside Silas.

Then, the unexpected. Cameron shoves him. Full-on two-handed and, bracing himself with his feet, he heaves into him.

Unfortunately for Cam, Silas has that whole immortal, super-strong thing going on, so he doesn't budge.

It only adds to both of them being more pissed.

"You don't touch me." Silas raises his arm.

Deghan and I rush between them, not wanting a total fight to break out.

"Hey, snap out of it," I urge Silas.

Deghan grabs Cameron's shoulders. "Come on, buddy."

I understand they're all stressed out but, um, my hand is still on fire over here.

"He's not wrong," Deghan cautiously says. "You're being a dick. More so than you normally are."

And now there is another reason to suspect that something out of the ordinary is going on with Silas.

Not to mention, what the hell is going on with Cameron? I've never known him to react that way either.

My injury takes me completely away from whatever the hell they're doing, my body urging me toward the sink. I turn on the cold water and plunge my hand under. It adds to the pain but somehow eases it a little, too.

Silas vamps over and reaches out for me, but I shut off the water, wrap my hand in a stray towel, and disregard his every attempt.

"Willow, please. I need to see it," Silas begs.

I leave the room, holding my arm to my chest, and go straight to the one person who I trust to think rationally right now.

Sydney.

I rush down the stairs carefully so I don't faceplant again. I don't exactly need another incident added to the already shitty week I seem to be having.

A guy and a girl I've never met look up at me from across the library.

I avoid their stares and continue on, heading toward the supernatural side. Once I'm out of earshot from them, I call out quietly, "Sydney."

I take in a deep breath. I can do this. I've done this in the past to find him. I close my eyes and ponder, "Syd, where are you?"

Like fucking magic, the light flickers, and a strange buzzing sound emerges.

I spin to locate the source and settle my sights upon a bee, gold and black stripes along its furry body.

It hovers in front of my face then whips its body and heads down the hall.

I follow it without question.

A minute later, the bee pops into a room and then buzzes out and away.

I glimpse inside and see Sydney. I turn and quickly thank the vanishing creature.

Did that really just happen?

"Willow." Sydney looks up, panic and confusion trailing his features. "What's wrong?"

I hold out my towel-wrapped hand. "I burnt myself, and everyone is acting like complete psychos. I should have gone to the infirmary, but I wanted to find you first."

"Jesus..." He's around the table in a hurry. "Can I see it?" Sydney's concerned gaze meets mine. He pulls the covering back a little and flinches. "It's blistered. We need to treat this immediately."

"Is it bad?" Tears well up, and I'm not sure if it's from the pain or the sheer exhaustion of this overwhelming day.

Sydney cups my face with his palm. "No, sweet girl. We'll get you fixed up in no time."

He's lying, but his kindness helps ease my nerves.

"Tremont, I'm fairly certain he has healing abilities." Syd wraps his arm around me and leads me out of the tiny room.

Abigail secured such a big space for me. I've definitely been taking it for granted. It makes sense now why people prefer it.

"You said everyone is acting crazy, what did you mean?"

"Silas came in and raged out on Cameron, then Cam all but punched Silas in the face in response. Something is *wrong* with him."

"With who?" Sydney faces me.

"Silas."

He huffs. "Tell me something I don't already know."

I sniffle. "I'm serious. Deghan even said that Silas was acting worse than usual. He feels *off*."

"Maybe he's stressed out..."

I want to believe that's all it is, but part of me is fully aware it's not that. The connection Silas and I share allows me to *sense* those types of differences.

"I wonder where Tremont is," Sydney whispers, almost like a thought out loud.

"Teacher's lounge," I say confidently.

He side-eyes me but doesn't ask questions.

We approach the north wing hallway, and the man himself exits the lounge with a steaming cup of coffee. Tremont squints and tilts his head. "What's going on?"

"We need your help." Sydney motions to my hand.

Without skipping a beat, Tremont says, "Here, this way." He takes us to the infirmary.

The door clicks shut behind him, and it's only me, Syd, and him alone in this silent and sterile room.

My body gravitates toward the comfort of Sydney.

He puts his arm around me like he can sense my concern. "She burnt her hand. It's blistered. I'm guessing second or third-degree."

"I see. Now, may I?" He steps closer, his own palm outstretched, waiting for me to deposit the wound. He unwraps the cloth carefully, the skin tugging in an attempt to stick to the fabric.

I look away, not wanting to see whatever is under there.

Sydney rubs circles on my back.

"Go ahead and have a seat." Tremont pushes a chair in my direction. He grips the little table on wheels and rolls it over to us. "I'm going to start now. You'll feel some cooling, but it shouldn't be painful, okay?"

I nod, keeping my eyes away from what he's doing.

Sydney kneels next to me, his hands tucked around my free one.

A chill courses through my entire side, starting at the base of my neck and rolling down my arm, onto where the burn lies.

I do my best not to flinch and make things any worse.

"You doing all right?" Sydney presses his lips to each one of my knuckles.

I've never seen him so...romantic? Is that the word that fits what he's doing?

He's never babied me this way.

I can't say I hate it; it's definitely helping keep me from freaking out about my melted skin.

On second thought, though...except for Deghan, all of my guys are acting differently, what the hell?

The door creaks open, Silas appearing on the other side. He doesn't say a word, just shuts it behind him and stands firmly in place.

A few moments pass, and Tremont finally speaks. "Are you experiencing any pain?"

I don't dare glance his way yet. "Not really, no." It's not a complete lie, but the throbbing ache that is still present says otherwise.

"Because of the severity of the wound, we will have to do multiple treatments to make sure it heals properly. Possibly twice a day for the next few, and then we'll go from there."

"Is there an issue?" Sydney asks.

"I can't say I expected it to be normal, but it's not working like I had anticipated. There seems to be a barrier disallowing me from giving proper healing. I'm confident in a full recovery, it may just take a little more time than normal."

Tremont rustles around with a package of some sort.

"I'm going to dress it with a bandage you can keep on for one to two weeks. We'll be able to continue the sessions without removing it. I encourage you to tape a bag around your hand when you shower. Try to get someone else to help you wash your hair. Avoid putting any pressure on it, and do whatever you can to not pop those blisters."

My hand is going to be wrapped for two weeks? We have a formal *this freaking weekend*. I'm going to look like an idiot.

Why am I surprised? Everything seems to be going to shit these days, anyway.

"Here." Tremont holds his closed palm out. "For pain. It'll help reduce swelling, too."

"What is it?" Silas asks.

"Mr. Harlow, it's simply an anti-inflammatory." He swivels in his chair. "Do you want to see for yourself?" He opens to reveal two pearly-white pills.

Silas squints from about ten feet away. "Very well."

I pop the medicine into my mouth and swallow it without taking a drink from the random cup Tremont hands me. I know by now that I should be wary of a clear liquid from a stranger.

Professor Tremont is helping me, so why do I have such a strange gut feeling about him?

He pokes at his watch, and the screen lights up. "How about meet me here at about nine tonight?"

"Okay," I say, finally peeping at my now wrapped hand. It's not so scary if I can't see what's under there. I've never been one to cringe so easily, but with everything going on, it's something I can't exactly handle at this time.

Sydney and I walk to the door, Silas following us out like a sad zombie.

We pause next to the garden.

"I'm going to clean up my mess in the library. You sure you're all right?" Sydney studies my face and flicks his attention to the sulking Silas. "I'll be up in a little bit. I'm going to see what kind of herbs I have that can help with your recovery."

I pull him in for a hug, desperate to cling to his energy for a moment. It's cool and warm and cloaks me with a temporary contentment.

I watch him until his head disappears in the stairwell to the basement.

"Willow." Silas touches my shoulder from behind.

I sigh, my mind going blank at what I want and need to say to him.

How can he possibly explain the way he's been acting lately?

And what if there is no excuse...and the reason he's being this way is because that's simply how he is. Maybe his feelings are changing or have changed toward me, and I'm no longer the person I thought I was to him. What if we were never fated, and I was a fool for ever thinking he might actually love me?

The conversation I was so ready to have with him now hangs over my head, all the unknowns suffocating me. What if this is the one that finally breaks us? Losing him isn't something I think I'm capable of handling. How could I ever possibly prepare myself for that to happen?

But what if I've already lost him?

CHAPTER 9

The walk to my dorm is silent aside from our footsteps on the elaborate stone floor.

"Are you hurting?" he asks once we make it into the private space.

I shrug, not wanting to lie but not quite wanting to tell the truth.

He keeps his distance, and that alone is more painful than the burn on my hand.

I make my way over to the window and attempt to distract myself from the overwhelming sadness taking hold.

The sky is darkening from a storm rolling in.

"What did you want to talk about?" His voice is still lingering near the door.

Now is my chance, the opening I've been waiting for. I need to ask him what's wrong, to figure out why he's so...shut off. But I can't. I clam up. I'm too afraid of the answer to say a single fucking word. If I go back to pretending everything is okay, it will be. It has to be.

"Willow?" He takes a step forward but stops.

Why won't he come closer?

If I was wrong, if all of this all along has been wrong, and we aren't actually fated to be together, what is this invisible force that binds us?

The way I can tell he's close without knowing it.

The way we can *feel* each other's pain.

His absence that practically wrecks me every time, like my soul is being ripped apart from him not being near.

What about the electricity that pulses between us with each touch?

Even his blood can heal me. Something he said had to do with our fate.

But what if all of that is some stupid mistake—a misunderstanding.

"I'm..." His voice cracks, a new level of broken showing through. "I'm sorry. For reacting the way that I did. And I understand if you don't want me around because of that. But you need to hear that I'm sorry. I hope you realize that I would never hurt Cameron. Not unless he hurt you. I shouldn't have freaked out on him. It won't happen again."

My mind does circles while trying to figure out what he's saying. I mean, at face value, he's apologizing, and that's great, but he really thinks *I* wouldn't want *him* around? I'm the one who's freaking scared to death *his* feelings have changed.

"I'll go. I won't bother you anymore, but I'll always be here if you need me." He sighs.

It crumbles my heart into a million pieces.

"Silas," I call out, turning to face him.

Rain pours down, pounding against the window in my room. Lightning strikes, and thunder crackles in its wake.

He stands there like he's not sure whether to retreat or come toward me.

"If I ask you a question, will you promise to tell me the truth?" My palm throbs and reminds me of the potentially long road to recovery ahead.

He swallows. "If that's what you want, yes."

"Can I also ask that you not shut down on me and leave?"

He averts his eyes to the floor and nods. "I'm sorry I do that."

I take a few steps, closing the gap between us. "I'm not mad at you because of it. But I want you to feel safe talking to me. If it takes time, all I ask is that you try."

He looks up, his metallic eyes glistening with something that resembles hope. "I will."

"Will you please tell me what's wrong?" I place my palm against his chest. "Something happened. I can't quite figure it out but I'm certain of it."

Silas draws at his lip with his pearly-white teeth. "You're right."

A huge wave crashes over me. Part relief, but then part panic over whatever he's about to say next.

"I'm not sure what it is, though. It's like a darkness has taken hold of me. I'm not...*myself* all the time. At first, it was subtle, but now it's constant, and I keep losing control."

Here I was, thinking he was having a change of heart, when in reality he's been facing a demon all on his own. How could I be so stupid to ignore the signs?

"How long has it been going on?" I lock my gaze on to his.

"It's hard to pinpoint exactly, but I'd say it started over the weekend."

So, something transpired in the past week? Okay...what happened then? Well, I went off campus with Sydney, got lured into a trap, battled and defeated a demon that spawned itself into a shit ton of Silases. Then, I ran off with Silas and had a magical time in a random cabin, went back to the school, sort of made up with Sydney after he nearly killed himself, and then we did the Reperio stone thing.

Was it something to do with us having sex?

Maybe the curse isn't my bad luck but something to do with Silas? But Silas isn't the one who's cursed, so how would that even be possible?

"And you have no idea what caused it?"

He shakes his head, but I don't totally buy it.

"You said you'd tell me the truth."

"I interfered." His words are so small.

"What?" I tilt his chin up to make him look at me.

"Sydney told me not to break the circle."

"The circle, what are you talking about, Silas?"

"I shouldn't have been there. It's sacred land. I fucked up, and I think I'm being punished for it."

Oh god, he means at the ritual when we tried to locate my mom.

"Shh...no, you didn't fuck up. We can figure this out. This is good. Talking is good. This helps. I'm going to help you fix this."

He shakes his head. "I don't think this can be fixed."

"Silas. Look at me. Remember not being able to touch. You told me the same thing. You said it was impossible. And the time I thought I couldn't get that demon out of my head, you told me *'nothing is impossible'* and reminded me of that very instance. If I'm capable of ridding us of both of those things, there should be no doubt in your mind that I can do this."

Hopefully, by convincing him I can assure myself, too. How in the fuck am I going to get something out of *him* that I know nothing about? I guess I had no knowledge of the other curses either and I still managed to break them. This one is different, though. It's in him, so I have to learn about it secondhand.

All while dealing with my own.

I can do this. What's one more thing to try to tackle?

"You're really not mad at me?" This time it's him who forces my attention.

"No, of course not. I've been worried sick thinking you didn't like me anymore."

At this, he pulls me into his arms. "Never in a million years."

And for some reason, I believe him.

"You understand we're going to have to tell the group, right? Especially Sydney."

He groans loudly and throws himself onto my little bed. "Do we have to?"

"Yep, transparency is important."

"But, I don't wanna..."

"Silas Harlow, stop being a baby." I hop onto the bed next to him and slap him playfully. "I just realized I have no idea what your middle name is."

He grips me by the waist, doing his signature move, flipping me over and landing on top of me. It's simple and yet so fucking hot. "Guess." His breath mingles with mine.

No way in hell can I think of a name right now with him *this* damn close to me. It feels like it's been a billion years since our bodies got familiar with each other.

I lean up for a kiss.

"Nope. You have to try first." A grin forms on his perfectly sculpted face. He traces his tongue along his bottom lip, teasing me that much more.

"Uh...danger."

He lets out a small laugh. "You are the worst, Willow Victoria."

"What, no fair. How do you know my middle name?"

He doesn't bother replying. Instead, moves forward and gives me exactly what I want, his plump lips on mine.

If he's going to avoid answering, this is one thing I'm willing to accept.

I weave the fingers of my good hand up under that black t-shirt of his, sliding up his chiseled chest and along his strong back.

He takes my face into his hands, pressing his soul into me through our kisses.

Never will I ever get used to this feeling. This complete fucking bliss, this drug-like euphoria when our skin touches.

He pauses with his lips on mine, but they're still.

No, no, no, please don't stop. I need more.

"We have company." His words murmur against my mouth, and he runs his tongue along my bottom lip before climbing off me.

"That is totally not fair."

A knock hits the door.

I close my eyes and drag my arms over my head. Uh. "Come in," I call out.

"Hey, sorry, didn't mean to interrupt." Sydney's shyness flows through the space.

Sitting up, I notice the brown paper sack he brought.

"Some stuff to hopefully help speed up the healing. I can leave it..." He scans the room until he finds the table. "Over here."

I scoot back to the wall, propping a pillow behind me. "We need to talk, Syd."

"Already?" Silas pleads with me with his eyes.

I hate to disappoint him, but the sooner the better with this kind of stuff.

"Okay..." Sydney looks from me to Silas. "We, as in, both of you?"

"Long story short, there is *something* wrong with Silas, for real."

"Geez, thanks, Wills." Silas huffs.

I toss an extra pillow at him. "Not like *that*, you brat."

"Please explain." Sydney drags a chair over and sits, leaning forward with his elbows resting on his knees, fully invested.

"He's been acting off, and it might be because of the Reperio stone. We think something happened during the ritual."

Sydney cuts me off. "You broke the fucking circle."

"Yeah," Silas confirms.

Sydney lowers his head and sighs loudly. "This is bad. Really bad."

"Why? What knowledge do you have on this kind of thing?" Silas practically begs.

Syd shakes his head. "Other than you now have a horrible entity consuming you, slowly eating away any bit of goodness inside your soul. Which, no offense, but how much was there to begin with? It will only continue to get worse and worse and worse until it basically drives you mad. And then there is the whole, it's fucking *impossible* to get rid of without..."

"Without what?" I ask when he doesn't continue. The silence is deafening.

"Destroying the stone," he says slowly.

"And destroying any chance I have at finding my parents."

"Exactly," he confirms.

"No, not happening," Silas interjects. "I'll be *fine*. See, I'm good. I'm not even repulsed by your presence now, Sydney."

"This power over you won't stop. It's wicked magic. Evil. If you're exposed for too long, you'll lose total control." Sydney shows actual concern, which is surprisingly terrifying, considering it's Silas he's talking about.

"We aren't for sure that's what it is. So, there is no need to jump to any conclusions or do anything irrational. Maybe it's only a vampire thing," Silas continues to defend himself.

"Where is it?" Sydney questions.

"The stone?"

Silas reaches into his black leather jacket, unzips a compartment, and pulls the gleaming red rock out.

"You keep that thing on you?" I shift to try to get a better look at it.

"Okay, first thing we need to do is get it *away* from you,"

Sydney demands. "I gave it back to you, and I told you to keep it safe, not put it next to your damn heart."

"How can I be sure that you won't destroy it?" Silas grips the stone firmly.

"I would never purposely do something to hurt Willow."

"That's what I'm worried about."

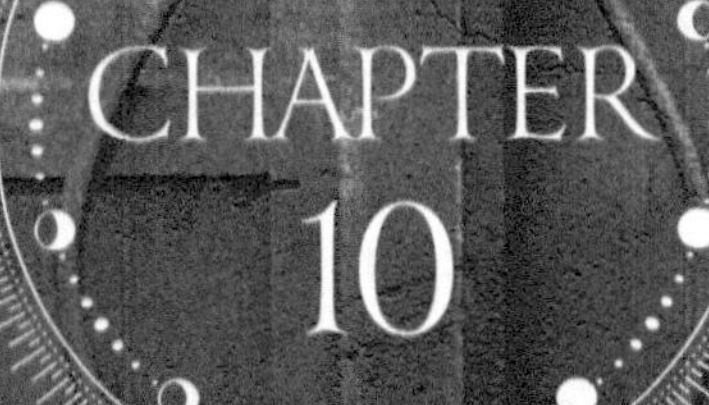

Silas let Sydney take the stone.

I have no idea where Sydney put it, and I'm glad.

I'm torn completely in two.

Of course, I want to smash it into smithereens and get *my* Silas back, but if I do, I might lose my mother forever. That's not a risk I'm sure I'm willing to take yet.

But what if I lose Silas forever by letting whatever is happening to him continue to get worse? That's unbearable, too.

So, for now, we wait. We count down the days and desperately hope that the stone recharges under the full moon this weekend, and I can search for my mom and dad again, and then destroy the damn thing and save Silas.

With my luck, though, I'm not so sure things will go to plan.

And that alone is what kept me up all night, leaving me tired as hell on my second day of the new term's classes.

I mean, no big deal, it's not like everyone is depending on me and Sydney to finish the realm repair today or anything.

Here's to hoping I can get through the morning without puking.

At least with the Silas distraction, no one is focused on me and my continuous accidents.

"How's the burn?" Walker asks from across the room. He strolls over, eyeing the bandage. "That's the wrapping you can wear for an extended time, right?"

So much for the diversion.

"Yep." I hold my hand out in front of me, turning it from side to side. "It'll be fine." I force a smile.

"Tremont is a talented healer. You're in good hands." Walker shakes his head. "Bad pun, sorry."

I should probably wait for a better time, but I find the question burning into me. "Any word on my parents?"

Walker shakes his head. "Nothing concrete yet."

It's like a knife stabs through me with every moment that passes. How is it possible that I've lost my mom? Will I ever get her back? The endless possibilities eat me alive.

"Here is your coffee." Sydney sets the cup on the desk next to me. "I put a couple extra ice cubes in it."

"Thanks, Syd." I take a long sip. It's perfectly warm and hazelnutty.

"You sure you're up to this?" Abigail holds the earmuffs out to me.

No, but what's the point in potentially ruining something else?

"Let's do it."

Sydney and I go through the motions. Headgear. Hands. Locking our gazes. The magnificent flow of magic. The bandage doesn't seem to stop it from coursing into one another.

Fluorescent pink and bright green sparkles cascade around us.

"Hi."

"Hey, you," I reply.

"How are you?"

"Better now."

"Yeah?" He grins.

"I enjoy our time together. It's a nice break from the rest of the chaos of the world."

"It is, isn't it?"

"What about you?"

Sydney shrugs. *"I'm okay."*

"Want to talk about it?"

"Meh, not really."

"I'm always here if you need me." I hate that he's internally dealing with things on his own. I understand it's a touchy subject, considering his parents have basically abandoned him after the whole demon debacle, but that doesn't mean he should have to deal with it alone.

Thirty minutes pass while Sydney and I have small talk in our heads together. It's not deep like some of the conversations we have, but it's good to sit back and get some one-on-one time with him.

I nearly jump when Abigail waves her hand in front of us.

We drag our hands away, breaking the connection.

"What's up?" I take the covering off my ears.

"We're ready to test it out." Her eyes are bright with true excitement. "Do you two want to do the honors?"

Us? Alone? Why does such a simple task seem so scary?

How has my brain not wrapped itself around the fact that we would be doing this very thing soon?

"Sure," Sydney answers. He takes my uninjured hand and leads me to the door.

Walker and Abigail follow.

"This is truly astonishing work you two have done. You

should be proud." Walker grips Sydney on the back. "To put it into perspective, with our calculations, this would have taken close to a year without your assistance."

"Wow," I mutter. No wonder they wanted our help.

All four of us stand on the outside of the classroom, and in unison, we say, "Infito grantum modem."

The purple haze appears in a normal manner, only stronger this time.

My mind takes me on a journey to the first day I saw the strange violet. I had thought I was going batshit crazy.

Now it's something I've grown used to. Along with the energy drain I experience every time I learn more about the supernatural world. Oh, can't forget about the non-stop buzzing that eventually died down once I familiarized myself with my *special* peers.

Sydney weaves his fingers between mine, and we go through.

Like in the past, I notice no change, my gaze immediately shifting to where the wall and ceiling meet. In confirmation of our success, a small flicker ripples at the seams, but otherwise it's fully intact.

"Holy shit," Sydney blurts out. "We actually did it." He reels me in, enveloping me into a hug.

I enjoy the embrace but don't dare take my gaze away from the joints keeping the room together. It's been some time since everything went down, but the fear is still very real, especially with this being the first time I'm stepping foot in the shadow realm since I thought I killed Silas.

A moment that broke me.

A moment I will *never* get past.

Walker and Abigail smile at each other and wander around the room, checking it over.

They mumble to one another, and they each take notes.

"We're going to run tests over the next twenty-four hours, which in here is clearly much longer, and if all goes well, we should be able to offer select classes in here, starting tomorrow."

Walker's eyes are lit up like Christmas lights. "I really am amazed, you two. This is incredible. The sheer power you share. It's inconceivable."

"Honestly, from my readings, I think the realm is in better shape than it was prior to the damage. More secure." Abigail puts her pen to her cheek and then writes something down. "Yeah, absolutely."

"Well," I say. "I'm glad we could help. It was my fault and all."

"You did us a favor, really." Walker looks back at me from his place a few feet away where he's examining the seam.

"I'm going to head back if that's okay. I'm feeling a little drained."

"Oh, yes. We'll be right behind you." Walker frowns slightly, his caring dad-ness coming to the surface. "There are snacks in the front desk if you need a pick-me-up."

"Thanks." I glance at Sydney. "You staying?"

"I'm coming with you."

Once again, we lock hands.

"Infito grantum hodem."

The words I spoke when I so frantically tried to get us out of the shadow realm during the attack by the evil demon.

Are there such things as *nice* demons?

We cross over into the normal plane, and a wave of relief washes over me.

"You okay?" Syd studies me with that concerned Sydney stare of his.

"It's a lot," I admit.

He nods like he understands and takes me back into his arms.

I breathe in his earthy scent and let his warming touch soothe me. "You smell good."

Sydney smiles into my hair. "So do you. Is that vanilla? It reminds me of these huge flowers that bloom behind my parents' house. They're this really pretty light purple and grow up these trellises."

"Clematis," I say.

"Is that what they are?" He takes another whiff and holds me tighter.

"Probably."

Sydney moves away, but only enough to look at my face. He tucks a strand of my disobedient silver hair behind my ear. "I'm proud of you."

I furrow my brows. "Why?"

He runs a finger down my cheek, his gaze trailing it and then back up to mine. "You've been through a lot. And here you are. Still going. It's admirable."

What other choice do I have?

I find myself speechless.

"I'm not so sure that I could have gotten through any of this without you," he admits.

"Syd..."

The moment slows down, our hug seeming to last forever.

His eyes flicker to my lips, and a second later, he slowly inches forward. Sydney's lips meet mine, and it's not rushed or full of heated desire, it's...meaningful. Like he's desperate for me to recognize that he needs me. His kiss speaks a hidden message that only he and I can understand.

Sydney breaks the connection to leave a kiss on my forehead, and then my nose. They're both so soft and delicate that my heart stutters.

A whoosh of air floats by, and Abigail and Walker appear from the purple haze.

Sydney and I quickly back away from each other.

"We, um, need to get our things," she says like *she's* the embarrassed one.

"I was just leaving," I add. "I need to get something from my dorm." A total lie. If anything, I need to process the feeling from that interaction with Sydney.

I snatch my bag and bolt from the room, not waiting for a reply. I press my fingers to my mouth and savor the memory of his touch.

The sound of footsteps follows me down the hall and up the west wing stairs.

"Willow," Sydney calls out quietly. With my back to him, he continues forward, stopping with his chest hovering against me. "Did I do something wrong?"

I shake my head but don't turn around.

His tone saddens. "You still haven't forgiven me." He exhales. "I'm sorry. I'll never tell you enough how sorry I am."

His weight shifts away from me and creates a coldness where he once was.

"I'll go. I won't bother you anymore, not until you're ready, even if that takes an eternity."

The thought of him leaving ruins me, the same way it did months ago when I tried to protect them all by distancing myself.

This is for the better, I had thought. Probably what he does right now, too.

I spin on my heel, grabbing on to his hand to stop him. "No."

His gaze falls to our hold and then rises to my eyes.

"Don't go."

He takes in a breath and steps close.

I reach back and open my door, wincing the second my bandage rubs the handle.

We stumble inside, mouths already finding a home with each other.

His kiss is like honey, perfectly smooth and sweet.

I bump into a bed, falling onto my butt. I grin against his lips and go to scoot back, giving him room to climb up, but he stops me.

Sydney kneels between my legs with his head down.

I run my fingers through his darky curly hair that falls across his forehead.

"What's wrong?" I whisper.

Those seductively green eyes lock on to mine, and he takes my hand into his.

"*Willow,*" his voice appears in my head.

"Syd..." I grow worried by each passing second.

"I..." His energy is potently scared.

His mind is a mess; his thoughts run rampant.

I can't make sense of it until all at once, the words become clear.

A tear wells in the corner of his eye from his admission.

"Say it out loud," I say in response.

He swallows. "I love you."

Happiness consumes me, and it's like a bolt of energy pierces through my body. My senses are heightened, and somehow, I feel more powerful than ever.

Love sure is a strange thing.

Would it be foolish of me to think that anything will ever be the same as it was before I thought he betrayed me? Absolutely. But maybe I should get over ever thinking that it should be that way. Sometimes, going through things with someone is what makes your bond stronger than ever. Maybe the rise and fall of our shared trauma will be the glue that keeps us connected, but not out of obligation or necessity, but because we really are good for each other and will overcome any obstacle thrown at us.

Because we love each other. Not superficially, but deep down, honest to goodness, the real deal...love.

With my hand still on his, I think into him, *"I love you."*

The smile on his face goes all the way to his eyes, and damn does it fuel my soul. He presses his finger to my lips.

"I love you, Sydney."

He takes my face into his hands, kissing me like he's afraid I might disappear. His body glides along mine, and we fall back onto the bed.

Taking his time, he removes every inch of my clothing, even my socks. He leaves a trail of kisses up my entire body on his way back, sending chills dancing over my figure.

I have to be cautious with my wound when I go to try to take his shirt off.

I flinch, and he hops off the bed and strips the shirt over his head, confirming that he, too, is a sight for sore eyes. The lines of his abs are much more subtle than the other guys, but definitely there and sexy all the same.

I rest on my elbows, waiting for him a little impatiently. Hearing his confession and watching him undress is enough foreplay for me.

He takes his time, inching his way on top of me, careful not to bump into my hand.

Once in place, his firmness tells me that he's as ready as I am.

"Are you sure?" he asks.

I reel him in for a kiss and reach down, stroking him at the same time, guiding him to my entrance.

He pushes himself so gently into me, easing himself in. He gasps into my mouth in pleasure. Sydney takes it slow, rocking himself back and forth into me with these lengthy and unhurried motions.

The satisfaction is nothing I've ever known and brings me closer and closer to the edge with each deliberately gradual movement.

Minutes and minutes go by this way. This never picking up, but consistent loving experience.

Once all the way in, he pauses, trailing my face with his gaze.

The pressure and angle of his body drives me wild.

"I love you, Willow Oliver."

His words are my undoing, and honestly, I have no fucking clue how it's possible, considering he wasn't even fucking moving. I come undone in a powerful mess of emotions, and it's everything I can do to bite back the scream that nearly leaves my chest.

He pulls himself out, and despite being in the middle of a forever-long orgasm, I take him into my hand.

Sydney licks his thumb and presses it to me, sending me over yet another edge and into round two of what I thought would never end. Without hesitating, he leans back down, pressing his lips against mine.

I don't stop the up and down of my hand until he finishes onto my stomach, my second release matched up with his.

Breathless, Sydney rolls onto his side next to me.

I'm panting and full of life as my gaze wanders to the clock across the room.

I sit up in a rush. "Shit, we're going to be late."

CHAPTER 11

"Willow," Professor Tremont calls out. He points to his palm and motions for me to come over.

This time, though, I grasp Cameron's hand and drag him along. I still can't seem to shake the strange feeling Tremont gives me, so I use Cam to ease the weirdness.

Cam's fingers wrap around mine and reassure me he's more than happy about the decision. His easy-going nature is what makes me care for him even more.

Speaking of, I need to talk to him about what happened when I burnt myself. It's not characteristic of him to react the way that he did with Silas. Maybe something is going on with him that he hasn't told us about.

"How are you feeling?" Tremont asks.

"Not bad," I lie. Don't get me wrong, the pain is tolerable, but holy shit does it not want to let up. Not to mention, if I accidentally bump into something, it sends pain shooting down my arm.

"May I?"

I hold it out to him, and he glances at the door. I assume he's checking to make sure the coast is clear.

He hovers his hand a few inches above mine and closes his eyes, a reddish power flowing from him and into me.

It's a cooling flush that eventually becomes lukewarm.

"That should do it for now. Make sure to find me this evening , and we'll do this again." He rubs right in the center of his palm with his thumb.

"Thanks," I mutter.

We get outside the room, and Cam speaks up. "Is that how he always is?"

"What do you mean?" I look over my shoulder.

"I'm probably overthinking it." He lets go but then quickly puts his arm around my shoulder, pulling me close. "That thing really doesn't hurt?"

I peek at him out of the corner of my eye. He totally knows I'm lying. "It doesn't feel great."

"Why didn't you tell him?"

I shrug. "He's supposed to be some great healer. Maybe I'm defective."

Cam laughs, and it's fucking adorable, his bright-white teeth showing. "If that's true, then what does that make me?"

"Perfect," I whisper.

He comes to a complete stop, spinning around and clamping on to my shoulders. "Willow Oliver, did you say that I'm *perfect?*"

I roll my lips inward to seal my mouth shut.

He grins wide and grabs my face, kissing me on the forehead, then the cheek, the other cheek, my chin, my nose, the top of my head. "You really know how to steal a guy's heart, don't you?"

Little does he know—he already has mine.

A few more smooches later, he finishes. "See you and the girls later for post-school snacks?"

"With you cooking, I wouldn't miss it." I attempt to wink at him.

Cameron giggles. "You really need to work on that." He starts walking backward, still facing me. "No getting hurt today, deal?"

"I'll do my best."

I make it to speech to find Silas standing near the doorway with his hands folded over his chest, looking grumpy as hell—his usual.

"Why are you always so mad?" I plant my lips on his cheek.

"I'm not. That's just my face."

I laugh. "Did you make a joke?"

"No, I'm serious."

Of course, he is, he's always serious.

The rest of the day goes by surprisingly well.

I don't spill, break, or hurt anything, and thankfully, I don't have the urge to puke. It's only day two of the new term, but classes are falling into place nicely. We're even beginning supernatural training tomorrow, and I'm hoping to get to bed early tonight to have plenty of energy tomorrow. All things considered, my luck seems to be turning itself around.

Maybe my misfortune wasn't the curse after all.

"You about ready to close up for the day?" Sydney asks me from across the table in the library. A large, old, dusty book sits in his lap.

A quick look at the clock shows half past eight. If I'm going to get any sleep tonight, I should meet with Tremont and get back to my room so I can shower. "Yeah, it's getting late."

We pack our stuff in silence; there's a calming comfort to his presence. It's really nice being with Sydney, it's like there are no expectations, we can simply exist around one another, and it's enough.

Walking up the steps from the basement, Sydney asks, "Any special requests for tomorrow's coffee?"

"Surprise me." I lean into him.

We go our separate ways, and it's not until he's out of sight that I realize I'm going to the infirmary to meet Professor Tremont alone.

Where is my stalker of a boyfriend, Silas, when I need him?

I turn the cold handle and step into the sterile room.

Tremont stirs from behind a desk in the far corner. "Wasn't sure if you were going to make it."

"Thanks for waiting around. I got busy in the library going over...some stuff." I shut the door behind me.

"Yeah? Have you made any progress on your latest curse?" He focuses on me.

I shake my head. "No, not yet. It usually gets worse before I figure out what it is."

"Interesting." His eyebrows rise. "Any theories?"

Why is he prying? Is he genuinely curious or is it something else?

"Nope. Everything has been going fairly smooth, minus this." I hold my bandaged hand up in front of me. Things obviously aren't going well, but I'm sure not going to tell him that. My circle of trust only extends so far, and he hasn't made the cut.

"Sometimes these types of things take time. From what I've heard, though, I have no doubt you'll figure it out."

Is that a compliment?

"That's the plan." I stand awkwardly by the door.

"Come on in. Have a seat. We'll get this squared away quickly so you can get on with the rest of your evening." Tremont waves his long, lanky arm.

"Listen, Willow, I'm aware that we haven't become very familiar with each other yet, but I wanted to tell you that I'm a bit concerned." Tremont flips my palm up and begins to do his work.

"Being an outsider, I can see all the effort you've given to those here at the school, and I want to make sure you're not being taken advantage of."

"What do you mean?" I keep my hand steady.

"I was part of the team that put together the computations on the shadow realm repair. That must have taken plenty of your and Sydney's resources to be able to do that in such a short time."

I cut him off. "We insisted. Both of us. It was my fault that the realm was damaged, and I, personally, felt obligated to do whatever I could to help."

He nods, and his gaze meets mine—his expression soft and kind. "I understand. I meant no offense. I'm sure you can make your own decisions. I only wanted to bring it to your attention in case you hadn't thought that way."

His red energy flows into my hand, the same chilling then neutral sensation.

"Regardless, you should be proud. It's quite the feat you two performed. Has to make you wonder, you know?" he adds.

"About what?" Consider my interest piqued.

"Oh, nothing." He glances down, slowly lowering his hand and then bringing it up, coursing the magic even deeper into my wound.

Is he really about to leave me hanging?

"What did you mean?" I pry.

"The connection between you and Sydney. I've heard stories of his family and their *darkness*. The way the magic bonds together to form such a powerful force, kind of similar to a yin-yang..."

"What are you insinuating?"

"Well, whether or not you have a matching darkness or a contrasting light." His eyes take their time adjusting, gradually rising from his healing process and up to meet mine.

I'm not sure if he does it on purpose or if it's purely coincidental. It fucking freaks me out all the same. "Oh. I guess I'd never thought of it."

Does he realize what I am? That I have angel blood? And if what he's hinting at is true, does that mean that Sydney has demon blood?

A lump forms in my throat. It's possible that a demonic witch cursed the Oliver bloodline. And considering the weird involvement with Sydney's parents, is it probable that the LeBlancs are the ones responsible?

It couldn't conceivably be true, could it?

Did Sydney's family curse mine?

CHAPTER 12

"**I** need help."

Deghan's smile upon my knock at his door fades away. "What's wrong?"

"Nothing, really. I, um...it's sort of embarrassing."

He stands back and lets me into his room. "What's up, princess?"

"So, I..." I shift my gaze to the floor and then raise my hand. "I can't wash my hair."

His grin reappears. "I'd love to be of assistance."

"I thought that...since we...already...you know...took a shower together. Maybe you wouldn't mind? I can figure something else out if you don't..." Why am I so freaking anxious to ask for a favor? The very reason I'm doing this is because he's already seen me naked, very specifically *in the shower*.

85

"Say no more." He immediately rushes to his dresser, flinging some stuff around and taking out a few articles. "Your place?"

The walk to my dorm is full of bubbling energy—my nerves mixed with his excitement.

You would have thought I offered him a ten-course meal, the way he's nearly beaming.

"Do you have something we can wrap that in?" He points to my hand.

"Ugh, yeah." I go to the small table to pick up the plastic bag and roll of tape.

Deghan strolls over, taking the items and making quick work of covering my wound. "There we go."

"Thanks, Deg. You're a lifesaver."

His lips turn up on one side. "Come here." He tugs me in and envelopes me into a full-on Deghan hug, melting away any of the uneasy energy I once had.

Why was I thinking this would be so tense? This is *Deghan* we're talking about. The most cuddly, welcoming, freaking sweet and awesome guy I've ever known.

I could have asked one of the girls to help me with my hair, but upon inspecting my faucet options, getting it done in the shower seemed to be the best choice. The sink is small, and I probably would have smashed my head in order to get rinsed off, especially considering how thick my hair is and how much water it takes to get all the shampoo out. I went so far as to sit on the floor and lean my head against the tub, but all the angles were wrong and would have royally screwed up my neck.

Not that I'm complaining about my decision, though. Taking a shower with Deghan is my idea of a good time.

The look on his face allows me to recognize he feels the same way, too.

"I'll get the water running," he says.

I follow behind him, leaning against the doorframe of the bathroom. "I really do appreciate this." I watch his muscles flex under his shirt when he leans over.

"You kidding me? I'd do anything for you, Wills, you should know that by now. I think it's pretty safe to say we all would." He comes closer, running his warm hand along my cheek. "It's like you have a spell on us."

I close my eyes and collapse into his touch, his words growing louder in my head. Could what he's saying be true? I want them to want me for me, not because of some stupid magical incantation.

Of course, that's outlandish, though, because I would never do such a thing, and why would anyone ever force the love of four unbelievably amazing guys on me?

"You ready?" Deghan pulls his shirt over his head, revealing his rock-hard physique. He tosses it onto the vanity and unbuttons his jeans, then pauses. "Let me help." Piece by piece, he removes my clothes, then takes my hand and leads me into the shower.

His movements are kind and gentle and tender, despite being the ferocious beast he sometimes becomes.

But, is he really? Even the time I saw him in his supernatural form, he still had those caring eyes and did what he could to protect me from the nearly rabid werewolf. The shock that was written across his face upon finding me the next day was heartbreaking. Deghan may be a werewolf, but I doubt he'd ever hurt a fly.

That *situation* was something we never really talked about. I'm still not sure who the rogue attacking wolf was...and I'm not sure if I want to know.

Although I've only seen him that one time, his wolf tendencies show through on occasion. His golden eyes radiate when his emotions are heightened, and his possessive and protective sides take turns displaying themselves.

He's incredibly accepting of the way all five of us are...but I'm not sure if any of the guys would be tolerant of anyone else attempting to break that barrier.

And that's something I'm completely fine with.

I never knew I could be *so* satisfied, and having each one of them in my life fills a space in my heart and soul that no one else could. We are like a puzzle, fitting perfectly together.

I don't want it any other way.

Well, obviously if I could get rid of the curse for good and finally get the chance to breathe and enjoy my life with these men, I'd absolutely choose that.

Sometimes I doubt whether or not I'll be able to make it happen. I keep surprising myself with how I'm able to overcome each hurdle that's thrown my way, but what happens if it's too much? What if the curse actually breaks me one day? What will happen to me? To the relationships I hold so close to my heart?

Will I lose them forever?

That thought alone is the fire under my ass to make sure that never happens.

"Lean back a little," Deghan says while guiding my head under the stream of water.

I close my eyes and let it cascade down.

His fingers massage into my scalp. A moment later, he mumbles, "Umm."

I open an eye and note his blank stare at the label-less bottles. "The one on the left is the shampoo."

He snatches it up and squirts some into his hand.

"I try to stay away from the ones with all the chemicals. Those are all-natural and homemade."

"Damn, you made this?" He lathers my hair, making sure to hit every spot.

Chills run up and down my body at how damn good it feels. I let out a laugh. "No, not me. But they're made in *someone's* home. I get them from this local farm market thing that Harper has. This super old lady sells a bunch of environmentally friendly products. I've used them for as long as I can remember."

"Mind if I try it?" He holds out the bottle.

"Be my guest."

"Let me take care of my girl first." Deghan nudges me toward the water again for a rinse. He turns me around and continues his task. "Other one is conditioner?"

"Mmhm."

He squirts some into his palm and then rakes his fingers through my hair to remove any tangles with his application.

Each motion is pure heaven.

Once he's done with my hair, he pumps some soap and foams it up with his hands. Starting at my neck, he rubs circles up and down and onto my shoulders. He gently massages his way around my back.

It's all I can do to not melt into a puddle.

He stops at my hips, pushing slightly on the dimples above my butt.

His hands are big, so massive they nearly wrap their way around my waist.

"Is this okay?" Deghan asks.

"I don't ever want it to stop," I mumble.

He leans in and kisses a spot on my shoulder where there's no soap. "You deserve to be pampered."

"So do you." I turn to face him, settling my gaze on his. I step forward, taking my good arm and dragging his face down to meet mine. I press my lips against his and pull him under the water a bit more.

"Willow..." He grips my face firmly, staring intently into my eyes. "I love you, you realize that, right?"

Like a bolt of divine lightning, something surges through my body, shocking me to life. Flowing energy consumes me, and somehow, without really fully understanding it, my power grows.

How the fuck is it possible to have two men, absolutely amazing ones at that, telling me they love me in such a short period of time?

And why is it that with each declaration, a new door is opened within me, unlocking some new hidden layer I was unaware of?

"Say something," Deghan whispers, running his thumb along my cheek. Desperation and fear seeps from his pores.

"Deghan...of course I know," I finally admit. I was so absorbed in my own thoughts that I left him hanging to think I possibly didn't feel the same. "I love you, too."

His sad eyes turn happy, a grin forming. He reels me in for a hug, lifting me off the shower floor and into him.

"You had me worried there for a second, Wills."

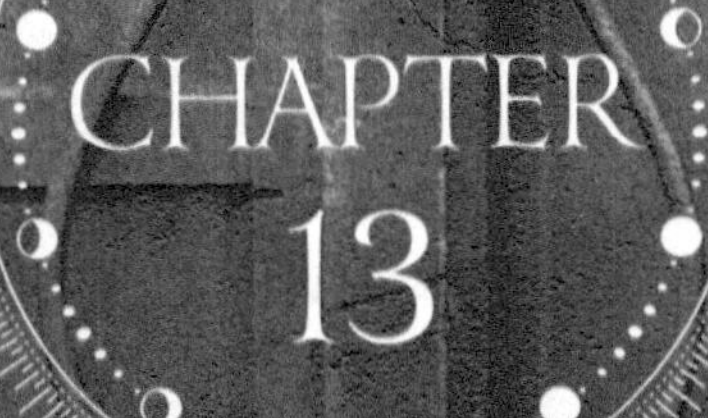

CHAPTER 13

Icannot fucking shut my mind off.

I lie here, staring at the pale-white ceiling, reliving the conversation with Tremont over and over again.

Maybe I'm overthinking the entire thing. Maybe he was purely curious about my progress, genuinely concerned I might be taken advantage of, and only thinking out loud about the connection Sydney and I share.

But whatever his intentions were, he got under my skin, and now I can't shake his words long enough to fall asleep.

I shift my mind to other parts of the day. To earlier when Deghan confessed he loved me. I recall the shape of his mouth, the way the words delicately rolled off his tongue and caressed me. For a moment, he was so afraid that I might not love him, too.

How could I not, though?

Deghan is strong and smart, hilarious, and thoughtful...he has one of the biggest hearts—next to Cam's. The two of them go together like peanut butter and jelly, and damn if I'm not the luckiest girl in the world for being able to share this thing called life with them.

Gosh, and then there's Sydney. The mere wisp of his declaration sent me spiraling into a world-class orgasm. I'll never wrap my head around how that's even possible.

Both men allow me to see these insanely vulnerable pieces of them, and I'll never understand what I did to deserve any of it. My relationship with all of the guys came so suddenly and out of nowhere, but it's as though I've known them forever. I'm safe with them, cared for, loved.

It's only been a handful of months, yet we all have this intense bond that I can't imagine not having. Losing them would be comparable to losing myself.

Kind of similar to what my mom had said about the loss of my father and her magic along with him. I can't comprehend how horrible of an experience that was for her. It's no wonder she shut down the way she did—I would undoubtedly do the same.

I flip the pillow I had laid on top of my head off to the side of my bed. I step into my slippers, heading to the one place I'm sure I have a better chance of sleeping.

I make my way to the door and fumble with the knob. I have to yank to get it to finally let loose and open. I should probably have that looked at.

Closing the door behind me, I tiptoe down the hall, careful not to wake anyone else up. Just because I can't sleep doesn't mean everyone else should be stuck with the same crappy fate.

The school is quiet, aside from the small huffing of energy from the supernatural side.

I wander into the north wing, glancing over at Sydney's door when I pass.

Upon finding my target, I knock lightly. It's only a tiny wait later until a familiar sleepy face greets me.

"You okay?" Deghan rubs his eyes.

"Couldn't sleep..." I should have stayed in my room and not woken him up.

He takes my hand. "Come on."

A figure on one of the spare beds moves. "Willow, is that you?" Cameron says groggily.

"We studied late so Cam crashed," Deghan admits.

"You don't have to explain yourself to me."

"Cam." He points to the beds. "Help me push these together."

In a matter of minutes, three mattresses are smooshed side by side. I claim the one in the middle, the guys on each side of me.

It's not long until Cam is snoring.

Deghan's warm arm flops over my body, grabbing me and yanking me toward him. "Come here, princess." He nuzzles his face against my neck and breathes in deeply.

I allow his warm embrace to soothe me, to consume my thoughts until it's simply the sound of his and Cam's breathing lulling me to sleep.

Headmaster Walker, Abigail, and Professor Tremont stand at the front of the semi-crowded classroom full of supernatural students.

Walker remains firmly in place. "We've called this rather sudden meeting to confirm that the shadow realm is now repaired to the point where we can resume classes."

A few murmurs leave the pupils.

"We are quite pleased with the quick progress and are even more excited to have you back to learning about your special skills." His gaze wanders the room. "We're going to be changing things up for this next term."

"How so?" a random student chimes in.

"This may come across a bit strange, but we're going to be pairing you with a different species for your training," Walker speaks right through a couple gasps from the group. "The goal in mind for this study will be to get acquainted with the other types of magic and learn how to properly function with them. One of our missions at Harper is to no longer have the divide between supernaturals, but instead build a bond to hopefully make the continuation of our kinds easier. We understand that there may be some prejudices already ingrained within you, but I'm confident that we can overcome them if we try. So, what do you say? Think we can give our best effort and come together?"

I glance around. There are a lot of faces I haven't met personally.

"This may be shocking to some of you," Abigail interjects. "But it will be a wonderful growth opportunity for each one of you."

"Do we get to pick our partners?" another student asks.

Walker shakes his head. "No. We feel it's better if we match you accordingly."

A communal silence follows.

"Shall we get started?" Walker takes a paper from Abigail. "I'll be naming the pairs, and their species, please wait until I've finished to cause any commotion." He takes a breath. "Sydney and Hopper, witch and vampire. Sampson and Clayton, witch and werewolf. Alexis and Jacob, witch and vampire. Noah and Sophia, werewolf and vampire. Deghan and Ezra, werewolf and vampire. Silas and Piper, vampire and werewolf. Willow and Ruby, witch and werewolf."

My heart seems to thud out of my chest. I didn't get any of my guys, but at least I got Ruby. But who the hell are Hopper, Ezra, and Piper? Goes to show how much attention I've been paying. Although, I do have an excuse, given I've been a *little* busy.

"Please get together with your partner and attempt to get

familiarized with them. We will be sectioning off more solid times in which you will be training in the shadow realm. For the next few weeks, you will be learning about your own magic—and your associates—to gain as much knowledge as possible. This first-hand experience with the other kind will be greatly informative, so please take advantage of this opportunity. Are there any questions?" He shifts his focus from face to face. "No? Okay then, get together, and we'll be around to tell you when you'll be meeting."

Tension fills the space immediately. I peek over my shoulder and find Silas not moving from his spot near the door. A shy, petite but strong-looking girl walks toward him. Not wanting him to bite her head off, I go over and place my hand on his shoulder, pushing my calming energy into him and pressing my lips to his cheek. "See you in a bit."

It seems to do the trick.

His shoulders relax, and he shakes his head at me, aware of what I've done.

"Guess we're finally going to get acquainted with each other, huh?" Ruby says.

"Yeah." I force a smile while I scan the room. "I'd say so."

"I'm not going to lie." Her voice gets quieter. "I'm just glad I didn't get a bloodsucker. I mean, no offense, I get that you're dating one and all. I'd rather not be stuck with one for a whole term."

I'm pretty sure any time anyone adds *no offense,* they absolutely know they're being an asshole.

"Ruby, Willow," Abigail interrupts. She examines the sheet attached to her clipboard. "You two will meet here first thing in the morning. Ten minutes before first period on the dot. You'll have one hour on Monday, Wednesday, and Friday, for now at least. Please make sure to wait for your instructor prior to entry. For the time being, I'll be joining you. Do you have any questions?" She checks for both of our reactions. "Oh, and there will be snacks in here, but eat breakfast first."

"Sounds good." Ruby puts her hands in her pockets.

"We have time for each group to spend about thirty minutes today, and you two are the opening act. So, whenever you're ready." Abigail pauses. "I'll be accompanying you, obviously."

"Oh, right now?" I blurt out.

"Yes, we want to test the waters and make sure everything goes to plan. Kind of a soft start to reacquaint the students to the shadow side." Abigail studies my face.

"That makes sense. Definitely. Yeah, I'm ready." I glance at Ruby. "You good?"

"Yep."

I take a deep breath, careful to keep it to myself as much as possible to not let on how nervous I am. Although I went to the shadow realm already since the *incident*, I was with Sydney, and there was some level of security knowing he was by my side.

Now it's merely me, Ruby, and Abigail.

It's moments like this that I have to remind myself that I'm an Oliver witch—strong and capable and fully able to overcome a little anxiety.

I check over my shoulder on the way to the door, scanning the crowd for my guys. An invisible string holds me to each one of them.

"Infito grantum modem," Ruby mutters and then slips into the other realm.

Abigail follows suit, and I'm close behind.

Every time I cross over, I expect to notice some weird shift in my body, but it never happens. My gaze flicks to the same spot I always look for, the upper right-hand side where the ripples of the seam connect this territory to the next.

To demons.

Deadly, terrifying, and ruthless creatures that want nothing more than to steal my power and rip me to shreds.

I swallow. I can do this.

I've battled numerous demons, what's one more time?

"The realm is stronger than it ever has been." Abigail points toward the wall. "See how the color remains the same? That means the connection is consistent and durable. In the past, we had a slight variation, which meant it was weaker then…vulnerable and susceptible to breaching."

Why in the hell were we risking coming here if it was so fragile?

She continues. "We weren't aware it could be at the level it is now. The combined magic between you and Sydney is unparalleled together. Your combined magic created a stronger bond than we knew was possible."

"Damn, Willow," Ruby chimes in. "I have my work cut out for me then."

Abigail chuckles. "You're not wrong, but you two have a lot that can be learned from one another. You are a great match, and I have a feeling that things will become very interesting with your training."

"Why does it seem you know more than you're saying?" Ruby adds.

"Because I do," Abigail admits. "I want you two to get familiar with each other's magics in time, but I will say, you two have a lot of things in common that I'm sure will benefit both of you to work on together. One of your strengths might be the other's weakness, and some are shared qualities that you both need to explore further."

One thing is for sure, we do not share the same mindset on vampires.

I hate the fact that I'm immediately judging her for saying what she did about *bloodsuckers,* but I don't see a difference between any of us. I mean, yeah, vampires drink blood, and werewolves shift, but we're all magical beings that deserve to be treated with an equal level of respect.

How would she feel if someone had said the same thing about her or other werewolves?

I honestly have nothing bad to say about any of the species— except for demons. Even the *bad* witches are descended by demonic kind, so it's hard to hold any ill will toward them, either. It's not exactly their fault.

We don't choose our family.

Which explains how Sydney was able to put aside his familial association because of what his parents did to us. It was an unforgivable act, and to abandon him the way they have and offer no explanation only solidifies the decision for him that much more.

"Today, girls, I want you two to jot down some of the things you feel confident about, in regard to your abilities, and then list some things you personally think you're struggling with. I want to go over these tomorrow when we meet and see which things we should focus on first. There's obviously infinite training, so developing a more personalized regimen will be best to make the most progress."

What do I excel at? I can come up with many of my weaknesses.

Like the lack of control I have over my abilities, my pathetic hand-to-hand combat, the fact that I'm freaking incessantly cursed and receptive to demon attacks pretty much at all times. Not to mention my mental block with actually realizing any of my strengths.

I allow my gaze to trail Ruby. What could she be good at?

She's fairly small. She seemed nice, up until she pissed me off with the vampire remark. What could she possibly bring to the table other than shit-talking people behind their backs?

I'm being petty, and I really should get the hell over it. But having such a fierce connection to Silas and knowing what a wonderful person he is, it hurts me that someone would treat him badly strictly based on *what* he is, not *who* he is.

He is a bit prickly on the exterior, though, so maybe her opinions are based on poor assumptions. Maybe if she got to know him a bit better, she wouldn't think the way she does. Not that I really care to let anyone understand Silas the way I do. And who's to say it would ever matter anyway? Some people are so close-minded that nothing anyone says or does could change their thinking.

"Go ahead and grab a provided notebook from over there." Abigail motions to a table by the door. "You can take that back with you, but bring it to each session."

Wasn't Silas the one who had Ruby check my room for intruders not too long ago? Why would she do that for him if she hated his kind?

CHAPTER 14

"Do you think you should tell the headmaster what's going on with you?" I study Silas's tense face.

"No."

"Why?"

"It's none of his business." His jaw is tense, more so than usual.

"And you don't see an issue training with the wolf girl?"

"Her name is Piper."

So, he's on a first-name basis with this female?

"Yeah, her," I confirm.

"There won't be any problems. I'm capable of controlling myself. I shouldn't have even told you." He walks across my room and leans against the wall. He's grumpy as hell, and boy is he bad at hiding it.

Or maybe I'm good at recognizing this isn't truly him.

"Is this you talking, or the stone?"

He rolls his eyes and sighs, confirming my suspicions. Silas is usually cranky, but not quite like this. "I'll see you later."

"Silas," I call out, but it's no use, he's already gone.

I rummage through my backpack and find the notebook from the shadow realm. I have about an hour until dinner and need to get started on my assignments for the week.

My hand throbs, reminding me of how slow of a process this healing is. Shouldn't it be better by now?

I flip open the page and put pen to paper.

I jot down the word **Strengths** and tap at the page.

Destroying the shadow realm? Does that count? Although, it was totally by accident.

I'm pretty good at improvising and working with whatever comes my way. Most of my magic comes to me at random and is never usually planned.

Which is probably a weakness. I need to work on control and how to harness it when I need it.

I guess my actual strength could be noted here, considering how powerful my magic is at times. I did partner with Sydney to do that repair in a fraction of the time it was supposed to take.

Apparently, I have a thing with nature, but I have little idea of how to truly tap into that either. Sometimes I'm really good at *knowing* things, too. Like the times I've asked myself something and I've been guided to wherever it may be.

Does that mean I have locating abilities?

Other than that, though, I kind of suck at being a witch.

A knock sounds on the door.

I perk up, hoping that it's Silas coming back to apologize for being a brat earlier, but it's not his energy that greets me.

"Hey, Will," Cam says from the other side.

"What's up?" I motion for him to come in.

"I thought we could study until it's time to eat. I already feel so behind, and it's only been a day." He waves the statistics book and then tosses it on the bed, plopping down next to it.

"Of course." I close the pad I was writing in and shove it aside. "Did you bring your calculator?"

He leans over and reaches into his back pocket, bringing out a massive device with a bunch of buttons. "Yep."

"Good." I smile.

I study his face, looking for the man I saw a few days ago who got angry. He's been replaced by the normal, caring, and adorable Cameron.

I've been meaning to get him alone and bring up what happened, but other than this very instance, I haven't totally had the chance.

What better time than the present?

I swallow. "Can we talk..."

His eyes narrow. "Yeah?"

"About what happened with you and Silas when I got hurt?"

"What about it?" Cameron turns to face me fully.

"You kinda reacted in a way I've never seen from you. Is everything okay?" I run my hand along his arm.

He looks to the floor and doesn't speak, so I continue.

"You're a wonderful listener, Cam. You always have been. But maybe it's your turn to do the talking."

His gaze slowly makes its way to meet mine. "It's my brother. He got arrested again. He was on his last strike with the paper factory, so now he's out a job. And without any money coming in, we're probably going to lose the house. We've used up all of our favors with the bank, and it won't be long. It's either that or I use what I have saved for school to pay the mortgage. It's a lot to handle, and I let it get the best of me. I'm sorry. Silas really does piss us all off, but I shouldn't have responded the way that I did."

Jesus, they're going to lose their house? I had no idea things were that bad for him. If anything, I'm mind-blown at how well he can keep his shit together despite his life falling apart. I could take a lesson or two from him in humility.

There has to be something that can be done, though, right?

Cam can't become homeless, and he shouldn't have to give up going to college to pay for his brother's mistakes.

Life is really fucking unfair at times.

Cameron, of all people, does not deserve this. He's good and pure and one of the nicest, most grateful humans on the planet.

"I'm sorry you're going through this, Cam, I really am. Is there anything I can do to help?" I ask, despite knowing there's not much I *can* do to help. I barely have enough money to cover what little expenses I do have.

"Not unless you have a shit ton of cash lying around you aren't using." He offers a weak smile. "Keep being you. And no feeling sorry for me. I'm a big boy. I'll be okay. I always figure it out. I just haven't thought of the solution for this one yet."

"You're admirable, you know that, right?" I shake my head. "There are so many layers of you that not everyone sees. Not even me. But you're always so happy and giving."

Cam shrugs. "What good does being pissed off all the time do ya?"

"Are you referring to Silas?"

"No, I mean, yeah, but he's misunderstood. I get it. He's had a hard life. Sometimes that shit is harder to hide than we think. I have no idea what he's gone through, but he's old as hell, right? He's probably lost a lot of people and dealt with his fair share. I'd hate to put my pain and suffering on anyone else. So, if I can be the reason someone smiles instead of feeling worse about their life, I'd rather choose that. We don't decide how people or the world treats us, but we can control how we react. I want to be part of the solution, not the problem. Does that make sense?"

Cameron is a saint, that's all there is to it. This world doesn't deserve his benevolence.

The next morning, I stand in front of the mirror and mentally prepare myself for the day.

First, I have training with Ruby and Abigail, and this evening, I'm signed up to go dress shopping with the girls. Don't get me wrong, both things could be a lot of fun, but they could be absolutely horrible, too.

Having that weird interaction with Ruby has thrown me a curveball. I thought she was friendly and accepting of the different supernaturals, but in reality, she's not. What's the difference between me and Silas? Does that mean she doesn't care for witches either?

It's my luck to get stuck with someone I don't click with. Why couldn't I have been paired with Silas or Deghan?

Sydney and I, magically, get along very well, but considering we're both witches, we never would have been put together.

I wonder how all the guys are going to fare with their partners. Deghan got a vampire named Ezra, who's damn near his height. She's long and lanky with sleek jet-black hair and a piercing glare.

Sydney was placed with a vampire, too—a guy named Hopper. He seems totally laid-back, not serious like Silas and Ezra. With his shaggy hair and chillness, he must be the hippie of vampires. Sydney doesn't seem to hate Hopper the way he does Silas, but regardless, he's not thrilled with his assignment.

And then there's Silas and Piper. The dainty werewolf who is as cute as a button.

Silas has a temperament to be withdrawn toward everyone, so I can't tell if he has an issue with werewolves the same as he does with witches, or, well, the Sydney kind. He's different with me than with anyone else, so it's hard to recognize for sure who he likes and dislikes.

I can only hope that whatever the stone is doing to him doesn't affect his training and cause any issues, let alone put anyone in danger.

"Blueberry," Sydney says while holding out a muffin.

"Cameron made them for you. Deghan said they're really good. I had an apple one, because, well...you know."

"Thanks, Syd. Shame your glitch is something so delicious." I take it and peel back the paper, biting the side. It's no surprise that it tastes like heaven. Cameron really is a master chef.

Which brings up a potentially good idea.

"Would you pay money for that?" I ask Sydney.

"The muffins?"

I nod. "Yeah, would you buy them?"

"In a heartbeat. I'm not sure how he does it, but everything he makes is delicious. It's like his magical power is being able to cook and bake." Sydney brings his cup of coffee to his lips and takes a sip. "Why?"

"I thought of something. I'll have to get him on board, but it might help a problem he has." I'm positive Deghan will help me get this going, too.

It's not much, but it's honest work, and maybe if things go the way I hope they will, Cameron won't have to spend his tuition money to keep his home.

CHAPTER 15

I suck in a breath, then let the words roll off my tongue. "Infito grantum modem." Crossing over the threshold, I note the way the air is slightly stagnant on this side of the plane. My gaze focuses on that spot in the corner, checking the seal.

Will this ever get any less fucking weird?

It's all fun and games until a demon penetrates the barrier, lures someone you care about into a trap, and tries to kill you and your friends.

No big deal.

And that doesn't even factor in the whole thinking I killed Silas thing.

Watching his body fall lifelessly to the floor because of something I did is not something I'll ever be able to fully get past. The entire experience was traumatizing, and going back to the very place where it happened is a definite challenge.

"Willow, would you care to take out your notebook and we can go over what you and Ruby came up with?" Abigail snaps me back to reality.

How long was I zoning out there?

I turn to the page I wrote on and hand it to Abigail.

She glances over mine and then Ruby's.

"Mmhm," she purrs. "Well, I think both of you have a lot more going for you than what you've been able to put on paper, but this is a start. Willow, it appears Ruby will be able to help you with your combat skills, and in return, Ruby, Willow can help you work on having patience with your studies."

Me, patient? She must have the wrong girl.

"How's your hand?" Abigail shifts her attention to my bandage.

"It's fine," I lie. "I have to keep this on for precautionary measures."

"Okay, well, good. These are both things that are going to take quite some time and a tremendous amount of work, but I'm sure we can make some real progress here." She flops the notebooks onto the table. "Why don't we begin with a little sparring for the day. Strictly human strength. We want to see what kind of skills we have without them, and then we'll incorporate magic over time."

I look to Abigail. "You want us to fistfight?"

"No. Sparring. It's the fundamental building block to pretty much any style of fighting. And if we want to work on your combat skills, this is exactly the first step." She points to Ruby. "You spar, correct?"

Ruby nods. "Yeah, it's a wolf thing. We do it multiple times a week to keep up our strength and endurance. It reduces the pain when we shift. By a fraction, but still, anything is better than nothing. We usually warm up first."

Abigail pushes a couple of desks out of the way and clears the middle of the room.

Ruby and I stand a few feet apart, gawking at each other.

What the hell am I getting myself into?

She's rather quiet today, but I don't mind her silence—it beats the alternative of her hating on vampires.

"If you want to get better at something, it's helpful to find someone more skilled than you, and train with them," Abigail says. "Hence why we're building on each other's strengths and weaknesses. Now, I don't want you to actually hit each other today, but over time, we'll work up to that. For now, let's get you two loosened up." She opens the door to a small closet and pulls out two black mats. "Here. Rubes, do you want to take over?"

We both take one, laying them down in front of us.

"Sure," Ruby says. "Jumping jacks." She glances down at her watch. "And go."

Ruby's body moves immediately, and it takes me a moment to catch up.

I fling my arms through the air and jump up and down. Several seconds later, I'm already out of breath.

Who said this supernatural thing was going to be easy?

I'm just glad that I typically dress like a bum, because if I was in jeans instead of leggings, I doubt I'd be moving this freely.

"And stop." She points to the floor. "Twenty push-ups."

I crouch to the floor, wincing at the pressure on my hand. I haven't even put my full weight on it yet.

It's everything I can do to get through them without letting on that I'm in pain.

Why didn't I tell her the truth about my injury and then maybe I wouldn't be flopping all over the place in preparation for fighting Ruby?

But in reality, I really do need to work on my combat skills, especially with more demons to come. I have to be able to protect myself from whatever shit life throws my direction. I can't always count on the guys to bail me out, not that I have, but I need to be fully sufficient.

I don't want them to have to worry that I won't be able to take care of myself.

"Let's focus on some stretching now, about five minutes' worth." Ruby sits on her mat and brings one leg toward her, lengthening the other. She leans forward.

I follow her motions, not quite being able to stretch as far as she does.

"And switch." A few movements later, she lies flat on her back. "Extend your arms all the way behind you against the floor. We're trying to open up our shoulders with this one. Press your body flat and take a breath. With each exhale, try to relax."

I do my best to follow her direction, despite my wandering gaze floating to the corner of the ceiling to verify the closure.

"Okay," she finally says. "Now stand. I want your feet staggered, slightly wider than your hips but no more. Keep your feet and knees facing the same direction and your weight distributed equally." Ruby places herself in front of me. "Watch me."

I repeat her exact stance.

"Good, you'll want to keep those knees slightly bent. Now, I want you to try to hit me."

I rotate at the waist to get a look at Abigail. "I thought you said no hitting."

Ruby interjects. "You won't land one, trust me."

"Go ahead," Abigail confirms.

I step forward, noting Ruby's completely unprotected body. Without continuing to second-guess, I shove my arm forward.

Although I'm damn sure I'm going to whack her, she moves her body with ease at the right moment to avoid contact.

"See," she verifies. "Again."

I don't hesitate, going in for another jab, failing with each new attempt.

I swing, and my fist goes slicing through the air.

Looks like Ruby really does have something I can stand to learn.

A short while later, I'm out of breath and damn near chasing Ruby around the room trying to hit her.

"That's time for the day, girls." Abigail cocks her head toward the door. "We have about five minutes until we have to head back."

Ruby stops moving to pay attention to Abigail, and I take the opportunity to sneak one last attack in.

Somehow, though, she anticipates my move and escapes it.

"Damn, I really thought I had you there." I laugh.

"I give you extra points for effort. It was clever, but not clever enough." She winks. "It's good to attack when your opponent is preoccupied, but if they're skilled, they'll see it coming."

This whole experience makes me wonder how the hell I defeated the demon in my head. It was like the made-up version of myself was infinitely stronger, faster, agile, and totally more capable of fighting than this sloppy person I'm stuck with.

"I understand that we aren't presently using magic, but I don't encourage this type of training outside of the shadow realm. We don't want to give our *other* students any reason to be suspicious of our behavior." Abigail stands near the doorway. "There will be some things you'll be able to work on out there, but this isn't one of them."

"What if we have a private space?" I insist. If I'm going to get any better, I need more than an hour a few days a week. Especially if some of that time is going toward helping Ruby with her skills.

"I advise against it, unless you have proper supervision."

***

The rest of the school day goes fairly well. I don't trip or spill anything or cause any disasters. It's almost like I'm a normal, living and breathing, functional college student.

But I'm not, at least not the *normal* part. I'm a freaking witch. One that attends a secret academy for supernatural people.

And there are more people similar to me, and others who are different...the vampires and werewolves that I barely understand anything about.

Plus, the demons that lie in wait on the other side of our realm, eager for any weakness to hop onto our side and cause chaos.

There are fairies, too. According to legend and word spread through the wolves, though.

Has to kind of make you wonder what other creatures are out there.

"Is that what you're wearing?" Remi puts a hand to her hip and looks me up and down.

I cross my arms over my chest. "What? You realize we're going *shopping, not* to a beauty pageant."

She groans. "We never leave campus. Don't you want to put on something nicer than that old tee?"

"I love this shirt." I grab ahold of the bottom of it and bring it to my nose, breathing in the scent of Silas that still remains. I tuck a portion of it into my pants. "You're lucky I put jeans on for this."

"Whatever." She rolls her eyes. "Where's your boyfriend?"

"Which one?" I blurt out.

Remi laughs. "Syd. He's loaning us his car."

That explains how we're getting into town.

The realization that I'm going to be the farthest away from all of my guys I've ever been since we met dawns on me. A strangely crippling anxiety attempts to wreck me, but I push it aside. This is the first time we'll be apart, so of course I'm feeling not so great about it.

Would it be too much to ask Sydney to go with us?

I shove that thought away, too. I need to be okay with doing things alone.

"There he is." Remi points across the foyer to him.

"Hey, girls." He scans the crowd then settles his gaze onto me. His gorgeous green eyes send me into another world.

My body seems to gravitate toward his, offering me the security and comfort I so desperately need here and now.

"Keys." Sydney holds out his hand to Remi. "Please be careful and have fun."

Remi snatches them from him. "We will. Thank you, again, you're a lifesaver."

"Yeah, thanks, Sydney," Kyra echoes.

Lillian, too, chimes in words of appreciation.

The girls head toward the main entrance of the school, but Sydney holds my stare, keeping me locked in place.

"You're nervous." He reads me like a book.

"Is it that obvious?"

"Maybe just to me." He takes me into his arms, completely enveloping me. "Be safe, please."

I'd be safer if one of you came with me, is what I want to say. I can't exactly tell the girls I have this never-ending curse thing going on and demons are popping up out of nowhere and threatening to destroy me.

But, for now, other than a couple of stupid accidents and Silas being even more of a grump-ass, things seem to be pretty okay. Which means I should attempt to lead an ordinary-ish life. Also known as go dress shopping with the girls for a dance.

"You'll be okay," he confirms. "But if you're not back in a few hours, I'll send out a search party." Sydney kisses my temple and slips something in my hand. "For protection."

The smooth surface rubs against my palm. I glance down to see a shiny black rock.

"Thanks, Syd." I stand on my tiptoes to press my lips against his cheek. "See you soon."

CHAPTER 16

"No freaking way," I insist.

"Pleaseeeeee," Kyra begs. "It's gorgeous. You would literally drop jaws in it."

"Try it on, you big baby," Remi adds.

I turn to Lillian for a little backup.

She shrugs and recoils when she says, "They're not wrong."

"Nope, I told you. Black. Various shades of black and grey. Nothing else."

Elegant is an understatement for this dress. It's decked out top to bottom with pale-pink sequins, but not the cheap ones, the totally stunning and perfectly sparkly kind. It's rose gold, with matching flowers lining the tasteful neckline. The back has a steep slope that goes damn near to the ass area. It's long and flowy with a wide train, but just short enough to still be able to get around with ease.

It's absolutely out of my comfort zone but fucking stunning.

And, there's no way in hell I'm trying it on. Regardless of whether or not I like it, the price tag is more than I can afford, so even if I entertained them by trying it on, I'd never be able to buy it, and that alone would make this whole experience suck that much more.

It's bad enough I sort of despise shopping and my anxiety keeps flaring up, but to find my love-at-first-sight dress and not be able to get it, totally blows on a whole new level.

"You should try it on," I tell Remi. "You'd look great in it."

She rolls her eyes. "You know my ass won't fit in there." Remi gropes her own body. "Do you *see* this thing?"

Kyra busts out laughing. "Put your booty away before they kick us out."

I seize the stunning dark-red gown situated behind the pink one of my dreams. "Lills, this would look killer on you."

"Damn, Wills," Remi says. "For being a *Plain Jane*, you have a pretty good taste for others."

Anything to take the attention away from me.

I shove the dress into the fitting room. "Lill."

"If I have to wear something bold, so do you." Lillian steps into the dressing room and tugs the curtain shut.

"Ky-bear, you have to try *this* on." Remi holds out a dark-purple, lace-covered piece. It's simple and sophisticated but sexy all the same.

"Um, yes." Kyra snatches it from Remi and hops into the room beside Lillian.

Remi and I fumble through the rest of the racks, waiting on the girls.

A few moments later, Lillian pops her head out. "Are you ready?"

She slides back the closure, revealing herself with a shy grin.

"Jesus Christ, Lills." Remi blurts out.

"Same," I say dumbfounded.

Earlier, it was simply some fabric on a hanger, but now it's this extension of Lillian that flawlessly fits her body. It's got this off-the-shoulder thing going on, the thick straps sitting along the middle of her upper arm. A long slit runs up the side, exposing her left leg in a seductive but still classy way. It cinches right above the waist, accentuating her usually hidden curves.

"Did you guys die out there?" Kyra calls into the space. She walks out, another complete stunner in front of us. She grabs on to the side of the dress, holding it out and doing a little twirl. The violet lace is see-through and beautiful.

"Damn, Lillian, I thought I was smokin', but look at you." Kyra circles her finger. "Do a spin, girlfriend."

Lillian does, and we all gasp at how spectacular she is.

"Yep, that's a winner," I tell her.

"Think so? It's not too dramatic?" Lillian examines herself in the three-sided mirror, twisting all around.

"Honey, dramatic is good. *This* is a no-brainer. You have to get it." Remi reaches forward and takes the price tag into her hand. "And it's only forty-five dollars."

Kyra studies her label. "Mine is, too."

Lucky—mine is out of my price range at a whopping two hundred dollars.

"All right. Our first stop was a score, but we have four more stores to get to, and I am picky, so let's get a move on it." Remi claps her hands. "Chop-chop, ladies." She shoves Kyra and Lillian back into their rooms to change. "We need to be on the lookout for shoes and accessories, too. Especially now that we're working with purple and red." She sighs. "And I guess black for you."

"What are you even trying to find? There were a few dresses here that you liked. What was wrong with any of them?" I skim the rack full of jewelry next to me.

"I'll know it the moment I see it, trust me. I haven't found it yet. Or, well, it hasn't found me."

Once the girls have changed and bought their formal attire,

we head to the next stop. Another consignment shop a few doors down.

Thirty minutes of scrounging through their selection, we come up empty-handed.

"I thought you invited a bunch of girls for the shopping extravaganza?" I take a granola bar from my back pocket and bite off a chunk.

"Did you really just have that on you?" Remi deadpans.

"What? I get hungry often." What I really mean is that I constantly have to restore my energy levels so I'm not vulnerable to a demon attack or pass out randomly from being a witch.

But I can't exactly tell them the truth.

"Everyone else flaked last minute. Said they were going to *the city* tomorrow instead with what's-her-face." Remi flips her golden-auburn hair and goes down another aisle of clothes.

"Who?" I trail my finger along a few hangers.

"That skeeze who's always trying to get under your skin. What the hell is her name again?"

"Allie," the rest of us say in unison.

Of course she would ruin Remi's plans, what a bitch.

"Ruby bailed, too?"

"She said she had something come up, and she'd try to find a way in town if she got free in time." Remi shakes her head. "Have you found anything worth trying on?"

"Nope." Nothing remotely close to the gown I already fell in love with despite it being everything I typically avoid.

"Let's go." She leads us out of the store.

Kyra puts her arm on Remi's back. "We'll find something, don't worry."

Remi eases into the touch.

Is Kyra aware she has this effect on Remi?

Lillian and I hang back, walking a few feet behind the girls.

"You think Ethan will like the dress I got?"

I turn to her. "Are you serious?" I loop my arm through hers. "He's going to pass out from how smoking hot you are."

She lets out a nervous laugh.

I push my calming energy into her to help ease her nerves. It's something I wish someone could do for me. It's not a big deal if I don't find a dress, I'll survive if I don't get all dolled up and attend the formal, but there's still so much other stuff that I can't get off of my mind.

For instance, what the hell is going on with Silas? Where are my parents? What happened to Sydney's? When is the next curse going to appear? Why does my damn hand still hurt so bad? And how are we going to raise enough money for Cameron to take away the financial burden his brother has dropped on him?

"Seriously?" Remi says loudly.

"Yeah, it's pretty common," Kyra replies.

"What is?" Lillian chimes in.

"Um, we were talking about Will and all her guys," Kyra says over her shoulder. "Polyamory or whatever."

What I have with them has a name? I kind of assumed it was a fluke, and I got really lucky with having this unspoken under-standing between us all. None of them have ever shown any kind of jealousy toward each other, not even Silas and Sydney, and they despise one another. Deghan walked in on me and Cam all hot and heavy in the library and didn't bat an eye other than to laugh at us for getting caught in such a public area.

Kyra lowers her voice. "Do you all...you know...hook up together?"

"No, we haven't."

"Is that something you'd do?" she continues to pry.

Remi lightly smacks her arm. "She doesn't ask you about your sex life."

Which is funny, because Remi totally asked me the same thing not too long ago.

I hadn't really thought about it honestly. Most of my experiences have been one on one, and being that sex is so new to me in general, I hadn't fully thought of the possibilities, especially now that I have multiple partners.

"If I'm being honest, I think it's great," Kyra continues. "Not the sex part. I'm sure that's nice on its own…but I mean your relationship dynamic with them in general. You all seem to get along really well. They treat you right. Like, better than right. I don't see a damn thing wrong with that. If anything, more power to ya, girl."

"As long as they're good with it and you are, I think it's great, too." Lillian rubs my arm. "Whatever makes you happy."

Not that I need approval from my friends, but it sure is nice to hear what they think about it all. The whole experience is foreign to me—dating in general—so to start off into it with four unbelievably wonderful guys is uncharted territory.

Things aren't really picture-perfect for me anyway, so why should I have assumed my romantic life would be either?

"Enough about me. What's going on with y'all?" I shift to Lillian. "Things with you and Ethan getting serious?"

She blushes.

"Did you *hear* what Ethan did?" Kyra draws out the words dramatically.

"No." I glance between them. "Is it bad?"

"He wrote…" Kyra looks to Lillian. "Sorry, it's your story to tell."

"He had Cameron bake me my favorite cupcake, red velvet with buttercream frosting. He had him write *Will you be my girlfriend?* on it."

"No way. That is officially the sweetest thing ever."

"Quite literally, right?" Remi adds.

Leave it to Cam to help plan something so romantic.

"I'm really glad things are going well for you two." I cling on to Lillian tightly, so relieved that my friend is coming back to me. I had thought I'd lost her forever the second I betrayed her and the girls and up and left them the way I did. I understand that I have a way to go before they trust me again, but to be given the chance is more than I deserve.

Remi leads us into another shop, this one a thrift store. She heads straight to the dress section and does a quick once-over through the selection.

"Nope." She turns on her heel. "Next."

"Really? That quick?" Kyra finally catches up to her. "What about this one?" She pulls a turquoise sparkly thing out and holds it up. "You'd look amazing in this."

Remi crinkles her nose. "Not my color."

"How? You legit have a blouse this shade." Kyra shoots out her arm to stop Remi from walking by. "What is going on with you?"

"Nothing. You know I'm picky." Remi's gaze nervously averts to the floor.

"Whatever." Kyra lowers her hand. "You're running out of options, though. Beggars can't be choosers."

Remi doesn't answer, just goes the rest of the way through the store and out the door, on to the next shop.

My chances of finding something I like continue to dwindle. Not that it's a big deal, I should focus on other things than going to a silly dance.

The next place is much smaller and smells of cedar and rosemary.

A kind-faced older woman greets us. "Can I help you ladies find anything?"

"Could you point us toward your formal attire section?" Lillian smiles at her.

"Why, sure. It's right over there. My name is Ruth if you need anything." Ruth points toward the back of the store with her feeble wrinkly finger.

The girls and I make our way in that direction.

Kyra pauses to ask, "What about shoes, ma'am?"

Ruth rotates her still lingering hand to the other side of the store. "Over there."

Lillian and Kyra go that way, and Remi and I the other.

A couple feet away, Remi stops, clutches her chest, and gasps.

Panic courses through me in a flash. "Are you okay?"

Her eyes go wide. "There it is."

"What? What's wrong?" I frantically shift my focus from her, to around the store, back to her.

Silently, she walks forward, reaching her hands out to caress the hanging black fabric.

"Did you really give me a heart attack over a freaking dress?" I let out a breath.

"I'm sorry, but isn't it perfect?"

She takes it off the top rack, eyeing it with such scrutiny.

I adore the modest long sleeves and simplicity.

It really is gorgeous, but it seems much more my style than hers with its solid black design. Although it's much shorter than I'd typically wear.

"I don't even need to try it on." She brings it to her and hugs it tightly.

It's then that I see the two shades of purple tulle poking out from the sort of scalloped and flared-out bottom. Two colors that match effortlessly with Kyra's dress.

This whole time I thought Remi was being a pain in the ass, but really, she's been trying to find an outfit that matched with Kyra's. My heart nearly sings at how freaking adorable this gesture is.

I glance behind me and lower my voice. "When are you going to make your move already?"

Remi looks away bashfully. "It's only a dress."

"It's so much more than that, and you know it."

"I'm not sure if she's into girls." Remi's gaze wanders to where Kyra stands and examines a rack of sunglasses.

"I think it's safe to say she's into *you*, and that's all that matters."

Remi's eyes brighten. "You think so?"

"Yeah, absolutely. She's the one who is turning down boys to go to the dance with *you*."

"I thought it was a friend's thing." Remi doesn't take her gaze off Kyra.

"Listen, Rem, I have more dates than I can handle. Lillian is going with Ethan. Which leaves you and Kyra. You may assume it's a friend date, but until one of you makes a move, neither one of you will see for sure how the other one feels."

Is this how oblivious I was about my guys liking me?

At first, I thought they were all being nice to me for no real reason, but in reality, we all shared a deeper connection that pulled us together.

Kyra and Remi are constantly exchanging glances, and not how me and Lillian do, but with googly eyes the way lovers do. It doesn't take a rocket scientist to see they have massive chemistry.

Now, if only they would realize it themselves.

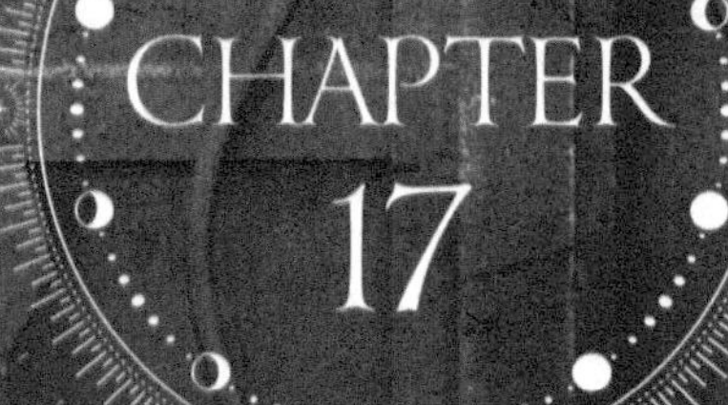

CHAPTER 17

We arrive at the last store and go through the entire selection, coming up empty-handed once again.

"What about this one?" Lillian holds up a shiny reddish thing.

"Too vibrant."

"How about this?" Kyra points to a metallic gold dress.

"Too short."

"I'm telling you, Wills. You have to go try on the one from the first store. The light-pink strappy gown." Remi leans against the wall, her garment bag tucked under her arm.

"Even if I did like it, it's expensive." I flip through a few hangers to see if anything else catches my attention. "So, it's a no."

"I can be quite persuasive." Kyra steps in front of me. "If it's *the* dress, I will barter the shit out of it until you *can* afford it."

"Who knows, there might be a sale going on that we missed. It's worth checking out, Will. Please, try it on for me." Remi presses her hands together and bats her eyelashes.

"Fine. But don't be mad if it doesn't work out. We have to get back soon," I add.

Remi jumps up and down and squeals. "Sorry, I'm excited. Totally thought you were going to be a hardass about this."

I nudge her. "Don't make me change my mind."

Of course, I want to see how it looks on. If it weren't for that price tag, I would have already. I just don't want to be let down by falling more in love but not being able to have it because of the cost.

"Come on." Remi weaves her fingers around mine and nearly drags me out of the store.

A few giddy moments later, we walk into that familiar store and head straight to where we were not too long ago.

Remi releases my hand and frantically shoves clothes to the side. "Where is it?"

"It was right there." I point to the exact spot it last hung.

"It's fucking *gone*."

"Miss," Remi calls out to the worker. "Can you tell me where the pink sparkly dress that was here earlier went?"

The tall teenage girl pulls out a notebook, flipping through a few recent pages. "It sold about a half-hour ago."

"It *sold*? You can't be serious. Do you know who bought it?"

The girl sighs and checks the paper. "Nope, paid with cash."

"You're telling me you didn't *see* the person who bought it?"

"Listen, lady, I got here five minutes ago." She blows a bubble in her chewing gum. "Can I help you find something else?"

Remi furiously shakes her head. "Uh, Willow, I'm so sorry. I dragged you all the way here for nothing."

"It's fine." I fake a smile. "I told you, totally out of my comfort zone. And anyway, I'll see if Sydney will run me to my house tomorrow to rummage through my mom's stuff."

My mom. She would have loved to tag along on this shopping

trip and try on dresses with us and be silly and drink copious cups of tea from the little coffee shop on the corner where I used to work part-time.

A pang of guilt flashes through me. I shouldn't be here. I should be studying, researching my curse, doing everything I can to locate my mom and bring her back safely. Not playing pretend and browsing for an evening gown.

"Ruby," Kyra calls out. "You made it."

I turn to Ruby walking through the narrow and crowded path to us. Overstuffed racks of used clothes billow out into the aisle.

She gets caught on a hanger and takes a second to dislodge it from her shirt before continuing on. "Sorry, I'm late."

"No worries. We were getting ready to leave but we can hang around." Remi repositions the bag in her arms.

"Seems like you had some luck," Ruby confirms.

"All of us except Willow. She hasn't found anything yet. There was this *stunning* dress, but someone scooped it up while we were at another store."

"That's a bummer." Ruby gives me a sympathetic glance. "Don't let me hold you up, though, if you were going to head out."

I speak up. "I'm going to grab some fresh air. You girls find something for Ruby."

I go to leave, and Lillian chimes in.

"I'll go with you." She latches on to my arm.

"Okay, we'll find you." Kyra immediately shifts to Ruby. "So what color are you thinking?"

"Thanks, Lills," I say on our way out the door. "You want to get coffee?" I point to the end of the street.

"Sure."

The crisp autumn breeze flows through the open area, blowing a trail of leaves in its wake. The sun casts a golden hue on the horizon on its way down. A child throws a tantrum in the backseat of a slowly passing car.

I hope Deghan is enjoying tonight's sunset.

We walk along the wide sidewalk. One that was built a long, long time ago when brick and mortar stores were the up-and-coming new fad. Now, online shopping has killed nearly all of these mom-and-pop businesses.

In Harper County, though, shopping here has been ingrained in the DNA of residents, so everyone puts their best foot forward to keep money flowing into what is left of the local economy.

I open the squeaky door to our destination, and the aroma of freshly ground coffee beans assaults us instantly.

"Willow," an old voice greets me.

"Mr. Price, how are you?" I beam at the old man.

He clears the phlegm from his throat and then speaks. "I'm just swell. Oh, it's such a pleasure to see your beautiful face. How's your mother?"

I avert my gaze, biting my lip to hold back the emotions flooding in.

I should have anticipated this type of questioning, but all I had on my mind was getting the hell away from those dresses and securing a fresh cup of joe.

"She's good," I force the lie. How has word not already gotten around town that she's missing? So much for the sheriff's department being of any help. Mr. Price is rather old, though. It's possible if someone told him that he's already forgotten.

"That's wonderful to hear." He shoots Lillian a look. "Who's your friend?"

"This is my friend, Lillian. Lillian, Mr. Price, the owner of Harper Café."

"Nice to meet you," Lillian says shyly.

"Pleasure is all mine." He smiles, but not in a weird creepy old man way, in an *I haven't seen a new face in a while* kind of way.

Mr. Price was always well-respected and generous in our town. One of the longest-standing business owners.

"I'm tickled to death that Danny is back in town. He picks up his chai latte nearly every morning." He clutches his cane firmly in his hand and points toward the counter. "Help yourself, child. I'm sure you need your fix."

Thankfully, he's not one to pry. "Thank you, Mr. Price."

"Mmhm," he groans. "You're onto bigger and better things now, Miss Oliver, but if you ever need a job, our door is always open."

"I appreciate that." I lift the little wooden gate to go to the work area. I scan the way whoever is working here now has arranged things. It's a little disorganized and massively inefficient, but who am I to judge?

I never even worked up here, but still, efficiency has always been a priority of mine. In the late hours, when the shop would be closed, I would sneak up front and make myself coffee between going through receipts. On occasion, I would tidy the work area but never say a word about it, noting how my system would stay in place for a few weeks until a busy shift happened or a new employee got confused on where things would go.

"What do you want, Lills? Are you into regular coffee or do you want a latte?"

"Dark roast works for me." She climbs onto a stool on the other side.

I push the lever and fill her cup with the steaming java. "Here you go." I point to the small table a few feet away. "Milk and sugar and all that is over there."

"I'm good. Thank you." She holds the mug in between her hands, blowing on the piping drink.

"Do you want an ice cube?" I scoop up a few and plop them into my own cup.

"Sure, yeah."

A mid-twenties man comes out from the supply room, pushing the door open with his back, a case of syrup bottles in his arms. He turns and practically jumps. "Jesus, you scared me."

I step back to give him space. "I'm sorry. Mr. Price said I could help myself. I'm Willow." I hold out my hand, only realizing too late how dumb that is, considering he's preoccupied.

He hurriedly sets it on the counter and extends his palm. "Jackson."

Our skin meets, and there is a slight simmer of energy that flows from him and into me. He's definitely not human.

Do other people notice that, too, or is it only me?

I study his figure. Most of the vampires I've encountered are rigid and have hardcore textbook posture, and he's kind of a slouch. Witches usually give off more energy than he did. So, if I'm not mistaken, he could be a werewolf. Despite his sagging stance, his shoulders are wide, and he's solidly built, strong. His brownish hair brings out his chocolatey eyes.

"I used to work here." I make my way to the customer side of the counter, pulling my drink to the seat next to Lills. "This is Lillian."

She gives her typical Lillian wary smile.

He nods her way.

"We have to go, right?" I glance at my wrist, despite not wearing a watch. God, I'm an idiot. "We'll take these to-go." I stand on the bottom rung of the stool to reach over the counter and secure two paper cups.

"We can..." Lillian starts.

I cut her off. "We have to meet the girls, remember. It's getting late."

"Uh, yeah. Okay." She gradually picks up on what I'm putting down.

"Nice to meet you, Jackson." I clutch Lillian's arm and all but drag her from the shop, waving goodbye to Mr. Price on the way out. "Thanks again."

Once outside, Lillian says, "What was that all about?"

"Something was off about him. Can't quite put my finger on it." I peek over my shoulder to find Jackson peering out the front window at us. I hastily look away.

"Only thing I saw was him checking you out. You're a total babe magnet, Willow. He was super-hot." She takes a drink of her coffee.

We walk up at the same moment the rest of the girls are exiting the store we left them in.

Ruby rearranges the large garment bag in her arms.

At least everyone else found the dress they wanted.

Maybe I really should see if Sydney could run me to my mom's house at some point. I'm sure whatever is in her closet isn't nearly as fashionable as what the girls found, but it's better than nothing at all.

CHAPTER 18

A wave of comfort caresses me the moment we cross over onto the school grounds.

Granted I haven't attended here long, it's become a home to me, and I long to be here when I'm away. It's where some of the scariest and best moments of my life have happened. It's where I found out I was a witch, where I met Silas, Deghan, Cameron, and Sydney. Where I met the girls. Where I've cried and grown and evolved into an entirely new person, constantly shedding my skin to make way for a newer and better version of myself.

I came to Harper Academy expecting to have a normal college experience, but what I've been handed is so much more, and honestly, I wouldn't trade it for the world. Well, sans the curses and all.

But all things considered, how terrible the curses have been, each one of them has taught me something new. I've matured from them, I've overcome barriers I didn't know existed, let alone thought I was capable of.

The darkness has allowed me to appreciate the light.

And without those gloomy trials, I wouldn't fully understand how lucky I am to experience the good parts of my life.

Things are tough, and although sometimes I'm not sure how I'll make it through another day, I continue to persevere and prove to myself that I'm worthy of the Oliver name.

"You zoning out over there?" Lillian pokes my arm.

"Yeah, sorry." I blink a few times, the school parking lot coming into my vision.

"Do you want to talk about it?" She rests her fingers on the door handle.

"About what?"

"Whatever is bothering you. You don't have to shut me out." Lillian's gaze seems to plead with me.

"I don't want to, either. There are some things I can't exactly say. It's a lot all at once." I reach out and put my injured hand on top of hers. "I'm not going to disappear, though. Okay?"

"I'm here if you ever want to get it off your chest. If you're ever *allowed* to." She exhales. "I don't understand why you can't tell me. But I want you to recognize that I'm here. You don't have to go through whatever you're going through alone."

Her words bring me immense joy. Not too long ago, I was worried I had lost her forever. But here we are, sitting in the back of Sydney's car, having just gone dress shopping together, and her being a kind and caring friend.

"Thanks, Lills. You really are the best."

"I know." She beams and shifts to serious. "But I refuse to wear this thing without you there, so you better figure out what the hell you're wearing." She hauls the clothing bag out of the back of the car.

Out of nowhere, arms consume me.

"I missed you; you were gone forever." Deghan picks me up and spins me around. "Why do all the girls have stuff, but you don't?" He sets me down on the gravel lot.

"I couldn't find anything."

"Dude, what the hell. The formal is in a *few days*. What are you going to do?" Deghan's eyes are wide.

I didn't realize the dance was so important to him.

I shrug.

"She's going to have Syd take her to her house tomorrow and try to find something of her mom's."

"Really?" He stares at me like he's trying to examine to see whether or not this is a true story. "Okay...that works."

I lean into him, and we walk toward the big stone academy.

"You hungry?" he asks. "I could eat."

I laugh. "Why am I not surprised?"

Deghan weaves his fingers between mine. "Let's find Cam."

"Hey," I blurt out. "Speaking of Cameron."

Deghan's brows crinkle. "Oh no, what did he do?"

Smiling, I quickly say, "No, nothing. Not bad. I had an idea I wanted to run by you."

"Ooh, ideas." He reverts back into light-hearted mode.

"I thought that maybe we could help him plan a bake sale." I'm not sure how much Cameron has told Deghan, but regardless, we're all aware Cameron pays his own tuition, so it's not far-fetched for him to need some extra cash.

"That's genius, actually." He lowers his voice. "Has he told you what's going on?"

It's a relief that Cameron has Deghan to talk to.

I nod. "Yeah, a bit. I was hoping that maybe this would help."

"Absolutely. Everyone who's had anything he's made has loved it. No doubt it would go over well. I wonder if we could have a booth set up at the formal."

"That might work."

Deghan squeezes my hand. "This could be a game-changer.

Give him that validation he needs to finally realize how freaking amazing he is."

"It makes me unbelievably happy that you're so supportive of him."

"Cam's my best friend. I'm a little biased but I have no doubt he's going to be a world-famous chef one day."

"And what about you? What do you want to be when you grow up?" I glance up at him and smile.

He meets my gaze. "Happy. I think I'd settle with just being happy."

"Me, too."

———

Cameron's face remains expressionless.

"Sooo...you on board?" Deghan hops onto the metal counter to sit next to me.

Cam takes the nearby white hand towel and folds it, something he's done twice now. "But what if—?"

"There are no what-ifs," Deghan cuts him off. "It's going to be a hit, and you know it. And we're going to help you. All of us. I'll even drag Silas in here to ice cookies or wash dishes. Whatever you need. We're your family. You need help, and we have your back." He takes a breath. "And, people are going to go apeshit once they find out."

"You seriously think people are going to *pay* for this stuff?" Cameron folds his arms over his chest, crinkling his navy-blue tee. He leans against the cabinet.

"I have no doubt." I jump down, making my way over to him. "Have I ever lied to you?"

He glances down at me, his gaze searching my face. He lets out a sigh. "No."

I stand on my tiptoes, pressing my lips to his cheek. "It's going to be a success."

His mouth turns up at the sides. "Okay. Fine. But if no one

shows up, it's all on you." Cameron moves quick, stealing a kiss before grabbing a notebook. "What should I make?"

"Brownies," I reply immediately.

"No-brainer." He looks up from the paper. "What else?"

"Cookies, muffins, cupcakes, those tiny round things that are a little crunchy but have the cream in the middle," Deghan rambles off.

"Macarons?" Cameron asks.

"Yeah, sure, that."

"Okay, I can work with this. I'll see what else I can come up with. I'll have to talk to Walker to make sure I can use the kitchen and figure out supplies."

"I can talk to him." I may have broken the shadow realm and all, but fixing it was no easy feat, and it's safe to say it's pretty obvious that Walker feels like he owes me one. "Consider it taken care of. I second what Deg said, whatever you need. We'll figure this out together. We aren't going to allow you to struggle on your own."

"I love you, guys." Cameron's eyes glisten.

"Awwww," Deghan draws out. "Come here, big guy." He pulls Cam in for a hug.

I walk over, wrapping my arms around them.

They both wiggle a bit, shuffling me amongst them for a smothering embrace.

I allow it to consume me and disregard my lack of oxygen between the two gorgeous guys. I could think of worse ways to die.

I jog up the west wing stairs, a sort of cheerfulness flowing through me with this newfound project of helping Cameron with his *situation*.

With my stomach and heart full, I grip the handle to my dorm and pop myself inside. The shower calls to me, whispering sweet nothings of comfort and relaxation. I could definitely use it, considering this hectic day.

It totally sucks I wasn't able to find a dress, but at least I have Cameron and Deghan on board with the bake sale to raise Cam some bill money.

I grip the hem of my shirt, bringing it over my head and tossing it on the bed nearest to the bathroom. It's pretty much become a catch-all for my laundry, regardless of whether it's clean or dirty. I'm usually more of a clean freak, but life has been a bit hectic, and I haven't stuck to my normal standards.

Something shiny catches my eye in my peripheral. Instinctually, I raise my arms to my chest to cover myself. I slowly make my way toward the new-to-my-room thing, gasping when my eyes completely focus.

There, laying on my bed, the thing that nearly ruined my day with disappointment.

Light-pink and flawlessly glittering, absolutely elegant in all ways, my fucking dream dress.

But how?

I hadn't tried it on. How would the person know it fits?

The only people who knew I had looked at it were with me, and it sold while we were at another shop.

Shortly after we left, though.

Which tells me that someone else was there. Watching, and waiting.

CHAPTER 19

Friday morning rolls around, and no one will admit to delivering the dress to my room.

The girls don't seem to care *who*, only rather that I actually have a dress and won't be using the excuse that I don't have anything to wear to get out of going.

Lillian is especially pleased. "You can't back out now." She takes a bite of a muffin she grabbed off the sample tray.

Deghan and I thought it would be a good idea to tease people's taste buds with what Cameron has in store for everyone at the bake sale. So far, it's going over wonderfully. His treats are the talk of the academy, and not a single person has said one negative thing about them.

The plan is to start selling on Saturday morning until about midafternoon. Then we will collectively break to recharge, get some more things cooked up if the supply is diminished, get ready for the dance, then take turns manning the booth at the formal.

Walker had no issue with allowing us to use the kitchen. He had joked about something regarding the health department, but then laughed it off and mentioned how we have a hidden shadow realm for supernatural students.

I guess that is a much more pressing issue than some college kids trying to raise a few bucks.

The headmaster said he would front the bill for the supplies and Cameron could pay him back from the proceeds.

All in all, the entire thing is going smoothly—too smoothly if you ask me.

With my shit luck, I'm a little skeptical something catastrophic will go wrong. Like an oven catching fire or me burning my other hand, or someone getting food poisoning.

I pray to the angels that it all goes well, for Cam's sake.

He's been anxious about pulling this whole thing off, but he's had this truly contagious optimism.

I haven't seen much of Silas, which tells me the stone is doing its job of putting a wedge between us.

Deghan managed to fulfill his promise of getting him involved, though, sending Silas off on errands to get Cam the materials he needs to make his goodies. And because Silas is so damn quick, he gets it done in no time.

"Are you ready for class?" Sydney asks from across the table.

I glance at the big round clock at the front of the room. "Yeah." I shove the last bit of my muffin in my mouth and swallow it down with a gulp of my cinnamon latte.

Another one of Sydney's wonderful creations.

"You should totally sell coffee at the bake sale." I point my finger at him. "Guarantee people would pay money for that, too."

"Look at you just pimping us all out." Deghan winks at me. "What could I possibly offer?"

"Hugs! Definitely hugs," I respond without hesitation. "I'd give the big bucks for that."

A wide grin befalls his face. "But they're reserved for you." Deghan scoops me up, smothering me the way he always does.

I relax into him. "Yeah, this is heaven." I breathe him in and let his warmth consume me. "Pretty sure these could cure cancer."

He laughs and ruffles my hair. "You're losing your mind."

"Been there, done that."

Sydney walks me to class quietly.

It's hard to not recognize something is on his mind. "Penny for your thoughts?"

He stops his pace, facing me and dragging me out of the line of traffic. "Listen, I know Silas is important to you, and despite me *really* disliking him, this stone is doing him no favors. I'm not sure how much longer he can hold on in there."

I don't understand. Silas has been distant, but he's still been pushing through. And I'd be lying if I thought it wasn't *him* who followed me and the girls into town and saw that I fell in love with that dress. Only Silas would have been able to *feel* the way that I did when I simply saw the dress. And only he would have been able to be stealthy enough to make it happen and keep his mouth shut about it.

How could it be possible that he's slipping away?

Maybe Sydney is wrong. Maybe he's exaggerating and getting worked up over nothing.

"What makes you think that?" I study his face.

"He's different, Willow. Bad. Worse. I don't want to stress you out any more than you already are, but I wanted to be transparent with you." The dark circles have reappeared under Sydney's eyes, letting me in on the secret that he hasn't been sleeping well again.

"We only have to get through what, two more days? The full moon is Sunday? The stone will be charged by then, and we can use it, find my parents, and destroy it. What's two more days?" I swallow the lump forming in my throat.

Sydney averts his gaze. "Yeah."

"Hey," Ruby interrupts our now silence. "You heading to class?"

I nod. "Be right there."

"Go ahead. We can talk later," Sydney says.

He walks away without another word. The weight of his absence fills me. It's so unusual for Sydney to be *worried* about Silas. I have to hope it's only an overreaction. Sydney is on edge with everything going on, maybe he's taking Silas's natural disposition too seriously.

"Everything okay?" Ruby asks on our journey to the end of the north wing.

"Yep."

She points to my still wrapped up hand. "How's that doing?"

"Better," I continue to lie. "Tremont works on it twice a day. He's making great progress."

Okay, so it's a *tiny* bit better, but only in a *healing naturally* not a magical kind of way. I'm continually baffled at how everyone praises his healing abilities despite not noticing them whatsoever. Perhaps it's me and how weird my magic is. It could be preventing him from healing me like it had hidden my magic from Abigail the time she scanned me all those months ago.

"Morning, girls," Abigail greets us. "Let's get right to it."

All three of us walk to the entrance, whispering the same words. "Infito grantum modem."

The haze appears, we step through, and in a millisecond, we're in another realm.

It never gets any less strange that these types of things exist.

Shadow realms and witches and vampires and werewolves and demons.

I focus on the upper right-hand corner, checking those all-too-familiar seams that remain intact. I have no clue what the hell I would do if they weren't, but it somehow puts me at ease to be able to see their seal.

"I've been thinking, and I want to try a new approach. Ruby had mentioned she wanted to work on tapping into her personal power, and I thought that we could help her with that." She looks at me. "Willow, you have quite a few *natural* talents, and that's a great asset to be able to tap into. I'm hopeful that we can work together to assist Ruby in finding hers."

"You have *multiple* abilities?" Ruby's eyes go wide.

My shoulders rise in a total *I don't know* manner.

"Willow is quite gifted, yes. It's truly astonishing, and it's safe to say she hasn't even tapped into her full potential yet. Only time and practice will continue to show what kind of power Willow holds. But Ruby, you struggle with tapping into those types of things, and I believe this will be a great learning experience."

Yeah, sure, I have this big, wonderful, strong power, but I have no clue how I access it. The magic just *comes* to me. I desperately need it, and it's there. And sometimes, it's not. So how is that something I can teach someone else?

If I'm being honest, I could use a teacher of my own for this kind of thing.

"Willow, I don't expect you to have black-and-white instructions on this, and you're still learning, obviously, which is why this will be a great experiment for both of you to figure out these things together. Build off one another. Do the whole trial-and-error thing." Abigail sits against the desk at the front of the room. "And I'll be here every step of the way."

"I...I'm not sure where to begin," I say quietly. It's a little embarrassing that everyone sees me as this powerful witch, and I don't have a clue what the fuck I'm doing half the time.

"Let's go back to the basics," Abigail speaks gently. "The times you've found these powers. How did they come about?"

"Well." I recall the time in the woods. I had run out of the school, utterly overwhelmed and needing some fresh air, only to get lost in the woods like an idiot. I had closed my eyes, cleared my head, and whispered to myself how I was going to find my way out. Then, the flowers lit up, leading me toward the school. "I asked for them."

"Can you be more specific?" Abigail encourages.

Ruby stares at me as though I have fourteen eyes.

"I'm telling you, I focused on nothing but the problem.

Allowed my mind to be totally free, and it came to me." I'm not sure how else to explain it. "I was lost, quite literally, and I couldn't find my way. I summoned some inner part of myself, and it showed me a path. Honestly, I thought I might be losing my mind." Something we accused my mother of doing. "But my gut told me to trust it, to follow it. And when I did, I was back."

"Intuition is an incredibly powerful tool for supernaturals, witches especially." Abigail hops off the desk she's leaning on. "I have an idea." She pokes at her chin. "What if we do some yoga meditation? Free our minds, loosen our bodies, and give room to whatever may flow in. Plus, it's known to reduce stress and anxiety, so it's a win-win either way."

"Uh, I guess," Ruby says hesitantly. She accepts the rolled-up mat from Abigail, the ones we used the other day, and places it on the floor.

I get mine and do the same.

"Go ahead and have a seat." Abigail collects one for herself and settles down, too. "Let's start by closing our eyes." She lowers her voice. "Relax your bodies...unclench your jaw, release the tension in your shoulders...take a breath in, and then out...with each one, continue to put your body at ease. Keep your mind from wandering by focusing on only your breathing and that alone. If your thoughts happen to stray, gently pull yourself back to the here and now."

I have five billion things going on in my life, how am I going to get all that out of my head?

"Take a deep breath in through your nose. One...two...three... and then hold it two seconds. One...two...and exhale through your mouth for one...two...three...four. Good job. And again. Inhale...hold...exhale." Abigail does the exercise as best she can while instructing us.

I peek through one eye when I notice Ruby shifting her body.

She repositions, a sense of annoyance seeming to float off her.

I close my eyes and go back to the exercise, breathing in, then out.

A few minutes of this go by, and my body truly does feel more relaxed. Although my mind keeps wanting to meander.

The face of each of my guys pops up into my head. A smiling Deghan, a serious Sydney, a cheerful Cam, and a broody Silas.

The image of Silas sticks, not wanting to leave.

I push it away, but it doesn't budge.

Breathe, Willow.

His face changes, his jaw tightens, his fists ball up, and he raises them to his face, gripping his hair and holding his head in his hands. Something is wrong with him.

I run through my mind to get closer to him, but he recoils.

He shrinks down, crouching into a small version of himself, helpless and terrified. The Silas in my mind flinches, like he hears something that might harm him. He puts his head between his legs and rocks back and forth.

Pure terror radiates from him.

No matter how hard I try to get to him, I can't. In this part of my mind, I'm only a spectator, unable to do a damn thing.

It's only a strange vision, but the thought of leaving him in here this way unsettles me to my core.

I remind myself: this is only the Silas in my head, not my Silas in real life.

I continue to painfully study him with each of his trembling motions until suddenly, his head snaps up, his eyes staring directly into mine.

Normally, they're a gorgeous shade of purple and grey, but only this time, they're blood-red and strained. A single tear rolls down his cheek, and he opens his mouth slightly to whisper a choked, "Help me."

My whole world shatters.

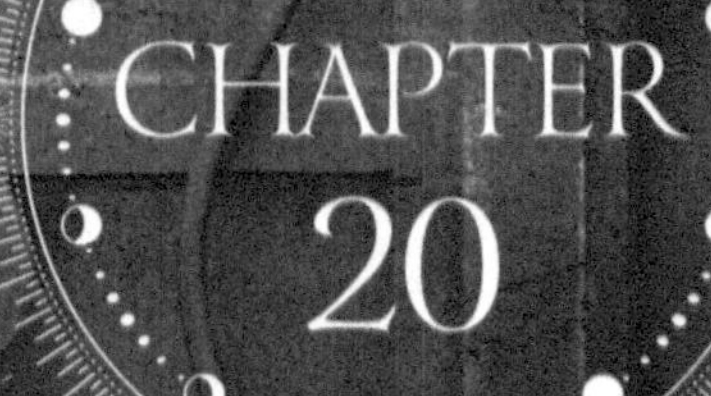

CHAPTER 20

"Willow," a frantic voice bellows

My body shakes—it's being shaken, something is rattling me.

"Open your eyes," the person urges.

I try to, but they're glued shut. The vision of Silas is burned into my line of sight.

I have to help him. I have to save him from whatever is hurting him.

"Get someone! Get help!"

A tremble weaves through my body. Pain, not my own, but someone else's, consumes me. It's Silas, it has to be him.

How do I get him out of this nightmare if I can't even get out myself?

Wind passes by my face; a familiar set of hands grip my cheeks. A gentle new voice. "Willow, come back to me."

Automatically, my lids open. Emotion overwhelms me, and tears cascade down. I continue to quiver uncontrollably.

My Silas scoops me into his arms, rushing toward the door. "Infito grantum hodem."

I don't dare break away from looking at his face, in fear that he'll turn into the other Silas. The frightened one.

"I've got you," he mutters into my hair.

"Silas, you..."

"I'm right here." The black T-shirt below his leather jacket shifts under my weight, revealing a wisp of his ink-stained collarbone.

A moment later, we're in my bedroom.

Silas sits on the small bed with me still tucked into his arms. "What happened?" He moves the hair out of my face to get a better look at me.

"You. I saw you. It was terrible..."

He smirks. "Tell me what you really think."

"No," I shake my head. "That's not what I meant. Silas, you were fucking petrified. I couldn't get to you no matter how hard I tried. You were...crying. Something was hurting you. I could feel it, too." I reach out and cup his flawless face. "You asked me to help you, and I couldn't save you."

He holds me tighter. "I'm here now. Right here with you. The *real* me. *Your* Silas. I'm fine, okay?"

"It was so real."

"But it wasn't. This is." He trails his fingers along my cheekbone. "Us. You and me." His gaze lingers on my lips. "This." He presses them to mine, bringing me back to reality with his touch.

There's no way this could be fake.

They're the same ones I've grown acquainted with. Firm and luscious, moving tenderly against mine.

I kiss him back, letting our mouths take me away from my brutal thoughts.

Now, it's just me and him.

His grip becomes tighter. His body shifts, letting mine fall gently onto the bed. Silas hovers over me, not breaking our fevered connection in the slightest.

"We're real," he says, assuring me.

Desire takes over in a desperate attempt to confirm what he's saying is true.

"Prove it," I mutter.

Silas grinds his body along mine, reminding me of our intimate times in the past.

I shove my hands under his jacket to try to remove it but end up flinching from the soreness of my still injured hand.

At this, he backs away. "Are you okay?"

"Yes. Please don't stop."

He studies me for a moment and then strips himself of his jacket, tossing it onto the floor.

I run my hands up his tattoo-covered arms and drag his face back down.

He makes quick work of removing my shirt. He returns to my mouth and glides his left hand down my body, slipping it inside my leggings.

Thank god for easy access.

From on top of my panties, he applies pressure, rubbing small circles with his palm.

I push myself onto him.

With my bad hand, I grip his neck, kissing him deeper. I take the other and follow the same trail down his body and into his jeans. I hold him as the firmness grows, stroking him gradually.

Finally, he floats his finger along the edge of my panties and shoves them to the side.

I take in a breath.

"This is real," he whispers and traces that same digit along my wet parts, teasing my entrance.

I groan in anticipation.

He slips inside but remains steady with his hand against my clit. The combination drives me insane with want.

I start climbing the mountain sooner than I hope but not daring to disallow myself the pleasure.

"Don't hold back," his sexy voice directs.

My eyes roll back, the bliss taking hold, the very same moment my door bursts open.

I bite down the moan that threatens to escape me regardless of my new visitor. My body trembles, but this time from an earth-shattering orgasm.

Silas continues to move, clearly not wanting to ruin what he started.

"Oh god, oh god, I'm sorry." Sydney's voice fills my ears. "I should have knocked. I'm leaving. I'm sorry."

I exhale, the intense ride coming to a stop.

Silas pulls his hand out, and I do the same.

He repositions himself and sits on the bed.

"Sydney," I call out. I should be embarrassed but the only thing I am at present is satisfied.

Syd stands with his back to us, almost exiting the room.

"What's up?" I glance down, realizing I'm topless.

Like he can read my mind, Silas vamps to get my shirt and tosses it to me.

"I, uh, I heard something happened. I was worried. I shouldn't have intruded." He doesn't turn around.

"She's okay," Silas answers for me. "Willow had an anxiety attack, but she's good now." He tucks a strand of hair behind my ear. "Right?"

I nod. It's safe to say I'm definitely not feeling anything comparable to how I was earlier. Not after his hand did that thing to my body.

I bite my lip. "I didn't mean to scare you, Syd." I go to stand, to walk over to him, and get him to face me, but he takes a step forward.

"Okay." He leaves my dorm.

Silas tugs at my hand to sit down. "Are you actually all right?" His brow is creased, and makes me think that if he were human, he'd have a wicked wrinkle there.

"For now, yeah." I walk across the room, making sure to turn the lock on the door this time. We don't need any intruders for what's about to happen next.

Silas watches my every move on my way to him.

I step between his knees, taking his face into my hands and tilting it up.

"What are you doing?" he questions.

I run my thumb along his bottom lip and lean forward, kissing him with everything I have. I dance my tongue into his mouth and cascade it with his. I break away for a split second to murmur, "Whatever I want."

I tug his onyx shirt, dragging it up and off him. I trail my hands down his chest and kneel on the floor. Without letting my first-time nerves take hold, I unbutton his pants and reach in to pull him out.

He's already growing hard, confirming that I'm doing something right here.

I lower my head, hovering right above his length. I trail my tongue along the tip and grip him firmly. I tease him until it's *me* that wants more. Not having any fucking clue what I'm doing, I open my mouth, sliding him in, a little at a time.

He groans and rakes his hand through my hair. He guides me gently up and down at the pace he wishes.

I glance up at him, our gazes locking on each other.

I swirl my tongue on the bottom of him and position my hand directly at the base of my mouth, moving the two together like they're connected.

He remains growing ever so slightly by the second.

Silas grips my head and gives a firmer push, shoving himself deeper.

Somehow, my body reignites, wanting another round of him.

In an instant, he stands, snatches me off the floor, and tosses me onto the bed. He digs his fingers under my bottoms and has them off and thrown to the side in a flash. He starts at my ankle, lingering his tongue all the way up my body, taking pause at my hips.

He leaves light kisses along my panty line, circling back to where his hand once was. "I need to taste you," he says, growling the words out.

And he does exactly that.

He blows cool air onto me and then takes his time, licking his way around my already soaked area. Silas grips my thighs and buries his face.

I wiggle around, not even trying to hold still. I thought what he did earlier felt good? That was nothing compared to this.

Minutes and minutes pass of him taunting me with his mouth until he decides to come up for air. He resumes his path up my body, pausing to pay attention to both of my breasts. He sucks and nibbles gently on each nipple.

Once he's close enough to my face, I grab hold of him and bring him to me, tasting myself with his kiss.

I shift my body, frantic to have him inside me. An idea strikes, and I pull away, flipping over onto my stomach. I long to feel him in a different way than I have in the past. I back up into him, sliding him into place.

He enters me and presses his body along mine, gripping my face to turn it to be able to kiss him.

Our tongues tango, and our bodies melt into each other.

He was already big, but somehow, he fills me more from this angle.

We find a rhythm that suits us both, a steady in and out that is so fucking right.

He lowers himself onto me more, smooshing my weight flat against the bed with him on top of me.

Having him touch so many areas of my body at once is a whole new level of pleasure.

"Is this okay?" he speaks quietly into my ear. His fingers weave their way around mine, holding on tightly.

I press myself against him in response. "Mmhm." With each delicious thrust, I manage to get closer.

I ache for him.

"Together?" Silas whispers.

"Together," I let out breathily.

Instead of picking up his pace, he slows it down, giving me long, deep strokes.

The new change of pace does exactly what he wants.

With our hands still locked together and our mouths tied, like he knows what he's doing, he shoves himself in one last time, sending us both over the edge.

He throbs inside me as I pulsate around him.

His body fully collapses onto the bed, only he doesn't let me go; instead, he drags me with him, turning our bodies to the side with him still inside me.

I don't ever want him to leave.

CHAPTER 21

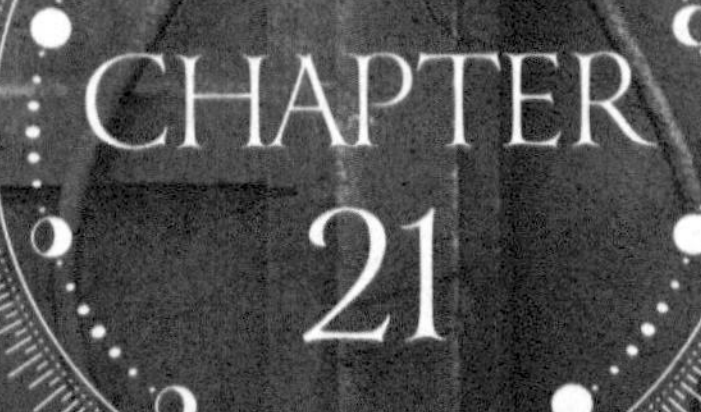

Once the high from our fun dissipates, the vision of him hunkering down onto the floor clouds my mind.

I may be back in the real world, with *my* Silas, but something was terribly wrong with what I saw. And if I've learned anything in the last few months, nothing is ever by coincidence.

It had to have been some weird magical omen or premonition...a warning of sorts.

"If you hurry," Silas says while putting on his shoes, "you won't be late for second period."

I grumble and bring the nearby pillow over my face. "I don't wanna."

He settles his weight onto the bed and uncovers me.

I sit up on both elbows. "Hey."

He cocks his head to the side. "Yes?"

"Um, are you going to the formal tomorrow?" I scoot up onto my butt.

He averts his gaze. "Why?"

"Well." *Because you haven't asked me yet.* "You haven't really mentioned it, other than to confirm you didn't drop off that dress."

He throws on his leather jacket. "It's not my kind of thing."

"Oh." I try not to let the hurt show through. Maybe I don't have as many dates as I think I do. I should have never assumed he would want to go with me anyway. Perhaps it wasn't him who brought me the gown after all.

He kisses my forehead. "I figured you would go with Sydney, anyway." Silas stands and tosses my clothes on his way to the door.

Sydney? He's never shown interest in going either.

I'm sure Deghan and Cameron are going together, so that leaves me totally date-less. I'm not going to barge in on Remi's plan to go with Kyra, and Lillian and Ethan are a couple.

I'll go alone if no one wants to ask me.

How stupid that an event that I have no concern with going to, I'm going to end up attending by myself.

Maybe I'll bail last minute and stay in my room and read and eat junk food. That sounds more appealing than spending a few hours getting ready and making a fool of myself in that dramatic dress.

"Earth to Willow," Silas says from his spot near the door.

"Yeah, that's fine. Whatever." I grab my clothes and head to my en suite. I should at least rinse off prior to heading to class. I don't bother saying anything else to Silas, so I close the door to the bathroom and lock him out.

When the rest of the school day is over, I skip going to the dining hall with the girls and go straight to the library. Studying is what I need to distract myself from the sad and terrified Silas who keeps popping into my head.

"Willow," Abigail calls from the headmaster's doorway. "Do you have a moment?"

I break from my path and head her way. "Sorry about earlier."

"No, no need. Silas informed me that you had a panic attack." She meets my gaze. "I wanted to apologize. It wasn't my intention to trigger you in any way."

"You didn't." I dig at my thumb with my index finger, a nervous habit I need to break.

"Please let me know in the future if I push things too far. I care about your well-being." Her energy is genuine and compassionate. She really is sorry for what happened earlier.

Although, I have no doubt that it wasn't her fault. Something else is in play here, I simply haven't figured it out yet.

"I will. I didn't sleep well last night. That probably had something to do with it." A lie, but hopefully one that will pacify her to stop thinking it was her doing that caused the episode.

"That'll do it. Witches are pretty finicky about eating and sleeping. We need all of both that we can get." She lets out a nervous laugh. "Anyway, you're free to go, just don't hesitate if you need anything."

"Thanks, Abigail." I offer a weak smile and leave the office. A few moments later, I arrive in the room in the library that has become a second home to me.

Books are stacked around, some toppled over haphazardly.

One, in particular, sits open where I left it from the last time I was here.

I go immediately to it, tossing my bag on a nearby chair. I snatch it up and sink into my usual seat.

I scan the page and realize I've already gone over this material. I flip to the next, and a picture of a pentagram comes into focus. For a millisecond, the five-pointed star glows a fire red but then fades onto the black ink on the page. Must be my eyes playing tricks on me.

I glance down to the origin section and read that the pentagram has been used symbolically by many, including those in ancient Greece and Babylonia, dating back thousands of years.

Various cultures have different meanings for the symbol, but in Wiccan practice, the points signify earth, sky, fire, water, and Spirit.

It is said to also symbolize the five senses of sight, hearing, smell, taste, and touch.

The pentagram's purpose is a little vague, but across most customs, it's used to either call forth, or ward off evil.

Seems simple enough.

Apparently, in Satanism, the design is usually with two of the points facing upward, often with a double circle around the star.

Satanic witches often summon evil spirits across realms using the marking.

Like demons.

A random chill trickles its way down my spine.

I go to the next page and find another symbol. This one is of a snake that is in the shape of a circle, eating its own tail. This design is sometimes known to be associated with reincarnation and immortality.

Next to this one is another that reminds me of an infinity sign but with two crosses coming out of the top of it. A quick scan of the text tells me it's a Leviathan Cross. It's said to be Satan's Cross, with ties to sulfur, which is a flammable element that helped alchemists rid unwanted substances. The guy that this thing is named by, Leviathan, is supposedly one of the Princes from Hell.

One? As in, there are more than one?

"Will?" Sydney pops his head into the library.

I nearly jump from my seat. "You scared me."

"Sorry." He rubs his neck. "Didn't want to interrupt you again."

"Oh, right. Listen, about earlier." My cheeks flush. How do I even explain myself out of this one?

He cuts me off and steps in. "You don't have to explain yourself, that's the point. I shouldn't have barged in like that. It's my fault."

"Are you...mad?" Dating multiple guys at once is completely new territory, and I'm not sure how this type of thing goes.

"No, not at all. Embarrassed. But I'm not mad. Maybe if it was some random guy. But it was just Silas." He wiggles his foot along the edge of the tassels on the rug.

"Do you hear yourself? You said Silas wasn't a big deal." I smile and shake my head. "You two are growing on each other."

"Now, I wouldn't go *that* far." He lets out a laugh. "I want you to be happy. And if that means Silas is in your life, then so be it."

"That's quite honorable."

"Speaking of...Cam could use our help. Can you spare some time?"

How could I be so stupid? I was so worked up that I had forgotten about the thing that *I* planned. "Yeah, duh. Of course." I grab my backpack and head out of the library with Sydney.

We arrive at the kitchen to find the place packed with people. All of my guys and the girls are here, preparing to help Cameron with his bake sale.

A grumpy Silas leans against the wall in the far corner.

Deghan waves at me from his post beside Cam.

"Where were you?" Lillian leans over and whispers.

"The library," I respond.

Saying the word while looking at Cam brings up old memories of a time not too long ago where we totally got caught making out, hot and heavy.

I'm not saying that I'm not satisfied, especially considering my double duty with Silas today, but considering Cam is the only guy I haven't hooked up with yet, my body is drawn to him.

I'm lost in the thought of Cameron taking me on that desk he picked me up and put me on when the door opens behind me.

Professor Tremont breaks my concentration. "Willow."

He motions for me to come over.

"What's up?" I glance back at the crowd.

"I have to go out and run a few errands. I won't be back until late tonight." He stops speaking.

Cool, why are you telling me this?

"So, I'll have to do your treatment now, rather than this evening during the time we normally do."

Ohhh. I really need to get my head out of my ass.

"Sure, yeah. Give me a second," I whisper to him.

I focus on the crowd. "I'll be back in a few minutes."

I scan the far wall, making eye contact with Silas on my way out the door.

Naturally, he's watching me.

"That's pretty great what you and your friends are doing," Tremont adds.

"Cameron is incredibly talented. He gets all the credit."

We walk the rest of the way to the infirmary, which isn't far at all.

Without turning around, I can sense Silas followed us out. It puts me at ease to know he's a bit of a stalker. His overprotective tendencies have saved my life on multiple occasions.

Not to mention, Tremont weirds me out from time to time.

It's not that he's a bad guy—I'm super skeptical of most people outside of my circle.

"How are you feeling?" Tremont holds the door open for me.

"Um." Oh, he means my hand. "Not terrible." Still not recovered, though, despite having a magical healer treating me twice a day.

"Would have hoped for a better reaction by now." He shuts us inside. "Perhaps my skills are weakening in my old age."

I laugh. "Old age, what are you, forty?"

"Ninety-three, actually."

My eyes go wide. How is that possible? He doesn't look a day over fifty at the most.

A grin spreads across his face. "Magic, my dear." He pats the seat next to his. "There are some rather wonderful anti-aging spells out there."

"Wow. I had no idea. Are you...immortal?"

He shakes his head and takes my hand into his. "No, although I can greatly extend my lifespan. I will, in fact, not live indefinitely."

"That's amazing." I don't bother studying what he's doing, rather I examine the features of his still-so-young face.

"It's possible to double, even triple your life expectancy if done correctly. But I don't necessarily encourage it."

The memorable cooling of his healing tickles my injured palm.

"May I ask why?"

"It's not favorable to watch everyone you love die of old age."

But what if those you love are mortal and immortal? How could I ever choose between living a longer life with Silas and Sydney, and living without Deghan, Cameron, the girls, and my mom?

I guess that's a path I'll have to cross when I get to it.

I exit the infirmary in hopes of finding Silas. I need to apologize for shutting down on him earlier. It's something that I'm used to him doing, but not something I want to get in the habit of, especially considering it's caused so much trouble in the past.

I walk out into the middle of the school, and he's nowhere to be found.

I close my eyes and try to absorb his nearby energy.

"Where are you?" I whisper to the universe.

A beacon in my heart calls me toward the forest behind the school. Maybe he needed to get a breath of fresh air?

I stroll through the dining hall, making a mental note to hurry the heck up and get back to help everyone out. I'm not going to be the friend who's a huge flake during their time of need. I just have to find Silas, tell him I'm sorry, and drag him back to help with the bake sale.

Easy peasy.

Once outside, the chill of the autumn air greets me. I look to the left and right, no Silas in sight. I recall the first day I arrived at Harper Academy. I hung out the window of my dorm and dropped my phone like an idiot. I had bumped into Cameron and Deghan and been baffled at how hot the guys at this school are.

Little did I know, I'd fall for both of them.

Plus, the whole weird instance of locating my dropped phone on the first-floor windowsill, perfectly unharmed. Silas saved the day and we hadn't even met.

I hop off the patio steps, leading myself in the direction my random intuition has told me to go.

I walk for a few minutes, the only sound being the light wind cascading through the trees and the fallen leaves that crumble beneath me. The breeze is cool and layered with the scent of pine and earth. The setting sun weaves ribbons through the trees.

I pause, taking in a deep breath and closing my eyes again to focus. "Are you near?"

Like a GPS, I'm drawn farther into the wooded area to the one who has the other portion of my soul.

My eyes take a second to adjust, but the second they do, my gaze settles on him.

Silas kneels next to a lifeless deer, his face buried in the neck of the animal he holds in his hands. He shakes his head back and forth, sucking the blood from its veins.

It's the first time I've seen Silas feed, and I find myself glued into place, frozen and unable to look away.

Moments pass, and finally I find the courage to take a step. The brown and gold leaves crinkle beneath my feet, and I stop again.

He whips his head toward me, barring his teeth and emitting a sort of hiss, almost resembling a warning. The red liquid seeps from his mouth and rolls down his chin.

His eyes narrow, and as though he registers who I am, his expression softens into something else. He shoves the being to the ground, and it thuds limply upon impact. He wipes at his face in a desperate attempt to erase what he's done. "Willow," he whispers.

I go to move, but my foot gets stuck. I try to wiggle it free, but the next thing I can comprehend is the world falling out from under me. I tumble into a heap on the ground, only barely breaking the fall with my hands. Pain tears through my already injured palm, the other stinging from the newly scraped skin.

I don't bother getting up. I just lie there, leaning my head onto the foliage and dirt-covered earth pillow. What's the point anymore when literally everything I do is a complete fucking disaster?

I need a stronger word than defeated, because whatever word that is, that's exactly how I feel...

It's like my life is a gigantic joke, and the universe is trolling me.

Silas rushes over without a drop of his feeding left on his face. "Are you okay?"

How did he clean himself up that quickly?

I close my eyes. "I give up."

"You're bleeding," he says tensely.

A strange wind rushes by, accompanied by a potently evil energy.

I sit up, but Silas puts out his arm to keep me down. "We're not alone."

"Shit."

CHAPTER 22

"Isn't this vampire territory?" the unknown person speaks. They whip by so fast I can't seem to make them out.

"Stay down." Silas grits his teeth and stands, hovering over the top of me.

"Do you have a little pet?" the person taunts from somewhere hidden away. "Can I have a taste, too?"

Silas goes to speak, but the guy cuts him off.

"Sweet, like honeysuckle. I can smell you all the way over here. What a delectable treat you'll be." The being rushes toward us, but Silas extends an arm and slams it into the guy's chest.

The unidentified body hits the ground, their face only a few feet from me.

Blood soaks through my bandage and onto the ground.

I move my arm, and Silas breaks his concentration for only a second, giving the guy exactly the opening he was looking for.

The tall figure rushes toward me with his jet-black locks billowing behind him. Time slows down, and his gaze meets mine, the undiluted rage, and hatred lining every bit of him. The cloak of his long, dark jacket flows with him, like it's an extension of his body.

Life comes back in full force when his hand grips my throat and lifts me off the ground.

In all the times I've fought demons and feared for my life, I've never quite been *this* close to death before.

Silas claws at his arm, but the person holds him back.

"Hi, little girl. My name is Kole...with a K. I'll be dining on you this evening. The pleasure is all mine." His nearly black eyes stare into me, and he licks his bottom lip, exposing his fangs.

I clutch at his tight hand around my throat, but all it does is get more of my blood everywhere, making things that much worse.

Kole lowers me and brings his head forward, licking some of the red substance off his skin. "Mmm." He closes his eyes in satisfaction. "I've never tasted such purity. No wonder you keep this one around."

"I'm going to murder you." Silas snarls. He attempts to break the hold the man has on him to no avail.

I take a breath, clear my mind, and focus. *Magic, don't fail me now.*

A bubble ripples through my body, the power stirring within me.

I drop my hands and summon it forward. I barely glance down, and the pink glow is forming already. I shift my eyes to Silas, and he nods, giving me the go-ahead.

I draw back my arm, creating an orb. Without giving the vicious vampire insight on what's going on, I waste no time and throw it directly into his chest, sending him spiraling back a few feet.

His frown widens into a grin, and his eyes go wild. "Oh, this will be fun indeed."

The broken contact gives Silas a clear shot to attack.

Somehow, Kole anticipates this and lobs a black ball of magic toward him, pinning Silas against a nearby tree.

I thought that summoning my power would be enough, now I'm not so sure.

"You're afraid." Kole stalks toward me. "I'm into that."

Repeating the motion from moments ago, I conjure another ball and slam it into him.

He digs his shoes into the ground as he skids backward a few feet. He winces from the pink explosion on his chest and then straightens. "Is that all you've got?"

"Willow," Silas calls out from his restrained spot.

"Hush," Kole screams. "You will be silent and watch the show I'm about to put on for you. And then maybe, once I rip apart your pathetic witch of a girlfriend, you'll come back to where you belong. Vampires don't mix with *their* kind." He spits on the ground between us and looks back to Silas. "What's wrong with you? You're an embarrassment."

"You don't know what you're doing." Silas struggles to break free.

Kole takes an unhurried step forward, like he's savoring this fucked-up game he's playing. His gaze wanders my body up and down, and he shakes his stupid head. "Although, I could always... turn you."

A newfound fear shatters my being. Turn me? Into a vampire?

I haven't even read that far into my research to comprehend what the fuck that entails.

I blast off two rapid bursts of energy toward him. "Good luck trying."

He staggers back again, but this time, when he rebounds, he uses his vamp speed to close the distance. Kole grasps my neck again and opens wide to extend his teeth.

This is it, I'm about to either die or become a vampire.

I'm not sure which is worse.

Not that I have anything against vampires, but I kind of enjoyed the little bit of being a witch I've gotten the chance to experience. And if this is in any way the same as the movies, I can't imagine I'd want Kole to be my sire.

If anyone gets to turn me into a vampire, it's Silas.

I scratch and claw and shove every ounce of magic I have into him to get him to stop.

But nothing seems to work.

A second flash of black appears in my peripheral. He must have a friend with him.

I'm for sure a fucking goner.

In my last moments, I lock gazes with Silas.

His purple eyes melt into me like the very first time I saw them. Although, currently there is much more fear and less of the longing he once had.

"Silas...I..." I mutter.

I guess if they're my last words, I have to make them count.

I don't get a chance to finish my sentence because the rogue figure whips by and tackles Kole to the ground.

The two of them tumble into a rolling chaos, and I can't seem to make either of them out.

I stand there for a split second, completely dumbfounded and in shock.

"Willow, help me," Silas pleads.

I rush to his side and put my hands on him and use the same tactic I had done on Sydney to siphon out the wicked magic.

A fierce hotness lashes at my skin, and somehow, it works.

Silas frees his arms, and a stressful moment later, his body is released from the tree.

He jumps down and places himself between me and the still-ongoing battle between the two creatures. "I'd tell you to run, but if he breaks free, he'll catch you. You're safest right here with me."

"I wouldn't have left you anyway." I close my eyes and bring forth the protective shield I had thrown on Cameron back in the shadow realm the time the first demon attacked. I inch closer to Silas and spread it around us.

He rests his back alongside my chest in response.

We become one.

Two souls, two beings, coming together to fight and protect each other at all costs.

I shift my body to look around him at the mess up ahead.

The dust settles, and a figure appears, a black-and-grey wolf standing atop the vampire who attacked us. The dog is massive, towering over Kole like he's nothing.

Another wolf appears, this one a familiar shade of brown with those to-die-for golden eyes. Deghan rushes past me and Silas, tilting his head back to glance at us on the way.

Deghan reaches the other wolf, and they do a strange stand-off, what I assume to be communicating in their heads to each other. I think that's a wolf thing.

Deghan nods and trots off into the woods. A moment later, he comes running back in his human form, barefoot and shirtless and in only a pair of black gym shorts. He makes his way over to us. "Think you can help me restrain him?"

"Why not just rip his head off and burn the asshole?" Silas demands.

Deghan rolls his eyes. "You know we can't do that."

"Given the circumstances, an exception seems reasonable." Silas sighs. "Give me sixty seconds." He turns to me. "Keep your shield up, okay? I'll be right back."

Silas rushes away, and sure enough, fifty-eight dreadfully long seconds later, he whooshes back in with a rope in his hand.

"That'll work," Deghan confirms.

"You're going to tie me up like some animal?" Kole spits. "Just get it over with and kill me already. At this rate, you'll bore me to death."

Silas roughly seizes one of Kole's arms and wraps the cord around it, securing it with a type of knot I've never seen done.

Deghan and Silas drag his body to a nearby tree while the unknown wolf snarls his teeth at the vampire.

Once secure, the wolf takes off into the woods and appears the same way Deghan had moments prior.

The person comes closer, and at first, I almost don't recognize his face.

Upon further inspection, though, I recall the dark-brown hair and chocolatey eyes. He's the guy from Harper Café—it's Jackson.

He shyly smiles my way and then double-checks the restraints on Kole.

"It's secure," Silas confirms.

"Doesn't hurt to verify." Jackson pulls the rope.

"Oh, you two hate each other," Kole adds. "The drama unfolds."

"We've never met, actually." Jackson grips it tighter and yanks Kole against the tree. "Yeah, you're probably right." He stands, shirtless and barefoot, identical to Deghan, and walks over to Silas. He extends his hand and says, "I'm Jackson."

Silas studies his palm, and I'm not so sure he's going to shake it. He grips it firmly. "Silas. I appreciate your assistance back there."

Jackson's gaze meets mine, and he nods. "Of course."

"Dude, I haven't seen you in forever. How have you been?" Deghan clasps Jackson on the shoulder and breaks the awkward standoff between him and Silas.

"Not bad. I'm back in town, though. Working at the coffee shop part-time."

"Wait, you two know each other?" I point from one to the other. It's then I remember how brutally injured my hands are.

"Yeah, we grew up together. Kinda family but not blood." Deghan grins and punches Jackson's shoulder.

Silas steps in front of me. "We should get that taken care of." He takes my arm and leads me a few feet away to a random fallen tree to sit on. "May I?"

"Mmhm."

Silas bites into his palm, drawing his blood and wiping it onto my unbandaged hand.

It's strange to watch, and I'm well aware it shouldn't be as seductive as it is, but the intimacy of the whole thing is next level.

The pain disappears within seconds, along with any trace of an open wound. All that is left is my blood mixed with his.

He unwraps my other hand, and for the first time since I burnt it, I see the mangled destruction of my skin.

"Angels, Willow," Silas nearly hisses. "I thought Tremont was healing you. This has to hurt like hell." He nips at himself again and gently rubs my injury.

Almost immediately, the dull ache I've had for days now fades.

"Holy shit." Kole's jaw drops. "She's...I had no idea. I'm..." He shakes his head. "I'm so terribly sorry."

"Wait." I focus on the stranger. "What are you talking about?"

"Don't," Silas demands.

"You're his Malachi."

"You mean to tell me you're not going to explain?" I plead with Silas.

He stops, puts his arm under my legs, and lifts me into the air into a bridal carry. "No."

"Let me down," I command.

"I have to get you back to the school and inform the headmaster of the intruder."

The beast who threatened to turn me into a vampire, the one who ended up apologizing moments later. For a reason, I'm still unclear of.

"You'll be safe now." Silas rushes us into the clearing behind the building. "He won't touch you ever again."

"You're telling me that this freaking psycho, who was about to turn me into his dinner, is all of a sudden not going to want to rip me apart?" I jump out of his arms once he slows down.

"Yes, that's correct." He grips my upper arm and continues to lead me the rest of the way.

"And it's because I'm your Malachi? What does that even mean? Why won't you tell me?"

Silas turns me toward him, bringing us both to a stop. "Because you don't need to know. Leave it alone. Please. Angels, Willow. Let it go."

I study his pained face. Why is he so insistent that I only have the minimal bits of information on him? He's always been secretive about our intertwined fate, and now this.

I'm his Malachi.

Whatever the hell that means.

I rip my arm from his hand. "Fine. Don't tell me then." I leave him standing there and stomp all the way to the bathroom to wash all the nastiness off me.

Next stop, the library.

If he's going to continue being so secretive, I'll have to find some other way to figure this out.

I head straight to my usual spot and scour the texts, desperate to find anything on the Harlows.

Five minutes later Sydney appears in the doorway.

"Um, Willow. We could really use your help. Deghan ran off and hasn't come back, and Silas is nowhere to be found." He leans on the wall and studies me. "This was your idea."

"Sydney, what's a *Malachi*?" I try not to sound as dumb as I feel.

His emerald eyes widen. "You found out?"

"What do you mean? You already knew about this?" My anger grows at how out of the loop I am. "Why didn't you tell me?"

Sydney rubs his temple. "It wasn't mine to tell."

"What about now? What is it?" I bite at my lip anxiously.

He sighs and shakes his head. "I shouldn't be the one explaining this to you. It should be him."

"I'm going to find out, you realize that, right? If it's not you, I'll comb every single book in the library until I figure it out." I lower my voice. "Please."

"I can't. I'm sorry."

Why is everyone so fucking reserved? Is the truth so terrifying that I can't be told? Does that mean this is bad? That has to be the only explanation for why they won't tell me. What could possibly be so terrible about what is going on between me and Silas?

"Willow, can we save this for another time? Cam really needs all hands on deck."

"Yeah, absolutely. You're right. This can wait." It was selfish of me to storm off in the first place to find Silas. And now, I shouldn't be focusing on something that's incredibly unimportant compared to Cameron's bake sale.

I've been in the dark this long, what's a bit longer?

Sydney puts his warm hand on my lower back and leads me up the stairs and through the foyer. "Holy shit." He stops and turns my palm up. "You're completely healed. Tremont really did a good job, didn't he?"

Little does he know, Tremont had next to nothing to do with the miraculous recovery.

"What aren't you saying?" He scans my face with his gaze. "Ohhh. I get it. Wait, what exactly happened?"

"Um, well." I glance around the room and lower my voice. "A random vampire attacked me, some were-dude named Jackson came out of nowhere and took him down. Deghan showed up. We got Kole tied up, and then Silas brought me back to the school."

"Kole? That's the vampire? Is everything under control now?" Sydney's energy fizzes over like he's about to take off.

"Yes. He's secured. Silas was going to get Walker and take care of it. Silas wanted to kill him, but Deghan said it wasn't allowed." I study my perfectly normal hand. "The vampire saw Silas mend this and freaked out, and then he said I'm Silas's Malachi and apologized for attacking me."

"Well, yeah, it's a not-so-secret secret oath. They can't touch another vampire's..." Sydney stops talking. "I'm saying too much."

"You're killing me. Please finish. What does this mean?"

"It means that Silas needs to man up and tell you himself. I'm not really sure why he hasn't, but there has to be some explanation. Maybe he's protecting you somehow. It's hard to say with him. But, if you're sure they have it taken care of, let's get to Cam. They'll catch up once they're done."

I hesitate. "What do you think they're going to do...with...the vampire?"

Sydney looks around. "Um, in this kind of situation? Probably stake him."

"I thought they couldn't kill him." Maybe they couldn't do it in front of me?

"No, it wouldn't destroy him, it would only immobilize him indefinitely. Vampires are weak to rhodium. It's a super-rare metal. They won't die, but if they're impaled with it, they desiccate." Sydney takes my hand gently and changes the subject like he wasn't just talking about serious supernatural stuff. "Come on."

We go through the doorway of the kitchen, and Cameron's face turns into a smile.

"I'm so sorry, Cam," I say.

"You're here now, and that's all that matters." He winks.

"Where the hell were you?" Remi carries a fresh-out-of-the-oven tray of cookies.

"Long story." I walk over to the sink and wash my perfectly fine hands. "What can I do?"

"Here." Cameron holds out a measuring cup. "Can you put three of those in here for me?" He motions toward a powdery white substance. Flour maybe?

I quickly get to work, pushing away all of my wandering thoughts and focusing on Cameron and what he needs.

"Hey," he whispers to me. "Is everything okay? Deghan ran out to watch the sunset but then never came back."

That explains why Deghan was outside when shit went down.

"Yeah, there was a bit of a snag, but it's being resolved as we speak."

He notices the lack of bandage. "Damn, you're good now?"

I shrug. "I guess so."

"That's great. I've been worried about that. Couldn't help but feel as though it was my fault." Cameron rolls dough between his hands and places the balls on a baking sheet.

"No way. That was all on me." I scoop the last level cup into the bowl. "What next?"

He points to a stack of spices. "Cinnamon. Two tablespoons."

A buzzer goes off, and upon turning around, Kyra is pulling another pan out of the oven.

Behind her, Lillian is fully absorbed on stirring something in a pot. She doesn't take her eyes off it for a second.

An hour goes by of helping Cameron measure things and getting him whatever utensils he needs, and finally, Deghan shows up.

No Silas, though.

Deghan comes over, but for some reason, it's not his normal gait. It's a little slower, maybe more sluggish than usual.

"What's wrong, Deg? Did something happen?"

He shifts his attention to the girls and back to me. "I'll tell you later. Everything is okay, though."

Does that include Silas, too?

The moment I'm about to ask, the man himself strolls in. He heads straight toward us, stopping in front of Cameron to ask, "What do you need me to do?"

We all work until sometime in the middle of the night. The only reason we stop is because half of the group has fallen asleep in random chairs in the kitchen.

"Thank you for the help, everyone." Cameron beams at us. "I couldn't have done this without you."

Silas doesn't bother sticking around and leaves the moment he's dismissed.

I was hoping we could have talked, but he probably anticipated that very thing and bolted at his first opportunity.

A few mumbled goodbyes later, we head our separate ways, the girls to their respective dorm, and us toward the supernatural side.

Sydney veers off and says, "I'll see you in the morning."

I follow his path to the basement steps. He must be going to the library.

"Do you mind if I crash with you guys tonight?" I ask Deghan and Cam.

"What? You kidding? You never have to ask, princess." Deghan wraps his arm around me. "I'm obsessed with cuddles; I think it's my love language or something."

"And food. Pretty sure if that was one of them, you'd choose that first." Cameron elbows Deghan playfully.

"I can't help it. I'm hungry all the damn time. I'm a cuddly bear. Hibernation and food. That's my jam."

"Can we stop by my room to get some comfy clothes?" Cameron yawns and stretches his arms wide.

"You can borrow some of mine if you want," Deghan offers.

"That works." Cam tugs me to him. "What about you? Do you need anything?"

"I gotchu, girl," Deghan interjects.

I melt into a Deghan and Cameron sandwich on our way to Deghan's room. It's soothing and exactly the comfort I need, considering the hectic day we all had.

Plus, I'm sure tomorrow will be full of stress, and I need all the relaxation I can get.

"Hey, why are you limping?" I swing my gaze to Deghan.

"Oh, right. Um, so, typically, I only shift on full moons, but I could hear Jackson's struggle and sort of prematurely changed. I'm fine, it's totally okay. I'll be sore for a few days, though. Usually, it gets easier with age, but I'm still at a point where it sucks a little bit."

"Damn," Cameron mutters.

"I'm so sorry, Deghan. It's all my fault. Is there anything I can do?"

He grins wide. "Looks like your hand is all better now, maybe it's my turn to get my hair washed?"

I nudge him. "Your wish is my command."

We arrive at Deghan's room, and he divvies out clothes.

For me, it's one of his T-shirts, which happens to fall all the way to my knees when I put it on. I hop onto the bed tucked in the middle and pull the covers to my chin. "It feels good to lie down."

Deghan flips off the lights while Cameron climbs in next to me.

Seconds later, Deghan is on the other side.

I lie flat on my back, reaching to each of them and taking their hands in mine.

It's not long until Deghan is sawing logs. He abruptly flips over, facing away from me, releasing my hand in the process.

I turn to face Cameron and take his hand into both of mine, holding it to my chest.

"Come here," he whispers and extends his arm toward me.

I scoot over and nestle into the wonderfully carved-out space.

Cam puts his lips gently to my forehead. He rakes the hair out of my face and tucks it behind my ear.

I tilt my head up to him, and somehow, despite the darkness of the room, his ocean-blue eyes light up my heart.

I inch forward and lay a soft kiss on his cheek.

He moves slightly, pressing his mouth onto mine.

All at once, the desperation and longing we shared in the

library not too long ago comes back in full force. Desire turns into a heated passion which turns into me climbing on top of him.

Quietly, though, in an attempt to not wake Deghan up.

I break away, bringing my finger to my lips to tell him to be silent while I check for the rising and falling of Deghan's chest. Instead, though, his loud snoring rings through.

Cam and I smile at each other and go right back to what we were doing.

He weaves his fingers up under the oversized tee, along my bare torso. His touch is fire and ice, and damn if I don't want more.

I grind my body against his growing hardness until I can't wait any longer.

I waste no time, reaching back to tug his gym shorts off.

He takes the opportunity to snake his hand along the front of my body and into my panties. He dances his finger teasingly on my opening and then hooks my undies and pulls them to the side.

I rub my exposed parts up his and finally, I position him in place. Swallowing my moan upon his entry, I glance over to make sure Deghan is still asleep.

Cameron grasps my ass and thrusts himself inside me.

I bring myself back down, crushing my lips into his and sliding my way onto his shaft.

He guides me in and out with his hands on my hips, but for the most part, I'm in control, riding him like there's no tomorrow.

It's a fucking miracle we haven't woken up the sleeping beauty beside us.

I guide myself along his length, hitting just the right spot. I pick up the pace, and he grows even more solid.

His fingers dig into my sides, reeling me in and begging for more.

Sitting straight up, I grab on to his hands, track them up my body, and then interlace our fingers. I shove them behind his head and pin him in place. I continue to wiggle my body onto his. The motion brings me so close I can almost taste it.

The moment I'm about to come undone, he gets himself free, reaching across my waist and flipping me onto my back in a move so smooth I barely knew what was happening.

This time, it's him who traps both of my wrists with only one of his hands.

With my lack of mobility, he brushes his mouth onto mine, dragging his teeth along my bottom lip. He thrusts deeply and runs his free hand up my stomach and onto my breast. He takes my nipple between his fingers and twirls it.

The combined sensation is nothing I've ever experienced.

His next plunge sends me over the edge.

I clench around him, my orgasm extreme and rattling my body.

Cam puts his hand over my mouth to help muffle the moans leaving me, but he never stops his in-and-out movement. Which only adds to the intensity of my pleasure.

I finally come down from my high right as he pulls out and strokes himself finished onto my belly.

I exhale and revel in how fucking sexy he is.

He grins like he's doing the exact same, but to me.

I peek beside me, and having no clue how, Deghan is still fast asleep, none the wiser to the insane sex Cameron and I just had a couple feet away from him.

Part of me wonders what would have happened if he'd woken up.

After we've finished, I get the best sleep of my life.

Don't get me wrong, I was already wickedly exhausted once we finished in the kitchen, but my time with Cameron fully wore me out and breathed an entirely new life into me.

Somehow, every second I spend getting closer to the guys, whether it's physically or emotionally, I end up *feeling* stronger. Is that even possible? Maybe that's what happens when you fall in love.

"Girl, if you don't sit still, I swear I will leave your hair looking a mess," Remi threatens.

I spit out a sorry and sit up straight. "Although, I'm not opposed to leaving it."

She lets out a long breath. "Don't embarrass me, Wills."

Her shaking hands tell me she's nervous about the formal, given I'm pretty sure she's finally going to make a move on Kyra.

"Is there anything I can do to help you get ready?" I subtly extend my index finger and press it against her leg without her realizing it. I push some calming energy into her.

"Nope," she responds. Already with less harshness in her voice. "I want to get you finished so I can focus on myself." She twirls a strand of my hair around the sizzling curling wand. "What are the guys wearing?"

I shrug but immediately regret it the second my shoulder gets too close to the hot surface. "Not sure."

"What do you mean? You haven't coordinated with your dates yet?" Remi lets the warm lock of hair fall and grips another. "The dance is in a few hours."

"I'll figure it out." What I really mean is, I won't. I'll go to the event alone since no one bothered to ask me to go with them. I'd rather simply make an appearance and get the hell out of there anyway.

The hours are ticking down until the stone will be charged by the full moon, and being around a bunch of people only adds to that nagging anxiety.

Yay for being socially introverted.

The moon will be at its fullest mid-Sunday, so I don't have much more of a wait until I can attempt to locate my mother again.

Walker continues to have no updates on my mom other than the occasional 'the trackers are on her trail.'

But that's the same thing I've been hearing since this happened. And I refuse to keep letting my flesh and blood slip away. If I want something done, I have to do it myself.

Remi curls the rest of my hair and then strategically pins it up all over my head. With an ultimate mist of spray, she says, "All done. But if you screw this masterpiece up, it's on you to fix it."

"It's gorgeous." I stare at the loosely flowing locks around my face and onto the somehow beautiful bird's-nest-looking thing she created. It really is quite beautiful.

"Now, for makeup. I'm thinking subtle." Remi fumbles through her cosmetic bag. "Your hair is stunning, and your dress is killer, so we'll want to go for a natural face." She sets a small round container with a see-through top next to me.

"Gold is natural?" I study the shining eye shadow.

"Eh, it's only to add a little pop. Trust me."

And that I do.

Fifteen antagonizing minutes later, she tosses the stick of mascara aside. "Man, I'm good."

The door to the dorm opens, and I glimpse in the mirror to see Lillian entering.

"Just in time," Remi says.

"Good. I need to take a shower, and Cam could use some help."

Looks like it's my turn to clock into bake sale duty.

That has to be better than sitting here while Remi pokes and prods and tugs at me.

I spend the time between Remi's torture session and the formal measuring out more supplies while Cameron bakes his massive heart out.

He comes up with heavenly brownies, triple chocolate cheese-cake bites, decadent cookies, and beautifully designed cupcakes of all kinds—the white chocolate macadamia nut being my fave—mini apple pies, and macaroons.

And that's only to name a few.

The selection Cameron came up with is insane, but considering the turnout this morning, it's safe to say he made all the right choices.

"I need more blueberry muffins. People are going crazy over them." He grabs a large metal bowl. "I think we'll be good if we can get more of those." Cam stares off into space for a minute. "Yeah, we should be."

I place my hand on his shoulder to calm him down.

"Thanks, I needed that."

"Anytime. Now, what can I do?" I scan the room.

"Keep me company, that's enough. I have the rest under control." Cam gives me his signature wink. Those gorgeous baby-blue eyes sending shock waves through me.

I'm taken back to last night—to our sexy encounter.

"Can you believe we didn't wake Deghan up?" I shake my head and laugh.

"Right? I thought for sure we were going to." He adds a dash of cinnamon into the mixture and then dumps a bowl of blueberries inside.

"Did I hear my name?" the voice of a sexy man calls out.

Cam and I exchange a look of terror followed by busting out laughing.

"Nope," I lie.

"Aw, are you two keeping secrets from me?" Deghan frowns. "Is this a face you can keep secrets from?"

I pinch my mouth shut and try to stop giggling.

"Well, break my heart then." Deghan clutches his chest dramatically and then smiles. "But you're free to leave. I can take over from here." He runs his finger along the side of my cheek. "Beautiful."

I glance at the clock. There's only another hour until the dance. "You better hurry if you're going to have any time to get ready."

Cameron pours the batter into the tins. "These are fast. No biggie."

I take the opportunity to head back to my dorm and finish getting ready. Although, all that entails is throwing on the dress that mysteriously appeared in my room a few days ago and putting on the costume jewelry Kyra let me borrow.

I can't exactly walk in the four-inch heels that Remi insisted I wear, and since they're not even visible under my gown, I opt to wear my Chuck Taylors instead. She'll kill me if she finds out, but here's to hoping she doesn't.

I do everything that needs to be done and end up with another thirty minutes to spare. Not wanting to sit around and twiddle my thumbs, I head to the library and do a little research.

Maybe I can figure out what the hell a Malachi is and why everyone is refusing to talk about it.

I poke my head out of my room, and when the coast is clear, I head straight to my destination. Somehow, I make it all the way through the school without running into anyone I know. My friends must all be busy with the finishing touches to their outfits.

I clutch the train—I think that's what it's called—of my dress to not step on it on my way down the library stairs.

I end up finding my study room without needing the compass Abigail made for me. I'm getting better at navigating the hidden portion of the library, but I'm not completely confident.

I run my finger along the spine of a few books until I find one worth pulling out. I flip it open and scan the first few pages. Nothing. Just some talk of herbs and their medicinal powers. I shut the text and search for another. I check the time. Ten minutes left.

Rummaging through the few stacks sporadically spaced on the desks, I try to find the one with minimal information on the Harlow family. Maybe that one will have something useful to help me crack this mystery.

I scan the books once, twice, then a third time. That one is nowhere to be found.

Of course it isn't. That's my luck.

Defeated and annoyed, I sit in a chair. So much for using the spare time for something productive.

The ticking of the clock reminds me that not only is it time for the formal, but each passing second is one more that I lose my mom, and that I lose Silas to the stone that could potentially help me find her.

What a fucking contradiction. The thing that can help me find her, can potentially ruin Silas forever.

Two minutes go by, and I grow aware that if I don't show my face soon, everyone will come looking for me. The girls because they think I'll bail, the guys because they worry something bad will have happened.

I pick up the long part of my dress and leave the library behind, along with any chance I have of figuring out this Silas thing.

I round the corner from the stairs. Various couples make their way, arms locked together, into the dining hall.

I sigh. Guess I'm going to do this one alone.

Spotting a familiar back of the head, I stop myself from going any farther.

Cam and Deghan, both dressed sharp as hell, walk side by side behind Lillian and Ethan. What a gorgeous group of people.

I step forward, deciding that now is a better time than never. I take in a breath, holding it and getting in line behind everyone else.

A strange sadness consumes me. How is it possible to feel so full of love and lonely at the same time?

CHAPTER 25

"You're stunning," a voice whispers into my ear.

Sydney.

My heart seems to pound out of my chest.

"He's not wrong," another person says.

Silas.

Each of my guys weave their arms through mine.

"Here, let me have this." Silas takes the handful of dress from my hand and holds it himself.

"For you." Sydney extends a beautiful white lily with light-purple insides.

"Thank you." I blush.

Here I was thinking that neither one of them wanted to escort me to the dance, and now I'm walking in with both of them.

My sorrow is quickly whisked away by their presence.

They lead me into the room and toward a crowd of people.

Deghan's jaw quite literally drops. "Dude." He clasps his hand on his mouth and shakes his head. "I'm gonna pass out." He steps forward and grabs my waist, spinning me in a circle. "You are absolutely stunning, Willow Oliver."

Cameron grins from his place on the floor. "Total knockout."

Deghan sets me down, and I have to nearly dodge the assault from Remi.

"I am so mad at you." She swats at my arm with her small purse—this time actually making contact. "Those shoes are dreadful."

"No one will notice. It'll be okay." I escape yet another blow from her.

"That dress really is fucking perfect for you. It hugs your curves in all the right ways."

I take Remi's hand and twirl her in a circle. "And look at *you*. Absolutely fabulous."

"Right? That's what I said," Kyra chimes in.

Remi blushes, and it's the cutest sight ever.

Silas and Sydney stand a few very awkward feet apart, waiting and watching me.

They're both sexy as hell.

Silas's fitted black suit is simple but classically trendy. His white shirt is unbuttoned at the top, and if you strain to peek inside, you can see a glimpse of his inked skin.

Not that I know a damn thing about fashion, but I think the word I'm looking for is dapper.

Sydney is stylish, too, with his dark-grey ensemble and black shirt. He even has a matching grey tie to go along with it. His normally unruly curly hair is still bouncing around but much tamer than usual.

It's safe to say they put a little bit of effort into their appearances tonight, and it definitely shows.

Lillian shyly waves from her spot next to Ethan. The two of them go together adorably. Her off-the-shoulder dark-red dress complements her figure well. She has her hair down, and it falls in gentle waves at her sides. Ethan has a matching ruby shirt that pulls their look together wonderfully.

I walk over to her. "Lills, you're on fire."

"Thanks, Wills. I could say the same about you."

A slow song plays across the speakers.

Ethan takes Lillian's hand. "Let's dance."

She hesitates, but I insist, "Go ahead. We'll catch up later."

I turn to spot Remi approaching Kyra. She says something to her, and Kyra breaks out into a massive smile.

Holy shit, it's finally happening.

Remi holds out her hand, Kyra takes it, and together, they head to the dance floor.

Pretty sure my heart might explode from seeing my friends so damn happy.

Sydney appears next to me. "Care to dance?"

Instinctually, I search for Silas.

He turns and goes across the vast space and steps behind the booth with Cameron and Deghan.

"Sure," I answer. "Although I might be bad at it."

Sydney grips my hand gently. "You? Bad at something? No way."

I let him lead me the way to an open area. I step close to him, and he wraps his arms around my waist.

"I wasn't sure you were going to come," I admit.

"I wasn't sure you wanted me to." He swallows. "But then Silas came to me. Wanted to ask for sure if we were attending together. That's when we both realized how stupid we were being. Each of us thought the other was your date, only recognizing at the last minute that you didn't have one at all."

"Hey now, I could have been keeping my options open," I joke.

"I'm sorry we left you hanging." He holds me close.

I rest my head against his chest and soak up his steady heartbeat while we rock back and forth on the dance floor.

I glance across the room to the bake sale. Three of my guys stand there, exchanging money for delicious treats by Cam.

I focus in on the girl Silas is handing a cupcake to, her neon-pink dress standing out like a sore thumb. Her body moves as though she's laughing. She turns around, and I find that it's Allie. That stupid brat is flirting with Silas.

I shift my gaze to his face.

He seems unfazed by whatever antics she's pulling.

The song comes to an end, and Sydney and I back apart.

An upbeat one comes on next, and the crowd goes wild.

Remi and Kyra shake their butts dramatically, and a whole bunch of people join in on the fun.

"Thank you for the dance," I say.

"The pleasure was all mine." Sydney brings my hand to his lips and kisses it gently.

"I'm going to check and see if the guys need anything. Want to come with me?"

"Sure. Tonight is your night. I'm here for you." His emerald eyes glow.

I take hold of his hand and push myself into his head. *I love you, Syd.*

He grins and responds with a mental, *I love you more.*

Cameron and Deghan have on matching dark-blue suits, like they planned their outfits. Of course they would, being that they're best buds and all.

"What is up, party people?" Cameron shouts atop the booming music.

"Do you want any help?" I yell back.

"More the merrier." He winks.

Sydney and I squeeze behind the table with them.

"What was up with Allie?" I ask Silas.

He furrows his brows. "What do you mean?"

"I saw her over here, having a heck of a conversation with you." I try not to come across like an overbearing girlfriend. If it was anyone else, I wouldn't have given it a second thought, but considering Allie kind of almost murdered me...her entire existence bothers me.

"Nothing happened," is all Silas responds.

"Okay." Apparently, he doesn't care to tell me what she was laughing about.

"I'm going to go." Silas is out the door without allowing me a chance to stop him.

Part of me wants to follow him, but Cameron needs me more right now.

I guess I'll figure that situation out when all of this is over.

"Everything okay?" Sydney leans close so I can hear him.

I nod.

"Um..." A random guy breaks my concentration. "I'll have two of the cheesecake bites, please."

I shift my attention to him. "That'll be five dollars."

Not really surprising, the bake sale sells out before the formal is over.

Cameron shoos us all away and says, "Go have fun. I'll clean this up."

A newfound smile is on his adorable face, and I can't help but wonder if it's from the immense relief of now having enough money to cover the unexpected expenses he found himself having to pay.

I hope his brother at least appreciates him for stepping up and taking care of business.

"I'll be back, guys." I pick up the bottom of my dress.

Sydney grabs my elbow to stop me. "Want me to come with you?"

"No, it's okay. I won't be long." That's not my plan anyway. Although the last time I went to find Silas, it ended up with me getting attacked by a vampire and almost being turned.

I step out of the dining hall and into the foyer. I close my eyes and let his soul guide me to him. I'm persuaded to go out onto the patio, but rather than going back through the formal area, I go out the front door and make my way around the old stone building.

I round the corner, and the shape of him comes into my line of sight.

He's standing on the patio, hands clenched on the railing, his back to me, seeming to be staring off into the dark forest.

I get within a few feet of him, and he speaks.

His voice is just a whisper. "I saw you that day."

I approach his side and reach out to put my hand on him but decide against it. Instead, I plant my palms on the wood surface next to his.

"What day?"

"You were hanging out of the second-story window. Desperate to get a signal on your phone. I couldn't take my eyes off you." He shakes his head slightly. "For once in my life, I was terrified of someone getting hurt. I didn't know you, but some-how, I *knew* you."

"That first week," I begin. "It always felt like someone was watching me. It took me a little while to realize it was you. Until I recognized I could sense you. Now I could pick you apart from a crowd blindfolded."

Without looking my way, he says, "Will you dance with me?"

I turn to him. "Out here? There's no music."

"We don't need it." He finally faces me and holds out his hand. "Please."

His expression is dark and serious, pleading even.

It tears me in two.

I put my palm in his, and he pulls me close.

We do that thing we do best, become one.

Moments pass of our silent embrace. We barely move, almost like the world has stopped turning and we're floating here.

He breaks the silence with his cracked voice. "You didn't ask for this. None of it."

"What?" I study his fearful face.

"I'm no good for you, Willow." He lowers his gaze. "I'm bad. I should have stayed away in the beginning. Angels know I tried."

"What are you saying? You don't make sense." I grip his solid shoulders firmly. "Silas, you're not bad. You realize it as well as I do."

"I can't live this lie anymore." His eyes well up with tears.

He's so broken it kills me.

"Hey, don't say that. What we have isn't a lie." I cup his face in my hand. "This is real. We're real. Nothing could ever convince me otherwise. Whatever you're hiding from me, I promise it will be all right. We've gotten through so much together. What's one more thing?"

He lowers his gaze, grips my wrist, and pushes it down. "No."

I gawk at him. "What do you mean *no?*"

"We can't do this anymore. I won't do it." He doesn't bother to look me in the eye when he rips my heart apart.

"Are you...Silas, are you breaking up with me?"

"I'm sorry." He utters the words and then is gone in a flash, and I'm left there, alone, confused, and in shock of what just happened.

CHAPTER 26

After Silas leaves me high and dry, I rush around the side of the building and back into the school. I make a beeline straight for the north wing stairs, not bothering to walk all the way to the west wing ones in an attempt to avoid anyone who might spot me.

I rush across the glass ceiling and into the hallway of the girls' supernatural dorms.

Ruby exits her room the same moment I'm running past, and we slam right into each other.

"Shit, I didn't see you," I spit out.

She bounces back up. "When I told you to attack me, I wasn't expecting this." She lets out a little laugh. "Are you okay? Why such a hurry?"

"I, um…" *Come on, Willow, think of a lie.* "Started my period."

"Oh gosh, don't let me stop you then. You don't want to ruin that stunning dress of yours."

It's then that I take in her attire. A humble dark-green gown with thin straps and a billowy bottom. Her shoes are gold, and she has a matching gilded necklace with a small moon.

Similar to the rest of the girls, she's a total ten.

"You look great, Ruby." I back away toward my door. "Again, so sorry for bumping into you."

She gives me an awkward smile like she's trying to read why I'm being so freaking weird. "See you down there."

"Yep." I shut the door behind me and sink to the floor.

What the fuck is my life.

You know that scene in *New Moon* when Edward leaves Bella and she sits in that chair in her room, by the big window, and time just passes and she's miserable and cries and doesn't understand why someone who pretended to care so deeply for her would up and vanish? Well, that's my fucking life right now. And how ironic is it that Edward was a mother fucking vampire, too.

Except, for me, it's only been a couple of hours.

I don't totally realize that until a knock rattles the door to my back, and I snap to reality. My body aches from sitting on the floor this long.

"Willow, are you in there?" Sydney's voice sounds afraid.

"Yeah." I fumble with the knob and scoot out of the way to let him in.

"What the hell? Why are you down there? Are you injured? Did he hurt you?" Sydney's hands magically scan my body.

"Yeah," I say again.

"Where? Show me where you're hurt?"

I bring my hand slowly to my heart.

"Willow, you're not making sense. What happened?" He pulls me up and off the hard surface.

I lean into him, not giving a shit about standing on my own.

I'm being dramatic, but damn if this doesn't hurt.

Sydney drags my limp body over to the nearest bed. He lowers me down onto it and rests my head on a pillow. He lifts my legs and sets them gently on the comforter and then removes my sneakers. "Talk to me, please. The last thing I saw was you and Silas dancing on the patio. You two seemed good...happy. Then I got word that Silas was on wolf territory. Which is super dangerous this time of the month. I was praying you weren't with him...but I didn't expect to find you this way."

"Is there something wrong with me?" I grab Sydney's wrist and demand his direct attention. "Am I ugly or do I have a crappy personality...oh no, am I bad in bed? Is that it?"

Sydney lets out a breath. "No, Willow. I promise none of that is true."

"Well then, what is it? Why would Silas break up with me?" The last few words come out choked.

"He did what?"

I rip the pillow out from under my head and smash it over my face. "Uhhhh."

Sydney tries to tug it away, but I hold on firmly.

"Listen, Will. I really do *not* care for Silas. For quite a few reasons. But I'll be the first to say this isn't him talking. It's the stone. You realize that, right?"

Without uncovering myself, I mumble, "What if the stupid rock is simply making him say what he already feels?"

"Then Silas is hands down the dumbest guy on the planet."

I peek out from under my concealment. "Really?"

"Yes. Without a doubt. Now, we have about ten hours until the full moon. Get some rest. You're going to need it. We'll sort Silas out tomorrow." Sydney shifts his gaze to my body. "You probably shouldn't sleep in that, though."

I sigh and then stand from the bed. "Can you help me?" I

reach clumsily at the fastener. It's a freaking wonder I managed to zip it up earlier.

Sydney's skin touches mine and sends chills over me. He brushes the hair away that's fallen from my once cute bun and frees me of my restraint.

"Thank you." I let the dress fall to the floor, not really caring about it being rumpled. I sluggishly walk to the nearby pile of clothes and seize a T-shirt off the stack. It's not until I put it on that I remember I wasn't wearing a bra under my gown.

Oh well, it's not like Sydney hasn't seen me naked.

When I turn around, he looks as though he's in shock.

He blinks and snaps himself out of it. Syd collects my discarded outfit and finds a place to hang it up.

I climb into my actual bed and snuggle under the covers.

Sydney sits at my side and presses his palm to my face. "You deserved a better night."

I push my hand against his, eager to soak up his comforting touch. "You were wonderful." My heavy eyes close despite my failed attempt at keeping them open. "Will you stay?"

Sydney takes in a breath. "Um..."

"It's okay. You don't have to." I grip him tighter.

"I'd love to." He slowly pulls away, and the sound of him undressing fills my room. Syd goes around to the other side and climbs in next to me, his warm body doing wonders for calming my nerves.

I reach back and run my hand along his nearly naked physique.

He's only in his boxers.

I position myself closer to him and move my legs so they're entwined with his.

He shoves his arm carefully under my head and wraps the other one around my torso.

He holds me tight like he may never let go, and it's all I could ask for right this moment. Well, minus the whole Silas suddenly hating my guts thing.

That will be a battle for tomorrow, though.

I awake to screaming, but the most startling thing of all is, it's me.

Sydney is shaking me and trying to wake me up. His face is afraid. "Willow. Are you okay?"

I close my mouth. "Yeah. I'm sorry. I think I had a bad dream."

"More along the lines of a hardcore nightmare. It sounded like someone was trying to murder you."

A strange pit fills my heart, and an intense sadness consumes me.

I reach for the nightstand to find my worthless phone. All it seems to be good for anymore is checking the time and setting the occasional reminder. The clock reads ten on the dot.

"Damn, we slept a while." I stretch and rub my still sleepy eyes. "What time is the full moon?"

"Eleven thirty-seven, to be exact."

I whip my head around to him. "Seriously? That's soon."

He grins and I take in his puffy morning face.

Damn, he's adorable.

"I'm going to take a shower." I hop from the bed. Although I'd rather stay there all day and cuddle with Sydney, big stuff is happening today, and we need to be prepared. I glance back on my way to the bathroom. "Do you want to join me?"

A grin forms on his handsome face. "As tempting as that sounds, I need to head to my own room and get ready."

I frown, and he continues.

"I'll bring you coffee when I'm done."

"Deal." I give him a smile in return.

Sydney throws on his suit pants and jacket, leaving his chest exposed.

I thought he was fine last night, but this bed head and shirtless look take him to a whole new level.

"I'll see you shortly." He presses a kiss to my forehead.

The moment he's gone, the gaping hole in my chest opens up.

What the fuck is happening to me?

I brace myself against the bathroom vanity and close my eyes. The vision from my nightmare fills my line of sight.

Silas. On the ground. Begging for mercy. His cheeks are dirty and tear-streaked. His fingers claw at the earth. His dark-grey tee is riddled with gaping slash marks. He brings a hand up and tries to conjure his magic, but it doesn't come. He's left there, defenseless and scared.

I shake the fictional Silas out of my mind.

This can't possibly be real. Silas is the strongest, most feared person I know. No way in hell would he let himself get into a situation he couldn't get out of.

I let the hot shower water cascade down my aching body.

I replay the image in my head while I go through the motions. Shampoo. Rinse. Conditioner. Rinse. Wash body. Shave legs.

A terrible possibility comes to me.

What if Silas didn't accidentally fall into this trouble?

The more I replay mine and Silas's evening, the more I realize Sydney was right.

Silas wasn't quite himself last night. Although, parts of him were frantically trying to show through.

Perhaps this was something he brought upon himself...to end his suffering.

CHAPTER 27

I'm towel-drying my hair when Sydney comes into my room, two steaming cups of coffee and a brown paper sack in hand.

"We need to find him." I throw the wet cloth onto my counter. "I was going to go but I don't know what I'm up against. Thought it would be better to wait for you."

"Okay. Yeah. Why, though? Did something happen?" Sydney hands me my drink and studies my face.

"I keep having these weird visions. It's almost like he's trying to reach out to me. Or maybe he's not, but whatever our connection is, it's showing me these horrible moments. A warning maybe?" I take a cautious sip and let the goodness flow through me.

"That could be possible." He sets his cup on the table and

opens the bag. "Eat this. You'll need your energy." He hands me a blueberry muffin. "Cam had a special stash I robbed from."

I peel back the wrapper and shove what I can of the delicious thing in my mouth. It's unattractive and a bit extreme but it does the trick.

Sydney's eyes go wide, and he laughs. "Hungry?"

"Not really," I say between bites. I wipe at the crumbs dangling from my chin. "Just want to hurry."

Sydney glances at his watch.

"Do you have the stone?" I toss the empty wrapper into the bag.

"No, but it's somewhere safe."

I down more of my coffee and leave the cup behind. "Let's go."

Arriving in the big open area in the middle of the first floor, Sydney grabs my arm. "Do you know where he is?"

I hold out my finger and close my eyes. I take in a deep breath and focus on Silas and only Silas.

Where are you? I think.

I let the vision of his chiseled jawline float forward, and then slowly, the rest of his face comes into view. His pale lips are cracked, and for once, he looks so...human. Fragile.

My heart thumps loudly, and I comprehend in an instant where he is.

The invisible thread connecting us to each other navigates me through the dining hall, out onto the patio, and into the forest behind the school.

"Willow, wait, you..." Sydney calls out.

But it's too late, and it doesn't matter.

Silas needs me.

I break into a run, picking up the pace with each fretful step.

I skid to a stop the second my gaze lands on him.

He's crouched on the ground, shriveled into himself. Alone and at the spot where I fainted into his arms that incredible moment we touched for the first time.

"Silas." His name rolls off my tongue gently. I take a few cautious steps forward and then kneel beside him.

He tries to shrug me off, but I don't allow him.

"It's me." I attempt to push my calming energy into him, but a weird resistance doesn't let it go through.

Silas moves onto his backside and scoots away. "Don't come any closer." His eyes are rimmed red. His hair drenched in sweat. A sickening sensation flows from him. "I don't want to hurt you."

How could I have been so stupid to think the man who has part of my soul could be so heartless and leave me the way he did?

That wasn't *my* Silas. That was some twisted, sick version of him the stone fucked with.

Sydney comes rushing to my side, and Silas flinches at his arrival.

"Dude, you look like shit."

A rogue tear falls down Silas's cheek. "Take care of her for me."

"Now, now. Don't be so dramatic." Sydney stoops to the ground. "Come here, bud." He reaches out his hand.

I've witnessed a lot of crazy things in my lifetime, especially in the last few months, but never did I expect Sydney to come to Silas's aid in this manner.

I guess miracles really are possible.

Silas exposes his fangs and hisses at us. "I said, stay back," he growls.

A flash of something red pokes out from Silas's clenched fist.

"What is that?" I point to it.

His gaze slowly shifts down, and he brings his palm to face us. His hand is quite literally steaming, and a red flower I've never seen before is tucked inside.

Sydney gasps. "Is that what I think it is?"

Silas snaps his arm away like he thinks Sydney might take the blossom from him.

"What is it?" I ask Sydney, not quite understanding the significance.

"A middlemist red. Rarest flower known to man." He pauses. "One of the very few things that can kill a vampire."

All of the breath is sucked from my lungs.

I shake my head. "No. No. No. It can't be." I drop to my knees. "Silas, please. Listen to me. Give me that."

He scoots farther and clutches it tighter. His hand oozes a gross gooey liquid.

Howling sounds in the distance, reminding me of the time and whose property we're on.

Shit.

"Sydney. Get the fucking stone. *Now,*" I urge through gritted teeth.

"But I can't leave—"

"So help me, if you don't stop wasting time." I hate to be so cruel to someone so gentle and kind, but this is life or death, and no way in hell I'm letting the latter happen.

Like he can sense my urgency, he takes off running away from us.

I focus back on the broken man in front of me.

Each subtle effort toward Silas I make, he scurries a little farther.

I've always been terrified of him shutting down on me, but never in my wildest dreams could I have imagined that he would resort to this.

Watching him this way, it's as if my soul is being set on fire.

I stare into his tormented eyes and silently plead for any remaining piece of him to hold on just a bit longer. For me, Silas. For us.

Moments pass, and I don't dare move. If I can keep him still, he won't make any drastic decisions.

He's faster than me. Clearly. So, the chances of getting that flower from him if he decides to do something with it is slim to none.

Another howl, this one much closer than the last.

Please, Sydney, hurry up.

Did Silas come out here because he wanted the wolves to finish off what he started? Maybe he couldn't bring himself to take the poisonous flower and thought they could give him a release.

But he had to have known Deghan would be one of them and wouldn't let that happen.

Leaves crinkle nearby, and I pray that it's Sydney.

My luck, though, it's not.

A light-ashy-colored werewolf emerges from a spot between the trees about twenty feet away. Its teeth are exposed, and saliva drips from its growling mouth.

I stand slowly and hold my arms out. "Please. Whoever you are."

But the beast doesn't want to hear what I have to say; instead, it lurches forward and leaps through the air toward the man I'd die for.

I take in a breath and pull my strength to the surface, throwing it between Silas and the deranged wolf.

Like it slams into a brick wall, the creature squeals and falls to the ground. Slowly, it regains composure and gets back on all four paws.

I use the opportunity to place myself between the two of them. I will do whatever it takes to protect Silas, even if it means my own life. I could never live with myself if I didn't give it my all to keep him from harm's reach.

The wolf digs its claws into the earth and raises its head. It lets out a howl, as if it's calling in reinforcements.

Shit.

I glance over my shoulder at Silas and find him still crumpled on the ground. That blasted flower gripped tightly in his fist.

I sigh and pull myself together, readying for the next attack.

With a huff of its own, the wolf charges toward me with its vicious mouth wide open.

I slam another burst of energy into it and send it flying into a nearby tree.

It yelps and cries but quickly gets back on its feet, shaking its head. A bit of blood goes flying.

I've injured the thing, but it seems to want more.

I guess I'm going to have to stop holding back out of fear I might kill the creature. If it's kill or be killed...

Balling up a bright-pink orb of magic, I hold it in my hand and wait for the animal to advance. I don't want to, but I'm out of other options at this point.

The otherwise pretty wolf makes its move, launching at me at the quickest pace yet.

I go to throw my magic, but instead, a ripple of green envelopes the beast and holds it in mid-air.

The wolf tries to wriggle free with no success. It's stuck in a sludge of green magic that can only be one person.

I turn to see him with his left arm extended forward and an emerald wave of power surging from it.

His expression is saddened. "It didn't work."

"What?" And then it dawns on me.

The Reperio stone. It didn't charge. The one thing that was going to help me find my mother.

The thing that's ripping Silas away from me.

"Give it to me." I hold out my hands.

Sydney shakes his head. "Willow, there won't be another one." He glances to make sure his connection to the wolf is still strong.

I shift my attention to Silas and find his arm rising to his face.

The red flower just inches from his mouth. A frightened stare. A whisper of goodbye in his eyes.

"Sydney, NOW."

He reaches into his pocket and pulls out the glistening stone. He tosses it through the air, and it's like the whole world has gone into slow fucking motion.

I clasp the rock at the same moment the flower touches Silas's lips.

I realize all too late that I have no fucking clue how to destroy this thing.

Come on, Willow, get it together.

This can't be the end of him. Because the end of Silas Harlow would, sure enough, kill me—even if I'm left alive.

I hold the stone firmly between my hands and invoke every single last ounce of strength I have from my body. Bubbling power flows through me, and my arms erupt with an icy-pink and blindingly bright magic. I focus it all into the stone, willing it to do what I want.

I take one last breath and let out the biggest scream that nearly tears apart my vocal cords.

Leaves and branches whip around my face, and trees creak, but I don't dare break my concentration from this stone.

I grip it tighter, so snug that my hands bleed.

And then suddenly, it's gone. Like a puff of dust, the rock disintegrates into nothing.

My body grows weak, and once again, I fall to my knees. I shove whatever remaining strength I have into my arms and drag myself to Silas's side.

His mutilated hand lays limp in his lap, the flower nowhere in sight.

A choking sound gurgles out of his chest, and when my gaze lands on his face, I see a red petal is hanging from his mouth.

CHAPTER 28

No. This can't be happening.

There has to be something I can do.

Sydney's voice rings through. "Willow, I can't hold on much longer."

What do I do?

Please, Universe, tell me what to do.

A strange image of angel wings comes into my line of sight. It hovers above a nearby fallen tree, but upon further inspection, the beautiful flowy white is tainted a bright red.

The color of blood.

Angel blood.

Another rustle of leaves, and a second wolf, only this one a familiar shade of brown.

Deghan towers over the smaller wolf, despite it being held in mid-air by Sydney's magic.

The light wolf cries out and then is lowered to the ground.

Deghan snarls at it and nips its rear, sending the foul creature running away from us. He chases it and keeps it from coming back.

I turn my bloody hand over and do the only thing that comes to mind.

I press it to Silas's mouth, dripping whatever I can inside.

One drop, two...then another.

Tears ripple down my cheeks. Why isn't this working? This has to work.

Sydney comes to my side. He digs his fingers through Silas's mouth and pulls out any remnants of the flower he can find.

It's not much, meaning Silas consumed most of the deadly-to-him thing.

I push my palm into his mouth again, rubbing it along his fangs, desperate for him to latch out and come back to me.

"Silas, please," I whimper.

Sydney fumbles with something. "Try this." He holds out a small pocket knife.

I hurriedly take it from him and slice into my already cut hand, drawing more blood. I tilt Silas's head back and squeeze my fist just an inch above him.

The warm liquid rolls across his lips and down the back of his throat.

"I'm so sorry, Willow," Sydney mutters.

It's genuine but does nothing to repair the gaping wound to my chest. It's as though someone ripped my heart out and left me there to die a slow and agonizing death.

I drag my gaze away from Silas's face, not wanting him to see me, even in death, in the state I'm in. To call me a mess would be a fucking understatement.

A gasp.

A hand.

Cold and familiar.

Slowly, I look up...those piercing violet and grey eyes stare back at me.

With what little energy I have left, I jump on him, tackling him to the ground.

Like I'm being brought back to life, too, my heart beats again.

The infinite weight is off my chest, and I can finally breathe.

I could never live in a world without Silas. Of that much I'm absolutely sure.

Although now, I may have lost my chance at finding my parents forever.

CHAPTER 29

"**I** hate to break up this beautiful reunion, but we need to get the hell out of here. It's still very much a full moon, and I'm not sure how long Deghan can hold that little asshole off."

Silas stands, pulling me into his arms with him. A new sense of vigor courses through him.

I don't have the strength to walk, so it's a damn good thing Silas has enough for both of us.

"Are you good?" Sydney studies Silas.

Silas narrows his eyes. "Better than ever."

That naturally cocky attitude is back. *My* Silas is here.

Collectively, we rush out of the wolf territory and onto the school's grounds where it's safe. But we don't stop there, the guys make their way inside, through the dining hall and up the north wing stairs to Sydney's room.

Silas lowers me onto Syd's bed but doesn't leave my side. He bites into his palm and rubs the wounds on my hands, healing me within an instant.

"Hold on, let me get this straight." Sydney grabs a few crystals from his desk. He places them all over the bed in some strategic pattern. "She can repair you, too. But bringing you back from the brink...that was no ordinary thing. There's nothing about that concerning the text on Malachis. So, if that's not the case...it had to be something else. There is literally *nothing* that will bring a vampire back from middlemist."

Silas and I exchange a glance.

I push myself up onto my elbows and wrap my arms around his waist. I never want to let him go ever again. "You had me scared to fucking death."

Silas takes my face into his hands. "You can't get rid of me that easily."

"It's her blood, that has to be it. She was so insistent on using it. I only went along because what else do you do when the girl you care about is freaking out about her dying vampire boyfriend?" Sydney continues to reason his way through the situation. "What could be special about that, though?"

I squeeze Silas tighter and ignore Sydney.

If he figures it out, he figures it out. But I'm not going to volunteer the information. At this point, I think it's safe to say we can trust him, but it's hard to be completely sure.

Sydney did sort of consume his glitch to paralyze himself to prove to me that he wasn't a threat.

I should probably trust him, considering everything he's done to show his true allegiance.

"The only thing that would trump everything else...it couldn't be. It's not possible." Sydney suddenly stops, and his stare bores into me. "But then, it would make sense. *All* of this would."

I bite at my bottom lip to keep from saying anything.

"You're..." Sydney lowers his voice. "Descended from the angels." His eyes go wide. "It's no wonder you're cursed and your magic is suppressed and stolen. You're from *the* most powerful bloodline in existence." He hands me a small bag of herbs. "Hold on to these, they'll help you gain your strength back."

Silas stiffens. "You can't tell anyone."

"Wait a minute, you *knew*?" Sydney gawks at him then at me. "Did *you*?"

"I wasn't sure, no. But I stumbled on it a while back." I look at Silas. "We both did. And we agreed to keep it a secret."

Sydney nods. "For obvious reasons. Wow. This is..."

Energy steadily trickles its way into me but at an annoyingly slow pace.

"Take some of mine." Silas holds out his arm.

I press my hand against him and soak it up. Something that I've only ever done with him. Further proving our one-of-a-kind connection.

"Willow, I..." Sydney fumbles for his words. "I'm pretty sure I can help you figure out your curse."

I sit straight, letting go of Silas in the process. "How?"

"I think I know who is cursing you." Sydney's eyes glisten.

"Who?" Silas's voice is firm and demanding.

Angels, I've missed him. The real him.

"I'm not completely sure, but I'm almost positive my parents have something to do with it." Sydney holds up his hands. "I promise I wasn't aware. I would have put a stop to it a long time ago. But now, knowing what I do it all makes sense."

Dumbfounded and unable to find words, I scoot closer to Silas.

"Explain." Silas puts his arm around me.

"My folks have always been super cryptic, so the bits and pieces I put together were just from paying attention and over-hearing things. They've always tried to...how do I say it...prime me for some big change. Like a sacred rite of passage type thing. I always thought it was them being weird and claiming we had this all-mighty bloodline, but the real shocker is I've heard them refer to us having *dark* magic." He paces back and forth. "Now, duh, you might say. Because we're all made up of either light or dark, but to think about it in the sense of one side of the spectrum to the other..." Sydney points to me. "If you have angel blood, then maybe I have demonic blood."

Tremont sort of implied the same thing.

Sydney's face goes pale, and he sits in the chair at his desk.

"Go on," Silas insists.

"What if the only reason my family is powerful, the way they claim to be, is because they've stolen the Oliver magic all along. Because that sure as shit makes sense. And whatever they were trying to prep me for was to make sure the curse lived on." Sydney lowers his head. "They always told me I wouldn't have the stomach for it. That I was weak. Pathetic. I heard them whispering late at night how I would never be able to follow in their footsteps. How I'd never be *strong* enough to do what needed to be done." He raises his head. "What else could that all possibly mean?"

"Is that all?" Silas rubs my hand with his thumb.

Always gentle and sweet with me, and harsh and callous with everyone else.

"I read something about this actually," I speak up. "About demonic witches stealing others' power. I...I sort of had a hunch that's what it was. Even that it was an angel versus demon type thing. But never could I have imagined the coven cursing us would be your family."

"That explains why we're so powerful together." Sydney rubs his temple.

"Similar to a yin-yang," I confirm.

"Exactly." He shifts his gaze like he's lost in thought. "If we were able to create the kind of magic to do that...we have to be able to break the curse."

"I have no idea where to go from here." I caress Silas's hand.

I can't begin to process how thankful I am that he's alive.

Well, sort of. As much as a vampire can be.

"We've been studying your family this whole time, though. We've been looking in all the wrong places. Now we need to research mine." Sydney looks over at his cluttered workspace. "But first, we need to get both of you better."

Sydney insists we both hold, breathe in, touch, and consume various herbs.

He swears he knows what he's doing, and for once, I don't question that.

Within a matter of minutes, a new sense of life is breathed into me. I'm refreshed, like I spent a day at the spa. But not a day where you end up more tired than when you went there, one that actually rejuvenated you the way it's supposed to.

"Can we talk about the elephant in the room?" I set the cup of a random concoction down on the table.

"Uh, which one?" Sydney glances from Silas to me.

"The freaking vicious werewolf that attacked us. Who the hell was that? It's someone at this school, right?" Not that I have any clue what I'll do with the information. Putting a flaming bag of shit on their doorstep sounds ideal, but honestly, I'd rather avoid the asshole and watch my back knowing that someone *really* wants us dead.

"I wasn't familiar with that one. If they're randomly attacking in the way they were, it's probably a newly turned wolf. Unable to control their urges. We shouldn't have been on their property during a full moon, but it also shouldn't have attacked the way it did." Sydney stuffs a few supplies into his backpack.

Are the new vampires brutal like the new wolves? I haven't been at this school long and I've been attacked on numerous occasions. Maybe it's my own fault for being where I shouldn't, but these can't be isolated incidents.

"Going somewhere?" Silas growls.

"Hear me out. If you're both up for it. Not today, but maybe tomorrow when we're done with class. What are your thoughts on going for a little field trip?" Sydney tosses the bag into the corner by the door. "I have numerous family grimoires at my place. Let's sneak over there and grab them. It could be huge in helping us figure out what to do."

Silas huffs. "How can we be sure this isn't another one of your traps?"

Sydney shakes his head. "What do you want me to do to prove it to you?"

I push some calming energy into Silas. "I trust him."

"That's what worries me."

I smile up at Silas and study his still dirty face. "You're gross."

"Wow." He grins devilishly. "You really know how to kick a man while he's down, don't you?" He pokes my side.

I force a smile despite how broken I am inside.

I'd destroy the stone again in a heartbeat if it meant saving Silas, but that doesn't make the repercussions any easier to swallow.

I have Silas back, and we're all okay, but I may have lost my mother and father forever.

"Tomorrow?" Sydney asks.

"Tomorrow."

CHAPTER 30

The amount of dirt and nasty stuff that rinses off me and Silas is super gross.

We stand, facing each other, in my shower, hot water pouring all over us.

He reaches out and caresses my cheek. "You saved me," he whispers.

"Always." I close my eyes and lean into his palm. "I'm sorry I let it go on for so long."

"We're going to find her. I promise you. I won't let your sacrifice be wasted." Silas smooths the wet hair out of my face and pulls me to his chest.

Our bare skin touches, and it's magnificent.

Not too long ago we were both convinced that we'd never be able to do this. And now, we can't seem to get close enough.

"Did you mean any of the things you said?" I mutter with my face against his skin.

He sighs. "Some of it."

Agony rips through me.

My Silas was in there after all.

Maybe I was wrong, and I lost him, too.

"You're the best thing in the world to ever happen to me." He exhales again. "But I really don't deserve you. You're far too good. You should be able to choose."

The last word strikes a nerve. I break away to stare into his eyes. "But I did. You think that I'm with you for any other reason than *me* wanting to be?"

He swallows and nods ever so slightly.

"Well, you're wrong." I wipe at his dirty tear-stained face with my thumbs.

"It was dishonest of me to not tell you about the Malachi destiny. I thought that I was protecting you by keeping it from you. That maybe, you'd be able to make your decision regardless of knowing the truth." His face is tense, like he's forcing himself to speak these words.

"I'm not afraid, Silas. Nothing will make me change my mind about you, about us." Unless he kicked a puppy. Who in their right mind would do such a thing?

"Some time ago, vampires were randomly selected to be paired with their one true mate. The coupling was named Malachi, meaning that of an angel. A divine being that would fit perfectly with said vampire. The occurrences are rare, but in the Harlow bloodline, they're almost always certain. I've gone my whole life thinking something was missing from it, but I had no idea what or who until fate brought me to you." He studies my face. "I've tried to leave Harper countless times, but I've never gotten far, this strange pull always kept me coming back. And then finally, the moment I laid my eyes on you, I knew it was you. I had been searching tirelessly, and, in that moment, everything clicked into place."

"Why wouldn't you tell me this, though?"

"Because I was worried you would feel you didn't have a choice. That you were stuck with me. That the angels didn't care what you wanted, and that maybe you wouldn't choose me strictly out of spite to them. I was selfish. I realize that now. Because regardless of whether or not you know, there's nothing that can be done. Our fates have already decided."

I shake my head. "No, I refuse to accept that. Despite what you think, *we* decide our future. And I consciously choose you. I always will. Now, and forever. The angels may have given us a path to each other, but we are the ones who either take the opportunity they've given us or not. I will choose you a million times over. In any lifetime. Fated or not." I press my hand to his chest, where his beating heart should be. "I swear it."

He weaves his fingers between mine and tips my chin up. Silas stares longingly into my eyes

"Jace."

"What?" I say, a bit confused by his expression.

"My middle name."

I don't need to hear the words to understand for certain that it's true. I realize without a doubt that he loves me. It's in his actions, in everything he does to make sure I'm happy and taken care of, in his protectiveness, and selflessness when he puts aside his differences with Sydney to make sure I'm safe.

Like the shifting of an intricate lock, something opens up inside me. A shedding of skin leading the way to a new version of myself that comes into focus.

"I love you, Silas Jace Harlow." Yeah, that has a nice ring to it.

CHAPTER 31

The rest of the day is spent resting and eating the delicious food Cameron prepares for us.

I request that to-die-for pasta, and he beams at being able to help.

"It sucks, you know." Cameron stirs the veggies in the sizzling skillet.

I watch him from my spot on the counter.

"Sydney is an all-*mighty witch*, Silas is this badass vampire protector guy, and Deghan...don't get me started on him. Strong and fierce and loveable. And I'm over here like *want some food?*"

I grin at him. "You're as useful as anyone else. I mean, I'm pretty sure Deg would quite literally starve to death without you."

"That's because he has a tapeworm." He laughs. "Not really, but damn can he put down some food."

I can't help but wonder where he is, and what he's doing.

Sydney told me that werewolves typically shift for a few hours on the full moon, but sometimes up to a day. It all depends on the level of experience the shifter has, what their needs are, and how skilled a hunter they are.

Apparently, the creatures need raw, fresh meat to get them through the lunar cycles. And if they're able to replenish their stores quickly, they can switch back to their human form sooner rather than later.

They need their exercise, too. Their animal bodies get cramped and require vast stretching and running each time they turn.

And if they don't...they become vicious, violent beasts that will attack anything in their way. Including humans, vampires, and any other being.

My mind flashes back to that unstable light-grey wolf that threatened me and Silas.

Was it starving? In need of a workout? Or did it just want to murder us because it could?

"Something on your mind?" Cameron pokes me with the handle of a spatula.

I shake my head and force a smile "Nope."

We didn't tell him what happened with Deghan and the other wolf. Considering how close he and Deg are, we didn't want to worry or stress him out when there is literally nothing he can do right now. If we told him, it would only add unnecessary anxiety and drive him mad waiting for Deghan to return.

Deghan seemed like he had things under control. So, we don't think he's in danger in any way. Otherwise, I wouldn't have allowed the situation to continue without intervening.

All things concerning werewolves, that's Deghan's territory.

"How did the bake sale end up?" I ask Cameron.

"I can hardly believe this but, I paid Walker back for all of the supplies and *still* managed to have three months' worth of bill money left. It's a fucking miracle. That should give my idiot brother time to get his shit together, and even if he doesn't, the headmaster told me that I could set up a regular little spot and keep selling baked goods. All he asks is that it doesn't hinder my learning. How freaking amazing is that?" Cameron beams and pulls me into a hug. "I couldn't have done it without you."

I squeeze him back. "All you needed was a little push. You had it in you all along."

He kisses my forehead and goes back to the stovetop. "Deghan is always telling me how great everything I make him is...but I swear he'd eat anything. I hate that I needed it, but this weekend was a huge confidence booster and really put things into perspective for my future."

"That's awesome, Cam. You think it's something you'll consider as a career?"

Speaking of, I've been so focused on all the shit going on in my life that I never really considered my life *outside* of the supernatural world. I guess I wasn't sure if I'd make it out of this alive, let alone get a job.

"Absolutely." He takes a few plates from the shelf overhead. "Where's Silas?"

I close my eyes and concentrate on him. His presence right around the corner. "He's coming."

"That's so crazy that you can do that." Cameron distributes the food.

"Trust me, it doesn't get any less weird for me either."

Silas glides into the room and appears at my side. He kisses my cheek. "Cameron."

Cam holds out a dish to both of us.

"This smells amazing." Silas takes a long whiff of the steaming pasta.

"Whoa now. Was that a compliment?" Cameron brings his hand to his mouth in disbelief.

"Don't get used to it." Silas takes my hand and guides me off the counter and over to a small table.

We all sit down and dive into our delicious meal.

It's sometime in the middle of the night when Deghan comes bolting into my room.

I nearly fall off my bed from the surprise. "You scared the shit out of me."

His golden eyes are frantic. "You're telling me. What the fuck happened? Are you okay? Is Silas...?"

"He's fine. I'm good. Sydney and Cam, too. We're all right. Take a breath." I put my hand on his and press my calming energy into him.

He takes a deep breath and exhales loudly. "I kept trying to shift back but I couldn't. It was like my body was resisting it. That's never happened. I was stuck in wolf form. The more I tried..."

"How did you finally break free?"

Deghan averts his gaze. "I killed Bambi."

"Aw, Deg. You had to do what you had to, to get back to us." I guide his head to my chest and pat his back.

"It wasn't literally Bambi, but still. Uh, I hate that part of being a wolf. Don't get me wrong, I enjoy a cheeseburger the same as the next guy, but I don't exactly want to be the one butchering the thing."

"That makes sense." I rub circles up and down his spine. "Are you hungry now? Do you need to eat?"

He shakes his head. "No. I'm just really tired."

I flip open the covers to invite him in. "Come on."

A sly grin spreads on his sleepy face. "You're the best."

"Mmhm."

He settles in next to me and pulls me against his warm body.

I let the nerves of the day fizzle away and doze off with him.

Morning comes and Deghan latches on to me each time I attempt to get up.

"Five more minutes," he whines.

"It's been *five more*, ten times now. We're going to be late for class if we don't get up." I pry his comforting arm off me. "And I'm training with Ruby today, so I have to make sure I eat breakfast. Witch orders."

Deghan sits straight up. "You are?"

"Yup. Shadow realm lesson. Monday, Wednesday, Friday." I change my shirt and grab a pair of clean leggings from my dresser. "But hey, me, Syd, and Silas are going to Sydney's house once we're finished with school. Do you want to go with us?"

"You mean the place where his parents lured you into a trap and almost killed you?"

"That's the one." I kick his shoes toward him and toss him the pants and T-shirt he left lying on my floor. "Long story short, we think Sydney's parents have something to do with my curse, so we're going to try to find some of his family grimoires to see if we can uncover anything."

He slides one of his shoes on then realizes he still hasn't put on his jeans.

I giggle and hurry to the bathroom to brush my teeth and hair. I quickly wash my face and throw on some moisturizer. Remi and Kyra would totally kill me if they saw my skincare routine.

It could be worse, I suppose.

"Probably be better for us to stick together." Deghan leans against the doorframe of my en suite while I finish getting ready.

"That's what I was thinking. If they do some shit, at least all of us will be there." I flip off the light to the vanity. "Listen, I'm not thrilled about it, but it's our best chance at figuring out how to break the curse. If I can't find my mom, the least I can do is this."

Deghan frowns. "The stone didn't charge?"

I sigh. "Not only that, but I had to destroy it, too."

Deghan's eyebrows rise. "What the hell did I miss?"

"Oh, you mean, aside from Silas going mad, nearly committing suicide...actually, he did now that I think about it, and I brought him back from the dead, but only after I pulverized the one shot at locating my mother?" I circle the room and find the few items I need to put into my backpack. "Pasta, you missed some killer pasta."

"Wills, I'm so sorry." Deghan follows me out into the hallway. "Is there anything I can do to help?"

I reposition the bag on my shoulder. "Not unless you know where my mom is."

He wraps his arm around me and brings me to his side.

It's his sort of silent way of making me aware he's there, that he cares. The gesture is comforting but does nothing to ease my endless nerves.

I make headway on one thing—by saving Silas—and take five billion steps back with another—pinpointing my mom's location.

Plus, the whole looming Oliver curse that seems to have no end.

We step onto the ground floor of the building.

"Willow," Professor Tremont calls out from across the foyer. He waves me over.

"I'll see you in a minute, Deg." I stand on my tiptoes to press my lips to his cheek.

I hastily make my way over to Tremont, not wanting to cut into my breakfast time any more than I already have. If I don't manage to eat *something* prior to training, I'll be in no shape to go on our adventure when school is over.

"What's up?" I ask the professor.

He gawks upon my approach. "Your hands. The bandage, it's gone." A smile breaks across his face. "See, I told you you'd be good in no time."

Right, I totally forgot about our twice-a-day healing sessions, considering he's been a bit missing in action lately.

"Good as new." I hold the once blistered palm out for his

inspection. "Thanks, again." For nothing. It was Silas who healed me, and part of me thinks Tremont knows it wasn't his doing.

"That's quite incredible." Tremont turns it over and runs his thumb along the outside, where the most injured section was. "Nonetheless, I'm pleased with your recovery." His gaze scans my face. "Are you?"

His question seems much more complicated than it appears on the surface.

"Definitely." I slowly draw my hand away. "Listen, I'm a bit rushed on time."

Tremont cuts me off. "By all means, it was good to catch up."

I walk toward my friends in the dining hall, but I can't help but feel that Tremont is watching me in some incredibly curious and devious way.

CHAPTER 32

"I want you to attack me." Ruby's wild gaze meets mine. Something new, something dangerous shines through. Tempting me. Taunting even.

"Go ahead," Abigail calls out from across the shadow realm classroom.

I shift my focus to the rippling seam on the top of the wall and then back to Ruby.

"What are you waiting for?" Ruby demands.

I swing at her, and she ducks it like no big deal.

She's different today.

Did the full moon change her in some way?

I throw another jab, followed by an uppercut from my other hand. Both failures.

She bounces on her toes and slaps at my shoulders lightly. Just enough to irritate the fuck out of me. She clearly knows what she's doing.

This time I swat at her with my leg, but somehow, she sees it coming and dodges it.

How is it possible she can anticipate every one of my moves?

"You're thinking too much," she tells me. "I can see what you're going to do before you do it. Your eyes, about a millisecond prior to whatever you're going to do, they give you away." She taps my arms again. "Why don't you try evading my attacks? Defense is equally important as offense."

I look over to Abigail.

She nods. "Go easy on her, Rubes."

Ruby stops doing her stupid little bouncing back and forth and plants her feet. She follows me in whichever direction I move, until finally, she punches me right in the shoulder.

It's not hard, but it's enough to continue to piss me off.

"You good?" she asks.

"Go again." I clench my jaw. My heart pumps harder, and my anger level rises.

She slams into my other arm and a cocky grin forms on her face.

Why is she so hell-bent on making a fool of me?

Instead of waiting for her to make a move, I advance and let my body take the lead. Screw thinking things through and calculating my next attempt.

I throw my arm forward, my fist flying at her and grazing her biceps.

Holy shit, I actually hit her. Barely. But it still counts.

"Better," she confirms and then flings another blow my way.

I narrowly avoid it but end up getting hit from her follow-up punch, right in the abdomen.

Her eyes meet mine, and something familiar unsettles in my core.

Is it possible? It couldn't be.

Ruby is my friend. There's no way she would...

But it's still feasible that she was the wolf that attacked us last night.

This thought sends a spike of fear and rage through me. I shove my fist toward her, landing it and missing the next blow. My feet stumble, and it takes me an extra second to regain composure.

We go at it this way for at least ten minutes, back and forth, one blow followed by another. One of us landing a punch, the other missing, then vice versa.

"You're weak," Ruby tells me. "What are you going to do if something attacks you?"

Does she not realize that I've battled numerous demons and *won*? She acts like I'm completely helpless.

"Something bigger, stronger, more lethal than you." Ruby throws another jab my way.

I block it and pull my fist back and slam it into her face. Harder than I have all this time.

It's not until she's thrown back a few feet that I identify the pink flowing from my hand.

Shit. I used magic.

Abigail runs forward and reaches Ruby's side. "Rube, are you all right?" She turns toward me. "Totally uncalled for, Willow. You know better than that."

Ruby holds out her hand and shakes her head. "I'm fine. Really. Don't make it a bigger deal than it needs to be."

Abigail lifts Ruby under her arms to help her stand.

"You need to be careful who you mess with." Ruby wipes at her bloody lip. "You're going to get yourself into trouble one day, and there won't be anyone there to bail you out."

I can't determine whether her words are a threat or a friendly warning.

Abigail calls our session early for the day and instructs us to go get cleaned up for the rest of our classes.

The moment she dismisses us, I say the words and send myself back to the normal realm.

———

"You did what?" Deghan asks with his jaw damn near hanging open.

"She clocked her right in the mouth." Cameron hands me a blueberry muffin.

"I bet she was pissed." Deghan shakes his head. "You have to be careful with that one, she's a little firecracker."

Is that his way of admitting it was her who attacked us?

I've been too afraid to find out, considering Deghan knows for sure who it was, so I've kept the nagging question to myself.

Cameron still isn't aware of the trouble we ran into in the forest either. The less unnecessary stress we put on him the better. He doesn't need to know every little detail.

We told him about Silas, and having to destroy the stone, but the wolfy bits we left out.

"Is everyone ready?" Sydney glimpses at each of us.

I lean against Silas and nod my approval to Syd.

"It's going to be a bit cramped." Sydney unlocks his car. "But I think we'll drive most of it and then go the rest on foot. I don't want to go up the main drive, so we're going to take a little side access that I used when I lived over there. Except this time, we won't go all the way. I'll hide the car in the brush, and we can walk to my house. It won't be far."

"And you're totally good with me going? I'm not going to get in the way?" Cameron asks.

I grab his hand and weave my fingers through. "I'm glad you're coming with us."

"Same." Deghan winks at him.

Silas lets out a grunt that resembles something of support.

We cram into the small vehicle and buckle up.

Cameron is riding shotgun, and I'm between Silas and Deghan in the back.

"Can we listen to some tunes?" Deghan takes a sandwich

from the backpack between his legs. He holds it toward me. "Want a bite?"

I can't help but smile. "No, Deg. I'm good."

He shrugs and dives in.

Cameron fiddles with the radio until something resembling music comes into focus.

I slowly scoot toward Silas. "How are you doing?"

"Fine." He glances down at me but then goes back to stare out the front window.

"Syd mentioned that the Reperio stone often had irreversible effects. Even once the rock is destroyed. Are you still experiencing anything?"

He doesn't seem to budge. "No."

I study Silas's serious face, searching for any clues of a lie.

"Slow down," he says randomly.

Sydney does what he says, and a moment later, a deer runs across the road, right through our path. "Thanks."

Silas puts his hand on my thigh and grips it tightly. "I'm me. I promise."

I sigh and let myself accept his answer.

That doesn't mean I won't be on the hunt for any uncharacteristic behavior, though.

A short drive later, we pull off onto a dirt path that's only a little distance away from Sydney's main driveway.

This trail leads us into a heavily wooded area that's rather dark from the tree coverage being so thick.

Sydney takes the trek slow, considering the bumpy terrain. He parks the car near some tall bushes. "Okay." He rotates in his seat to look at all of us. "Let's make this snappy."

We funnel out of the vehicle and form a circle.

A strange chill overtakes me the moment I realize these are the woods where his parents attacked. Where demon Silases were mutilated by my hands. Where I yelled at Sydney and told him to leave me alone.

Like he senses my discomfort, Silas pulls me in close.

Sydney points up ahead. "House is less than a minute walk through there. We'll go in, grab whatever books I have, then rush back here and leave. In and out."

"Sounds good," Cameron is the first to confirm.

The rest of us offer a silent authorization.

The walk really is a short one. Once we bust through the overgrown foliage, the small home that Sydney used to live in isn't far at all.

We collectively creep our way toward the building.

I keep an eye on the mansion beyond Syd's place.

So far, no sign of life. No lights, movements, noise, nothing.

It's eerie and a bit unsettling if you ask me.

How could a family just abandon their son and their incredibly lavish shelter?

One by one, we approach our destination.

Sydney puts his hand on the door, but instead of turning the handle, he pushes the creaky thing open. He turns to us and puts his finger over his mouth to signal to be quiet.

We follow him in.

He locks eyes with Silas, and they share a mental exchange.

For two people who don't care for each other, they sure do seem to always be on the same wavelength.

Sydney flips the light switch on the wall, and once the bulbs are illuminated, I'm pretty sure each of our mouths drop open.

CHAPTER 33

The last time I was in this building, it smelled of Sydney—that familiar woodsy scent. Books and clothes were strewn about but in an organized kind of way. Sydney style. The apartment was nice and cozy and inviting.

But now? It currently seems as though a mini tornado ripped through the area.

His posh tables are overthrown. Couch cushions ripped apart and the stuffing scattered about. Dishes from his fully equipped kitchen are crushed on the floor. His bookshelves are toppled over, and a strange, unsettling putrid stench fills the air.

I go to his side and place my hand on his back. "Syd."

He swallows and steps over his personal belongings. "They must have known." His voice is quiet and broken. He clears his throat and snaps himself out of his shock. "Take a look around. See if they left anything behind."

The next few minutes are spent digging through the wreckage with not a valuable thing found. Don't get me wrong, there were plenty of monetary items like a rare photo that even Silas did a double take on, just not anything that could help us with our research.

"It's a lost cause." Sydney's shoulders slump with his exhale.

In a few days, Cameron regains his home while Sydney loses his.

"What about the bigger house?" Deghan asks from the entryway.

"If they went through the trouble here, there's no doubt it's taken care of, too," Silas answers. "Our best bet is to move on."

And that we do.

With a flip of the light, we leave Sydney's the way we found it —a disaster.

About halfway to the car, Silas holds out his arms to stop us. "Wait here." A second later, he's back but hovering at my side. "Someone slashed the tires."

"Shit," Cameron mutters.

"What do we do?" Deghan adds.

Sydney is still, but fearful energy pours out of him.

"This way," Silas demands. "I have a place not too far. It's protected. We can regroup there." Silas puts his hand on my back.

In preparation, I draw my magic forward and let it rest right below my skin, desperate to keep it there to the best of my ability.

Not thirty seconds into our voyage, a cloaked figure appears in our path up ahead.

If I didn't know any better, I'd say it was Silas, not Sydney, who was in on this ploy, considering he told us to go in this direction. But I do know better, and Silas would never purposely put me in danger.

"Deghan, go," Silas urges.

Without the figure catching on, Deghan disappears from behind us, his stealthy wolf-like tendencies coming in handy.

"Stay behind me." Silas maneuvers his body in front of me.

I grasp on to Cameron while Sydney closes in the back.

Cameron shakes slightly, his nerves taking hold.

I push my calming energy into him, careful to not be excessive and use too much of my reserves.

As a group, we hesitantly move toward the being and then stop.

It continues to close the distance.

About a hundred feet away, the thing reaches out and removes the cover from its head.

Sydney's body shifts from his spot. "Mom?"

"Only by birth. Don't flatter yourself."

Sydney flinches, the verbal wound cutting deep. Another one added to the stack of already low blows from his shit parents.

How could a mother be so cruel?

With a flick of her wrist, Silas goes flying from his spot and lands in the dirt to my right.

"Ophelia, you may call me. It's only fair that we're on a first-name basis since I'm so knowledgeable of you, Willow." The woman taps the air and somehow locks on to me, Cam, and Syd, and pulls us forward.

I draw a wad of energy up but find myself unable to conjure it.

"Fuck," I mutter.

"You children really are rather foolish," the grumpy yet lavish lady retorts. "There is no stopping us. You're wasting that precious energy of yours even trying." She sighs. "The energy that belongs to me."

Despite being restrained, I'm still able to spit on the ground and speak. "Over my dead body."

An evil grin covers her face. If she weren't such a hateful woman, she'd be rather gorgeous. But personality does a thing or two to the way one is perceived, and currently, she's uglier than hell.

"Be my guest." She holds out her hands. "And to think, I was going to do you the honor of keeping you alive, but if you're so willing, then by all means, please make this easier for us."

"Mom, why are you doing this?" Sydney pleads. "Don't you have enough? Can't you let her go?"

"The angels cursed us with you." She picks at her nails like she's bored of us already. "If you must have any explanation, your father and I have nearly pure demonic blood. One of the darkest known in existence. We've always wanted to take it one step further, and that's what we needed her for." Sydney's evil mother points to me. "But in some sick attempt to stop us from gaining the power we desire, they gave us you. A complete anomaly."

What could that possibly mean?

She goes to speak but is cut off by a flash of brown shooting through the tree line.

Deghan, in wolf form, tackles her and sends her spiraling away.

Thanks to his contact, our magical restraints are broken.

Immediately, I summon a ball of protective power and coat Cameron with it. "This should help." I take a split second to cup his face in my hands and stare into those gorgeous blue eyes.

I hope like hell this isn't goodbye.

Not only with Cam, but with all of us.

"Run!" Silas yells.

Deghan raises his gorgeous dark head to the sky and howls loudly.

Is he calling in backup? Wouldn't that add to how dangerous the situation is, considering what happened yesterday?

If we have to pick battles, though, maybe this is the best chance we have.

With my hand grasping Cam's, we take off toward Silas's cabin in the woods.

Silas significantly slows his pace to stay by our side.

I'm sure he'd rather whisk me into his arms and get there in an instant, but I'm not leaving Cameron behind. He can't protect himself in a supernatural situation this dangerous.

A whimper bellows out, and when I look over my shoulder, Deghan's wolf form is lying on his side next to a tree.

I skid to a stop. There's no way I'm leaving Deghan behind either.

Silas grabs my arm. "Come on," he says through his clenched jaw.

I shake my head. "We have to stay."

"Oh, Willow..." Ophelia teases playfully. "Come out, come out, wherever you are."

"You don't know what you're getting yourself into." Sydney's gaze meets mine.

He's right. I don't. But this can't continue to go on any longer. She has to be stopped. The curse has to be broken.

If she wants a fight, she'll get it.

This ends right here, right now.

CHAPTER 34

We lurk quietly in the shadows, and once the wicked woman is far enough from Deghan, we take the opportunity to rush to his side.

Cameron grasps Deghan's wolf face into his hands and places it in his lap.

Sydney hovers his hands above Deg's body while Silas stands watch.

I simply kneel there, painfully waiting for Sydney to direct me.

"Deghan, we're here. You're going to be okay," I attempt to comfort him.

"His ribs are crushed, and there is residual magic holding him in place." Sydney's emerald eyes stare longingly into mine. "We can do this, okay?" He lays his hand palm up, inviting me to take it. "I want *you* to focus on siphoning, I'm going to heal him."

I had no idea that was something he could do.

"I've never done this." He shifts his focus to Deghan. "This might hurt a little, but nothing like what you're feeling now."

"Faster. The bitch is coming," Silas informs us.

I peek over my shoulder, and sure enough, she's gliding—literally, without her feet touching the ground—toward us.

Can this woman be any fucking creepier?

"What can I do?" Cameron asks frantically.

"Keep him calm." Sydney takes a deep breath and interlocks his fingers with mine.

Within a second, the green and pink magic courses together and gushes out around us.

Sydney lowers his voice. "You're remarkably stronger. How is that possible?"

I shrug. "Magic?"

He shakes his head, and we both place our free hands overtop Deghan.

I block out everything except the flow of power and my task of removing the junk from Deghan.

But it's not quite that simple when a loud crack startles me. A nearby tree falls in Ophelia's path, buying us the smallest amount of time.

"Hurry up," Silas urges.

The bitter and vile magic courses through Deghan and into my own supply. It takes only moments before his wolf form can move.

Quiet whines leave him while Sydney continues to heal him.

Without really knowing what the hell I'm doing, I focus my mind on healing and press my hand gently to his torso.

Another loud crash. This time it's the fallen timber being thrown to the side.

Ophelia latches magically on to Silas, his body contorting under her grip.

How do I choose between saving one man versus the other?

"Willow, you're strong enough to do this." Sydney breaks away from my embrace. "Focus on Deghan. I've got Silas." Like he senses my hesitation, he adds, "I promise."

I take my now free hand and put it over Deghan's body, pushing both vessels into him.

I can do this, I tell myself.

Cameron smooths the fur between Deghan's eyes. "You're going to be okay."

Sydney stands. He doesn't allow his mother the chance to react. He slams a powerful blast of green energy into her side. Just enough to break the connection to Silas.

Words are exchanged between the two men, but I can't make them out.

I close my eyes, willing myself to be able to figure this out. I open them, and little flickers of light appear.

Gold, purple, blue, orange...every vibrant color you could imagine.

Floating speckles that float up from the ground and over to me.

I swallow, unsure of what it is that is front of me.

Then, as they come closer, I notice the tiny wings attached to their bodies.

A few of the creatures land on my hands, their pulsing colorful energy flowing into me, making me even more powerful. The rest of them take their place on Deghan's body, covering him in an unusually imaginative blanket.

Cameron gasps, but I don't dare stop.

My intuition reassures me of this extraordinary experience.

Thirty seconds pass, and miraculously, Deghan's wolf form fills out, his ribs snapping into place and the life being brought into his once feeble body.

I don't get a chance to say my thanks when the absolutely breathtaking Fae folk fly away, their beaming lights dimming until they are completely out of sight.

"Thank you," I say anyway, never meaning two words more in my entire life.

Deghan hops onto all fours and nuzzles Cameron's side and then mine.

I turn around to find Silas and Sydney, side by side, their arms extended, blasting off one ball of power followed by the next.

Ophelia manages to dodge each of their attempts, but the path of their firing leaves her unable to retreat from her position.

Good, that's exactly how we want her.

At least that's what I think, until two more hooded figures appear behind her.

We stand united and tuck Cameron to our backsides. There's no time to get him to safety. If we try to run, they'll only defeat us that much quicker.

So instead, I reinforce his protective barrier and summon my strength.

The bubblegum-colored power ripples off my hands and sends magical sparks flying.

Sydney was right; I am more potent.

But I'd be lying if I said I hadn't detected it happening the last week. Each moment I got closer to the guys, realizing their love for me, and mine for them, it was like I unlocked some hidden layer of my magic, making me stronger than ever.

Love fuels the Oliver witches.

That's why they took it away from us. They were afraid we would become too tough and resistant to their tactics to steal our magic.

But for me, I've broken curse by curse, *and* found love.

Four times over, not including what I feel for my friends.

I threaten their very existence and ruin their sadistic plans.

Smother the light, and there will only be darkness.

I am Willow Oliver, descended from the angels themselves, and I will not allow these vile beings to rule over us any longer.

The cloaked individuals step up next to Ophelia.

One lowers his hood, and Sydney gasps. "Dad?"

Ophelia grins and dodges another of Silas's violet orbs. "What did you expect?"

Anticipating her shifting her weight to avoid his blow, I send one right in the path she takes.

Her body shakes from the impact, and fear washes across her face momentarily.

Only long enough for another devious smile to form.

The third figure remains covered.

I can't help but wonder who it is. Taking things into my own hands, I send a burst of pink their way. I rapid-fire until I throw the person off their footing.

Their jet-black shawl slides back over their face, and this time, it's me who gasps.

All those weird feelings, those unsettling moments alone with this person assault me like an out-of-control wildfire.

My instincts were right all along.

"Tremont," Cameron whispers from his place behind me.

So much for passing that statistics class.

This whole time I was aware something was off, but I didn't quite expect it to be this. I had thought that his magic was just rather shitty, and his healing powers were nothing that people praised him for. In reality, he was only lengthening my injury to weaken me.

"How's that bad luck treating you?" His voice sounds thirty times more dangerous than in the past.

That's probably what happens when you find out that someone is actually a malicious and fucked-up person.

"Oh, you really thought I was trying to help, didn't you?" Tremont's stare nearly burns a hole through me. "That was only me ensuring the curse was still firmly in place. If anything, you did me a wonderful favor by burning yourself." He chuckles. "It was something similar to taking candy from a baby, truly."

Bad luck?

So it turns out I really was cursed with misfortune.

Part of me thought that to be true, but what a strange and silly thing to happen.

Spilling some coffee and oversleeping was supposed to drain me of my magic?

"Although, you are rather resistant. It's annoying, if you ask me. You aren't aware of your power, and yet it protects you all the same." Tremont slowly twists his hand.

I don't allow him to finish with the motion. I slam a hot pink ball of power into his chest.

"Enough!" Ophelia calls out. "We may be outnumbered, but it's impossible to defeat us. All you're doing is prolonging the inevitable."

She throws her hands up and tosses a net of glistening black magic toward us.

Sydney and I throw our own up, shattering her attempt to contain our little group.

"Give me your power," she says through gritted teeth. But she's not talking to me.

Each of the men to her sides places their hands on her shoulders. Their bodies are locked into place, and a current of energy flows into her.

Deghan bares his teeth and snarls at them. He raises his snout to the sky and calls out once more.

We need backup, and fast.

Two furry flashes whip by from the left and right.

The smaller golden one sinks its muzzle onto Sydney's father's leg and breaks him away from Ophelia.

The familiar light-grey one snags Tremont's torso, severing his tie, too.

I draw in a breath, unsure of having the wolf that tried to kill me and Silas not too long ago here with us.

But there is that saying, *keep your friends close and your enemies closer.*

Close but at a distance in this case. I don't want that deadly beast anywhere near me.

"What the hell is that?" Sydney stares off into the distance, seemingly at nothing.

"What are you talking about?" Silas grows annoyed when he doesn't see anything.

Sydney points into the trees. "Right there, glowing and flashing like a neon fucking sign."

"You're out of your mind. There's nothing there." Silas huffs and balls up his fist.

Upon further inspection, I gasp. There's no way he could be seeing the same thing I am. Unless...there's only one way that would be possible.

And if that's true, we got this all wrong.

CHAPTER 35

Sometimes I think I have it all figured out.

But nothing is ever quite what it seems.

And honestly, I don't mind being proved wrong, especially when the reality of things is better than the narrative we tell ourselves.

This whole time we had suspected Sydney of being descended from the Devil because of his parents and their darkness.

But putting together all of the pieces, like what Sydney has told us, what his evil mother said about them being cursed with an anomaly, and Sydney having the same very rare sight that I do—I realize now, Sydney is no different than I am.

It's no wonder she was able to cast him to the wayside so easily.

She never cared for him; she only wanted to use him until he was no longer of service to her.

Because despite being born from her womb, he's no child of hers.

She disowned him the moment she felt his light and knew that she could not control him.

Sydney isn't the yin to my yang—my opposite—he's my equal.

He has angel blood.

The realization fully hits me at the same moment a blasted bolt of power does.

I'm thrown to the ground, knocking into Cameron on the way down. I reach and grasp to stop my fall, but my hands come up short. My head rattles off the hard earth, and everything fades to black.

"Child," a voice calls out through the darkness.

A beaming light comes into focus. A familiar set of white wings appear, attached to a gloriously perfect being.

"You know what you must do," the angel sings.

"Please," I beg. "You have to help me."

Suddenly, an image comes into focus, and a strange and sudden epiphany floats through me. It's like I knew all along, but something helped guide me toward the recognition.

"That is all I may offer you. You must do the rest yourself."

I reach out toward the celestial presence but am snapped into reality by the shaking of my shoulders and Cameron calling my name.

"Willow! Christ. I thought you were dead."

I glance at his body, noting the lack of protection. When I was knocked unconscious, it must have broken the protective spell. I grip his arm and force it back into place.

"I need to get that woman's blood." I shift my focus across the forest where she stands, rocking back and forth to avoid the blasts of power from Sydney and Silas. "Where's Deghan?"

Cameron sighs. "Another person appeared, the one who hit you. Deg went after them."

I hop up with Cam's support and pull my energy to the forefront. "I'm going to have to get close to her."

"What do you plan on doing with the blood?" Silas asks between attacks.

"I'm going to use it to break the curse."

Sydney glances over his shoulder at me. "You know how?"

I nod and whisper exactly what I need him to do into his ear.

Out of breath and fatigued, Ophelia slowly retreats.

I take the opportunity to step forward. "How about we do this one-on-one? There's no need for you to hurt my friends."

She stops throwing her magic and dodges the last of the purple that goes her way.

"Trust me," I mouth to the guys.

How many times have I said that one, though?

Pretty sure the last time I did, I ended up dying inside my own mind.

Ophelia glides toward me until we're about ten feet apart. She raises an eyebrow. "Feeling a bit confident, are we?" Her eyes are nearly black, matching the color of her hair well.

"If it's me you want, it's me you'll get."

"Fair enough," she retorts.

"You think you understand anything about *fair*?" I watch her carefully to try to anticipate her first move.

"You think you're so smart, Willow Oliver." She shakes her head. "This started before me, and it will go on once we're both gone. This *feud* between the angel and demon coven, it will never end. It goes deeper than anything you or I could ever have control over."

I breathe in deeply, the scent of the earthy area filling my lungs. "You're power-hungry. That's all it is. You're naturally weak and you need powerful witches like me to leech off of. It's pathetic, really."

"If it weren't for your lowlife bloodline, this would have never started. The Olivers are to blame for this, Willow. Don't you see that? I'm strictly only carrying on the family tradition. Because I am *loyal*. Something the Olivers appreciate *nothing* about." Her jaw becomes tense with the anger setting in.

"Whatever. Project your blame if it makes you feel any better about being a shitty person. It's safe to say we're all aware of the truth." I glance over my shoulder. I part my lips ever so slightly and mouth the word, "Now," so quietly it's nearly inaudible. Only one set of ears will be able to hear me, and that's all that matters.

I slam two fistfuls of paralyzingly pink magic into her, and a split second later, Silas rushes her.

He glides by so fast the shock hasn't even registered on her face.

My magic rendered her motionless, while he ran by and sliced her arm with his fangs, leaving a pooling of blood on the ground.

Rage consumes her, and it's not long until she breaks free of my restraints.

But I expected that much.

I take a step back, letting her think that she's going to best me, but all I'm doing is leading her away from the mess she left on the bare soil.

Ophelia fires at me, and I narrowly miss it. Just like in my training sessions with Ruby, I forget to watch for the follow-up. The black sizzling power slams me in the gut.

That I did not anticipate.

I heave and nearly lose my lunch.

Another blow, knocking my shoulder this time. Pain rips through me, but I don't let her attention fall to anything else.

I slam a few rapid-fire orbs at her, missing each time.

All I have to do is keep her distracted.

A whoosh of wind, and Silas appears by my side.

"You have to help him," I urge.

"You need me more." Silas grabs my hand and places it on his shoulder. "Hurry."

I siphon some of his energy, already more revitalized with each passing pulse.

Ophelia laughs. "Wow. She's your Malachi. You're a special one, aren't you, Willow? Shame, though, that I'm going to kill you both, and fate has no control over that."

"Actually, Mother," Sydney chimes in. "Your fate has already been decided." Syd slams her over the head with a large branch, knocking her unconscious.

I guess a little old-fashioned human brawling comes in handy.

"We need to act fast. I'm not sure how many other goonies she has coming." Sydney takes the same stick and hands it to me. "You have to draw it."

I take it from him and drag it along the loose dirt-covered ground, forming a large circle, and then a five-pointed star in the center in one fluid motion—not breaking contact with the earth until I'm finished. "I need Deghan."

Silas nods and hurries away using his vampire speed.

"Are you sure this is going to work?" Sydney frantically looks from his passed-out mother to me.

"It has to." I gesture to one of the points. "Cam, you there?" Sydney and I claim the two points facing upward. Now, we wait for the other two pieces of my soul.

The spot of earth where Ophelia's blood coats the ground is smack dab in the center of the star.

The angel carefully weaved this plan into place, and I'm the vessel to bring it to fruition.

Leaves crumble, and in the time it takes me to blink, Silas is at my side.

"Deghan's on his way." He presses his hands to my cheeks and pulls my face close. "I'm so proud of you.

I lean in and press my lips against his, taking the very brief pause to savor something good.

Deghan runs up in his human form, covered in only a pair of gym shorts. "You rang, princess?"

"Stand there," I instruct him, then Silas.

He does what he's told, and together, we make up each section of the star.

I reach out for Sydney's and Silas's hands. They follow suit and take Cameron's and Deghan's. Each embrace slams a new burst of power through me, and when we're all connected, a new sort of fire takes hold inside me. A good one. An endless supply of pure magic.

Without really understanding them, words flow from the tip of my tongue. An ancient, long-forgotten language.

The four men who bring me so much love and joy, and the same ones who make me more powerful than I've ever been.

Love fuels the Oliver witches, and I hit the freaking motherload.

Ophelia LeBlanc had no idea who she was messing with.

My eyes roll back, and the chant continues. "Oh fallum unghur brota makler vartal." Nothing makes sense, but I let it flow all the same.

"Shit," Cameron mutters, distracting me momentarily.

The sound of grumbling fills my ears. She must be waking up.

I recite the words quicker, and a strong wind forms around us.

It goes up, up, up, and then becomes one in the middle above the blood sacrifice. A tiny little tornado threatening to break the hold we have on each other.

"Whh-what? How?" Ophelia blurts out. "No!" She rushes toward us, but once she hits the barrier of the circle, she's sent flying back from the invisible blockade.

The power whips through me, flowing a solid current from each of our hands into the next. Even Cameron. I don't understand how it's possible, but I give in to the blind faith that this is going to work.

Anything is possible in this crazy world we live in.

Ophelia lets out a painfully loud scream, but I don't break away from the ritual to see what she's up to.

I can't stop. I won't stop. Not until this is *finally* over.

The small but destructive twister grows stronger and stronger with each deafening octave she shrieks.

Until there's nothing at all.

No more crying, no windstorm, nothing. Just the silent forest around us.

"Willow." Deghan pulls me off the ground and into his arms.

A strange, freeing sensation floats through my body in a way I've never experienced.

But then, a sudden terrible pit forms.

Something that could only remind me of one sinking feeling.

I finally open my eyes and scan the vicinity like a madwoman. "Where...?"

Sydney lowers his head, clearly not wanting to meet my eyes.

I glance at Cameron, and he avoids my gaze, too.

Tears make their way down my already flushed cheeks. "Where is Silas?"

CHAPTER 36

Three days have gone by in a stupor of next to no sleep, barely being able to eat, and a painful sadness taking absolute control of me.

I haven't gone to my classes.

I haven't given any of my friends the time of day.

I lost the will to live the moment I lost him.

Silas.

The name I cry out at the rare moments I'm able to fall into a forced slumber. The flashes of weakness when my body decides it can no longer take the insomnia. But it's short-lived. The vision of Silas in a fiery inferno wrecks me every time.

He's gone.

And with him went a piece of me that I can no longer function without.

I gained all of this power for nothing.

I may have broken the curse, but at what cost?

I have won, but I am defeated.

Glancing around my disaster of a room, I take in the little bits of him left behind.

His dark-grey shirt draped over the chair at the table. The sweatpants he let me borrow that I never gave back...they are far more comfortable than any pair I own. The book on my nightstand that I only got a chance to read a few pages of before disaster after disaster hit. His scent, still lingering on the sheets that I refuse to wash in fear of losing him forever along with it.

A light knock sounds on my door.

"Come in." My unused voice is scratchy.

Cameron peeks his head inside. "Do you have a minute?"

Tears well in my eyes. Apparently, I have a limitless amount of them that I no longer have any desire for. I nod anyway.

He strolls over and sits next to me on the bed. Handing me a cup of what smells like coffee, he looks me over. "Will..." Cameron tucks a rogue strand of hair behind my ear.

I'm in desperate need of a shower, too.

I sniff the drink, but everything is different now. Things that once appealed to me no longer bring me the same joy.

I'm lost. Swimming in a fog of nothing. Desperately clinging to whatever shred of humanity remains.

Cameron's ocean-blue eyes meet mine. "I've uh...I've been in some pretty dark places in the past. Especially recently." He lets out a breath. "Nothing compared to what you've been through, but I've come to realize that it takes a kind of sadness to be able to recognize happiness, and you, Willow, you brought this to life for me. You're kind and caring and considerate and so fucking loving...selfless and strong. Despite everything you've been through, you still choose to put one foot in front of the other, and damn if you aren't an inspiration for me to be a better man. It is an absolute honor to be a part of your world.

"You've always been there for me. So, I hope that you realize

I'm here for you now. We all are. Whatever you need. We aren't going to give up on you...not now, not ever. We're going to get through this together."

Together...all of us...just without Silas.

What's left of my heart shatters even more.

How can I go on without him? What kind of person am I if I move on? Especially knowing this was *all my fault.* I'll never forgive myself.

And now, all I'm doing is bringing down everyone around me. Dragging them into this dark sadness they never asked for.

They really are better off without me.

With this pitiful realization, the door to my dorm bursts open.

I don't bother taking my eyes away from the random string I twist between my fingers.

Nothing can distract me from this infinite sadness.

"Willow." The voice is smooth and calm and comforting, belonging to only one person and one person alone.

Little bits of my heart get glued back together with the one welcoming word.

It's not Silas, but the other missing piece of me.

"Mom." I barely spit it out when the tears come raining down.

I'm on my feet and across the room, pulling her into a hug within seconds.

"This isn't real. Mom?" I continue to sob.

She pats my head and squeezes me tight. "It's me. I'm here. Oh, sweet Willow. Mommy is here."

And despite feeling like I had lost it all, her coming back into my life is exactly what I need.

Now, with this tiny bit of life breathed back into my lungs—I know what I must do.

Follow along with Willow in the fourth installment of the Harper Shadow Academy series, Ancient Magic.

Acknowledgments

Wicked Magic broke me. In ways I could never truly put into words. The story poured out of my soul, and I know for a fact that the next installment, Ancient Magic, will wreck me once more.

Consider this my formal apology for the way the book ended. Please don't hate me!!!!!! There will be two more books to tidy things up and hopefully bring you some smiles instead of tears!

Thank you for sharing this journey with me. For watching and reading along while I rip my heart out of my chest and bleed it on the paper.

To the few people that keep me relatively sane—my tiny human, Victoria, Kate, and Kelsey. I don't think I'd have gotten this far without you all by my side.

To the insanely wonderful people over at Patreon who support the behind the scenes—I will be forever grateful for your continuous support! Clayton, James, Dustin, Tyler, and Victoria —I appreciate each one of you so damn much.

My editor, Emmy Ellis. My design team, Mibl Art. Niki Trento-Spencer. Savannah Richey. You are what make these books really shine.

The entire RHRA group and the members of Luna Pierce's Paranormal Addicts, your encouragement has helped push this series to what it is!

To the readers of the **Harper Shadow Academy series**, I love you to the moon and back. Your support is what makes this all possible!